AF433475

Other works by S.M. Sykes:

A Dim Blue (book 2 of the Blue series)

Loss of Blue (book 3 of the Blue series)

It's my body, I'll haunt if I want to

Life of a Lycanthrope

Message on the Wind

Every review helps immensely. If you enjoy this book or not, please take the time to leave a review @ Amazon or Goodreads. See the Qr above for links.

Eyes of

Blue

(Book 1 of the Blue series)

S. M. Sykes

Ingram Spark:
ISBN 979-8-8691-7074-3(paperback)
          979-8-8692-9709-9 (ebook)

Amazon:

ISBN 979-8-8836-6813-4 (paperback)

      979-8-3234-9774-4 (widespace)

ASIN- B09X546562 (kindle)

S. M. Sykes Books
27196 Indian Meadows Cir
Millsboro, DE. 19966

Table of contents

Prologue

You have just done one of the smartest things you have ever done, you picked up this book and started to read it. Now, will you do the second smartest thing? Will you read these pages and heed my warnings?

If you do and you can comprehend my story through the ramblings and time jumps, you will see what I have learned and endured over the past couple of years. If you follow along you may learn how to keep yourself alive.

When I started out I knew very little about this new world and the dangers that existed in it. I have written down my story in hopes of passing this along to others that have lived a similar plight. I have done this so that the information that I have gathered will not be lost with me.

It shall live on for future generations to know what exists out there, or hopefully existed, and maybe gain a little understanding on how to survive. You have survived this long, and I do not know how you have lived, nor how much you really know. But maybe my words will give you information that you did not have before. Information that may keep you alive.

But even more than that. Maybe it will contain information that will help you live, not just survive in this world. Maybe we can get past this fallen world. A world where the apex predator has-Eyes of Blue.

Running

Running...Again with the running. Always with the running. Running for food or running because of fear. I could remember a time when I actually enjoyed running. I enjoyed the rush, the wind and the feeling of my legs propelling me towards the finish. Back then it was fun when I ran with my brother, with my team and for my school. I loved the competition and the feeling of getting stronger and faster every day. I could feel myself getting better and having more endurance. Reveling in the competition wanting to be better than the previous race. Looking for a way to shave precious seconds off my time, to keep that faster pace for just a few more steps. Saving enough to have that last burst of energy for the sprint to the finish.

But, that was then. Nowadays it's not fun. There was no getting stronger, no feeling of being better or of competition. Just fear, it's always the fear that drives me to run faster than before. The only competition here was life and death. If I don't run fast enough or far enough, if that one step falters when it shouldn't. If I didn't get to that next hill, or that next door to get to a safe place, then I was dead.

As if that wasn't enough, there was also the running that was surrounded by food. It was either to find food, or because I had food and others wanted it.There was no getting stronger because I was always weak from the fear and the hunger.

Before this endeavour, it had been a while since I had to run in fear. Most of the people had left, my refuge in this dark world. I used to love being around people. Now being on my own was the only way to be safe. Everyone had their own agenda, which didn't always align with you staying alive. I have not seen another human being in months. The winter generally kept people cooped up inside and away from the elements, but it also used to mean gatherings and parties. Now it just meant cold and making sure you found a heat source to stay alive.

Food was always on my mind. Not just how I was going to get food or what kind of food I would find, but remembering what food used to be like. There was never enough food now, hadn't been for years. I always liked to pretend that I was eating a big, juicy, dripping burger with pickles and mayonnaise, or a large McDonald's french fry with a Wendy's frosty to dip them in. It was always pretty much anything other than what I was actually forced to eat. That usually consisted of scavenged cans of beans and corn, or something that I could catch and cook.

But OOOH how food used to taste. Great, NOW I am Hungry and RUNNING!!

Okay, let me take a break from my revelry here and fill you in on a few things. I am guessing that there are two questions (at least) you are probably asking right now.

1)   *Why are you running?*
2)   *Who are you?*

Well, the first question is probably a two-parter.
Why am I running off at the mouth?
What is the reason that I am physically running?

For the first part of this question I never have been able to answer that. I am a talker. I would say I was born to talk, but I actually started speaking real words a little later in life than most kids. Don't get me wrong I was talking, but only my brother could understand me and had to translate it into English for those around me. Once I used my first real words though, I haven't stopped. People, like my Dad, used to say that I would eventually run out of words and I would no longer be able to speak. If that were true I am probably running on empty as I speak.

For the second part of the question, I was running from a pair of Deaders.

That answer your question clear enough? No?

Well, if you have lived in this world, the world after The Fall, that would have been all I had to say. For sake of argument I am going to assume that you have either lived under a rock or your reading this after they have all been killed and this is all just for entertainment. I will answer the question, what are Deaders? I was not sure about all the scientific terms and such, they used to be humans, but they aren't any longer. They are humanoid and still have the very essential features of being human. They have lost all of their humanity and have reverted to a more animalistic state of mind. As we know all humans die. Since the fall humans have died at an accelerated rate. It doesn't matter if they die by knife, gunshot, sickness, or a heart attack, once they were dead, they wouldn't stay that way long. A few minutes later their eyes would open and they would get back up. They would become a mindless animal-like predator. Every living thing and everything with an electrical energy source was their prey.

I guess one term you could've used was undead. Although these aren't the undead or zombies you are used to seeing on the television screen or that you read about in graphic novels. These undead didn't respond to sights and sounds. They responded to electrical currents, or something like that, I said before that I didn't know all of the science behind them. I did know that they could "see" lights and animals, including humans. All animals run on an electrical current of sorts. The brain sends electrical impulses throughout the body to your nerves to move your muscles.Our bodies are full of signal carriers that run up, down and all over. This was what Deaders could see. Now, I use the term "see" lightly because their eyes are completely blank, it must be like some kind of radar, or thermal vision.

Either way, I was pumped up with adrenaline and other endorphins so I was probably lit up like a Christmas tree to them.

I hate thinking about things from before. Now I'm missing Christmas. See what I mean, hateful world.

The biggest difference between the Deaders and a human, is their eyes. I told you that they are blank and dead looking. To explain that a little better it is kind of like how movies used to show seers, they are blank, no iris, and no pupil. Now their eyes aren't white , they are blue. They glow too, they glow a dim blue. I am not sure why or how, I just know that when I see that in the dark you run for your life as fast and as far as you can.

Another reason that I don't refer to them as undead is that all of you that were fans of "The Walking Dead" and "Night of the Living Dead" would probably assume that I am running from slow-moving reanimated corpses. That is not the case. These deaders can run as fast as they could prior to death. So an obese deader would still be slow, but if they were in any kind of shape in life they could be something terrifying to contend with. From what I understand, they absorb electrical energy from their surroundings and use that to "feed". This keeps their muscles and skin from deteriorating and slowing them down. This works very similarly to what I was explaining in the beginning, if I don't eat, I can't run because I have no energy. It was the same with these things. They use the energy of others to feed themselves so they could run for more energy.

Did you keep up with that?

It seems that if they don't eat then they slow down and the natural order of body decay starts to take back over. I didn't know if these things could die from starvation or they just lose the use of their muscles. That would have been a question for a scientist. I was good at math and English. Science was never my cup of tea.

I know there are people out there that would say "Why not just stab or shoot them in the head?" One reason was that I didn't have a gun. Another reason was that it didn't seem to work that way. I think I stated before that these aren't like the zombies you are used to. That type of thinking got a lot of people killed in the beginning. Real life is never like the movies, is it?

So these bastards are fast and their skull wasn't deteriorated and soft like in the movies. It was hard as mine and yours. This wasn't easy to pierce by hand. Even if you do, you are not too likely to get deep enough to do real damage. They didn't seem to use the same sections of the brain as we do. There was no love, compassion or empathy. I doubt they were pining for their lost high school love or remembering the dance moves for the Macarena or the Whip. Decapitation has seemed to keep the dead from rising, but anything less than that hasn't seemed to stop their need for energy.

Now if that wasn't scary enough, another difference was that these guys could communicate too. They aren't shouting German or using walkie-talkies, but they could coordinate their movements. If you aren't careful, they could box you in and then slowly come in for the kill. I had seen it, it was similar to a pack of wolves. It gave me the shivers just thinking about it.

Once they have you in their grasp they draw the energy from you. Some call it your soul, others your Chi. Either way, no matter what you want to call it, when they are done, so are you. A few I had seen didn't claw and tear, just drained you to the core.

Once you were kill by a deader, you don't rise again. Your energy is now theirs, there was nothing left to reanimate your corpse. Lights out forever. No glowy eyes and walking dead for you. I guess since they are draining all of your energy, there was nothing left. It would have been like trying to recharge a dead battery. No amount of juice in the world would keep it running right.

Now that we have gone over what the deaders are and why you should be afraid of them, let's get back to the story.

I was running because I had seen two Deaders. Typically, that meant there was more around. Luckily I didn't think they really "saw" me before I saw them. It definitely didn't seem like they were looking for me.

I was up on a dune, enjoying looking at the ocean and some of the first nice weather of spring, when I saw them come from behind another dune. Since I was laying on the sand I just rolled off the dune on the far side and stayed as low as possible. I think I got away clean.

I usually tried to make it as simple as possible when it comes to these jerks. AVOID AT ALL COSTS! That way I didn't have to find out any more nasty gruesome information about them. What I just shared with you was about all I know. While the curiosity of what they are and how they became a real thing was always gnawing at me, I really didn't want to try the scientific method out on these things and die in the process. Remember I really didn't like science anyway.

I remember when I wanted to know everything. Not just about the dead, but about everything. That was before all of this though. I always remember what curiosity did to the cat. And I was all out of satisfaction to bring me back. Now, I just wanted to know where my friend (singular) was and where my next meal was coming from.

So I guess that leads us to your second major question.
Finally, right?
Who am I?
Well, do any of us really know who they are? Do we really want to know? Philosophers have been researching and prophesizing this exact question for millennia. But you're not looking for the philosophical answer are you?
You want to know the, hello what's your name, kind of way.
Well, I am Ava Caroline Washington. Born and raised on the Eastern shore of Delaware.
Let me answer a few quick questions about that too real quick.
Yes, it was a state, the first one. You would know this if you paid attention in history class. No, it was not part of Maryland or Pennsylvania. There was a Delaware River, a Delaware Bay and

a city of Delaware in Ohio. None of these explain where I was from. If you had ever traveled to the beach, not the shore in Jersey, but the beach on the eastern shore. You had probably heard of Delaware. This was the small unknown state that I grew up in. More specifically I grew up south of the Missipillion River, in good old Slower Lower Sussex County, Delaware.

I grew up in a "normal" family. Mom, Dad, older brother and me. We went on family outings, ate dinner together and watched movies, not at the same time. We had a great understanding of each other and looked out for one another. My parents always asked about my day and truly loved my friends. There was always someone to talk to, even if they didn't seem to be able to keep up with my conversation all the time. I was not sure why, but they would get lost and eventually just let me talk.

I had just started high school when this all started, so I was about 15 years old, hard to remember anymore. I loved my phone and my friends. I was on every app possible if it interacted with other people. I would send thousands of texts a day to keep up with all of my friends and stay up with all of the new stuff on social media sites. My life was wrapped up in electronics, family and sports. I would stay awake worried about that pimple or if that boy in English class was going to ask me to homecoming. My brother, though we loved each other, would annoy me to no end. He was older, so he thought he knew everything and could boss me around. Little did he know, I knew everything, so I needed to tell him that every day to make sure he kept himself in check.

It was a pretty typical teenage girl's life.

That doesn't really answer your question properly though. That was who I was. I was not that person anymore. When the power grids went down there was no social media, texts or internet. Then there was no annoying older brother, no Mom, no Dad. All of my friends are probably dead or so far underground I will never see them again. There will not be any more homecomings or proms to worry about. Nothing from before.

There was no social anything anymore, let alone social media. I actually found it hard to believe that we used to get anything done with all those sites notifying us of the smallest detail in someone else's life. But taking the time to look back, we really didn't get anything done. We felt that we had accomplished things and worked hard, but it was usually nothing of note. We were all on these sites to stay relevant, to be in the spotlight and be remembered. But when it all went away, when it all came crashing down around our feet. None of it meant anything. They used to say the internet never forgets, That may have been true but even it was forgotten now.

I still carried my phone in my backpack to remember the days when that seemed to have been the most important thing in my life. Maybe one day the grid would come back up and life would regain some of the old normalcy. Something of the time before all of this, before mankind became the hunted. Before The Fall.

It's stupid, really, the fact that I thought it was important and the fact that I still carried it. I just thought about what i would do if I could have charged this thing one more time. If I could see the pictures of my friends and my family. Pictures and videos of all those that I have lost and would never see again. That was another downfall of our old all-digital society, when the grid went down we didn't even have pictures to remember our loved ones by.

Losing my family was the saddest part of all. We were all together in the beginning. As everything got worse my family started falling apart. Not that we turned on each other, just that we lost members, Dad, Matthew and then even Mom. I tried not to think about who I used to be and how things were. It just made the days harder than they already were. I just focused on the here and now.

You wanted to know who I am, not who I was, right?

Now, I am 17 years old… would have been driving if there were still cars. Well, there were still cars, just not working cars. There were cars blocking the highways, dead in the streets and cars used to block communities off when people thought that would keep them safe. None of them ran. None had the juice. That was one way Deaders kept themselves alive when they ran out of people. They would just rip into a car and take the juice straight from the battery. It would almost have been funny to watch if it weren't so damn scary. They were like tweekers looking for their next fix. Remember those memes with Dave Chappelle looking like a bum asking, "You all got any more of them Girl Scout cookies?" For these things, it would have been car batteries.

I had been on my own with just Andromeda for almost a year. I found a shelter in the old army bases at Cape Henlopen

State Park not long after I lost Mom. I have been living there ever since. It kept out most of the weather and has huge heavy doors that block any electrical signal that I put off. It also stopped any noise or light from carrying outside of the shelter. This wasn't a worry for the Deaders, it was for the other humans that liked to live off of others and take what they had. I could light a fire to keep warm or to cook the nasty stuff I call food. It had been pretty safe for a while, but nothing ever lasts for long in this new world.

Cape Henlopen State Park is in the town of Lewes, it was a pretty big town before this all started. A larger town, of course, caused more Deaders to be created. Once everyone was out of work and the area went into lockdown people resorted to looting and rioting in the streets. This led to a lot of deaths, which led to a lot of deaders. The population of Lewes was mostly retired people. People that retired and moved to the beach were not all that handy. They really never had to do for themselves, the world from before made people think sending emails and answering phones was important. It was at the time, for some reason, but that didn't give them the skills to survive after The Fall. They were at a loss when everything came crashing down around their ears. They made very easy targets for the looters and the Deaders.

Since this happened so fast and not many people left town with items in their cars I have been able to scavenge quite a bit to cover my needs. When that didn't work or it got too dangerous I would fish out at the pier in the park. I remember days before this all started that it didn't matter if we caught anything, it was just fun to be out there. Now, it was survival to catch something. I set traps and hunted in the woods along the park too. Between the food in town and the others I kept Andromeda and I fed pretty well. So in a nutshell I was pretty much just a forager now. Not much else for life to consist of.

Did this answer your question?

During this winter the Deaders seemed to have completely disappeared. I hadn't seen one for almost two months, up until two weeks ago I thought that maybe the cold killed them all off or that they starved to death with nothing to feed them. I had hoped that they could starve.

I guess I still didn't have the answer to that question.

I was able to take down a deer about 8 days ago with my bow. My dad taught me to hunt at a very young age. That was something else that used to be enjoyable but was now a life and death scenario. Come to think of it, animals may have been what was drawing the deaders here. The town was a ghost town, no life or energy forces to draw them there. They must have been spreading to the surrounding areas where there was still wildlife. Nothing like a state park to house the most wildlife, even during an apocalypse.

Andromeda and I were just trying to survive. We had a safe place to shelter and an ok food source for the most part, definitely better than most I was certain. I questioned sometimes if being alive was really all we should be looking for or was living what we should have strived for? In this new world, I think we had to settle for the former and hope the latter happened sometime soon. But hope was all that we had at this point. As I said before, nothing lasts long in this new world. Now here I was trying to get away from these creatures and get back to Andromeda and safety.

Stupid, I should have thought of this before and packed up weeks ago. These are not the only two I have seen. I saw a pack of them and heard them calling through the night a week ago. I thought they had moved through, guess I was wrong. The activity increase had me thinking I may have extended my stay too long.

In the back of my head, I knew this may come to an end, but comfortability and complacency made it hard to make any other move. I just tried to stay safe and stay alive. In all reality, I was lost on where to go, to be honest. I really didn't know enough about the country and the state it was in, or enough about these creatures to make more than a guess on what direction would have been safe.

Now, Andromeda and I were sitting ducks if these two bring more and we didn't move on. I had the freedom to go, to head out of the area. I had my bag and a lot of my belongings, though no real food or water, but I should have been able to find that on the road. But that would have meant leaving her, and that was not going to happen ever! I left Andromeda in the bunker while I went on the foray today. She hadn't been feeling 100% so I figured it would have been safe to go out by myself for one day. If I left she would die. She couldn't get out of the bunker on her own and she had no real way to find food for herself.

I had to get away from these two. I couldn't lead them back to Andromeda and the bunker, they were smart and could remember where they lost their prey.They would stay outside and we would be trapped. The only place that I could think of that may have been safe enough to wait these things out was the observation tower. The downside was there was no door and only one way in or out. There used to be an outer door and an inner door to the steps, but those had long been broken off. Maybe someone else tried this same thing and lost their bet? Maybe the weather just got to them and the hinges rotted away, or they were taken to be used as protection somewhere else. Too many different things could have happened to know for sure.

If I got stuck there it might be bad though. The only hope I would have was that the inner area was fenced off from the outer loop stairs. If I got inside there I may have been able to get to the bottom before they could. If I didn't break my neck in the process. Then I would have to hope that there were only the two of them that I had seen and not others waiting in the wind, out of sight. Since I couldn't think this all through any more while I was running for my life, that was the plan. Nothing like a long 3-4 mile run through the sand and then a thousand flights of steps to kill you.

Well maybe not a literal thousand, but tell that to my aching legs.

Stairs

Lots and lots of stairs.

My legs burned and complained greatly about running that far then having to do stairs. Even with the deer meat I didn't think I had gotten enough protein or vitamins to keep my body healthy. I stumbled up the steps and tried to stay away from the small windows. I had not heard the Deaders communicating around me, but that didn't mean they weren't. Sometimes you could hear them easily, sometimes they came out of nowhere. I couldn't find a rhyme or reason to their methods.

I wanted to believe that I was safe and that they were never anywhere near me, but I had to be sure and not rely on faith and belief. The observation tower, which was to be my safe zone, was 60 feet of pure metal and concrete. It was built during World War II to could keep an eye out on the coast and protect the bay and Fort Miles. It was built to withstand, a testament to the construction of that era. While there has been some reconstruction since then, of course, the bulk of the structure remained untouched. Metal only lasts so long in the salt air, but it was still in good shape. About six months ago I had come up here to see if there was anything left in the area to look at. It offered a great view of all of the surrounding area, even up to Lewes. But when standing there, you are too exposed, your electrical signal could probably have been seen for miles around. I had stayed away since then, thinking that it was not safe to be up there. Now, I was using it as my sanctuary, my last stand against these creatures of myth and legend. I wanted to go back to my hideout, my new home. But I couldn't risk leading these things there. I needed to make sure I was not being followed or surrounded. Not being set up by creatures that should not even exist.

The steps start out rounding the inner wall of the tower. They are large steps and it gave my eyes time to adjust to the darkness within. They then worked their way to the outside, so there are observation areas through the small windows from the metal platforms. The steps get smaller here but with metal platforms at regular intervals. It was hard to walk up these steps and be quiet.*Good thing these creatures aren't attracted to noise.* Every breath I took, every single step on these metal bongos, seemed to resonate throughout the whole tower. Though the windows encircle the whole tower, they are small and hard to see through. I guess you want that if ships are firing at you from the coastline.

I stopped by a couple of windows, trying to stay low and out of sight from the ground as much as possible. The area was nothing but trees and sand dunes. It was impossible to see even the smallest thing from the ground through these small windows. I could see the horizon well, which was what these things were designed for, but they are too small to look down at any good angle. I had to go to the top of the tower to peek and see if they were still in the area. It was getting dark as I got to the top. When it got dark, it would be impossible to tell if they were out there, although it would be easy for them to see me clearly. They seemed to be better nocturnal hunters, though they do move around throughout the day too.

I guess you didn't sleep much when you were dead. Which was actually the opposite of what one of my dad's friends used to say. He would say "you could sleep when you're dead." usually before they went out drinking or to a game.

If you were close enough, you could see the glow of their eyes at night but from this distance, they would have to have been looking directly at me for that to have been the case. Then I would have been screwed. I needed to see their bodies moving through the trees. The view from the top was spectacular, especially with the sun setting over the bay. It was behind the lighthouse on the rocks, or what used to be a lighthouse. It was wrecked and in shambles, but I could remember what it used to look like and I focused on that. There were a lot of famous photographers that used that lighthouse in this area for photos. A lot of them at sunset like this.

You could see for forever up there. I looked towards the town of Lewes, since I was there, still trying to catch my breath. There wasn't much but ruins to look at now. What wasn't burned and looted had been knocked down and flooded by the rising tides. It was crazy how fast nature could take back what we took from it. At least they were smarter here than in New Orleans where they built under sea level and used levy's to keep the water out. I bet there was nothing left down there at this point.

I needed to be careful at the top and focus on the task at hand. There was nothing up there to hide me. The only thing there was a chain-link fence and the posts.As I looked around I saw locks hooked to the fences. Things still here, left over from the time before. It was funny to see that someone would take the time to come up here to lock up their secrets. Did it help them leave it here and walk away a bit lighter? Not being weighed down by whatever secret they told to the lock? Were these people still alive to worry about that secret? I will never know for sure, but I hoped they were and that those locks took away some of the weight of the secret they held. As I was thinking about these things, I was also peaking my head slowly out of the tower to look the way that I had come. Down to the trees and sand, to see if death was following me, or if I had cheated it again, for now.

As I looked, I couldn't see the Deaders from before. I actually saw a lot of nothing around me. The state park was always a bit desolate, but with the thriving city of Lewes in the background, it seemed like an oasis from the noise and every day. Now it seemed like a deserted island that was keeping me from where I needed to be. I really had nowhere I needed to be, Andromeda could take care of herself for a while, but that was all I could think of as I was looking around. Where should I be? Where was I going? I know I can't stay here now, not with them so close. They caught me off guard that day. I didn't have Andromeda with me and it made me vulnerable. I needed to make a decision. Stay or go. If I left, where did I need to go? My head was swirling so I stopped thinking about it and worked my way back down the steps, waiting a while more.

I was sitting there on really uncomfortable steps trying to work the cramps out of my calves and wondering how cold it was going to get. Spring was on its way and you could feel it during the day, but the nights still got bitter at times. Maybe it would be a night where the temperatures stayed a little higher, but with my luck, I was not counting on it.

It was not a fun couple of hours. But it was better to wait for them to be gone and not have them follow me as I ran back to Andromeda. The animals move more through the night and might give me a little more cover. If the deer were out and the Deaders were chasing them, maybe I could slip through. I know I saw two, I couldn't stop thinking that there were more. That there was another walking towards my tower and more waiting for me to run. As I said before, these things hunt like a pack. Even though they are dead, they seemed to have been able to think and function as a unit. A trap being set was maybe a little far-fetched though. I got so amped up running from them to get here and worried about Andromeda that my fight or flight instincts were warring with each other. I was never much of a fighter; running away was always the better choice for me. But there were many times since the Fall that flight just wasn't an option. I had learned to stand my ground when needed and even make things go my way. With these things, pure fear kicks in and I run like never before. I just needed to sit back and relax for a bit, then I'd head up top and check the situation again before heading out.

I was really tired, but had to stay awake and aware. There was no one here to watch my back. No one to warn me if I fall asleep. Just like there would have been no one to take care of Andromeda if I didn't make it back to her. It wouldn't hurt to rest for a minute. Gather my energy in case I needed to run again. The steps were cold and hard, no way to relax enough to fall asleep. But man, when that adrenaline leaves your body, it takes all the energy with it.... I could just rest a bit and feel better.

Home

Matthew was running around the living room with my phone, teasing me. He kept getting yelled out by Daddy because he was stepping in front of the television blocking his view. Matt just laughed and moved out of the way, until I came closer and then he did it again.

Daddy was watching football. I was watching the game with him until Matthew decided he wanted to see what my notification was for.It was nothing but a snap from a friend. Nothing worth getting worked up about, but it's my phone and he was just trying to work me up. Mom was in the kitchen trying to be stern by telling Matt to give me my phone back. But we both knew Momma won't do anything if he didn't stop. She just wanted us to be quiet. Matt couldn't see the notification because he never figured out my passcode, Mattisajerk. You would think that would be easy. But he still refused to give me my phone. Uhhhgg so frustrating!

I got mad and yelled that he was being a jerk and jumped over the table at him. Mom and Dad were both yelling at me because I almost broke the table and tackled Matt near the TV. This caused Daddy to miss a play. Good thing we had DVR and he could record it, or he would have been really mad. Some penalty against the Bears, holding I think. We wrestled around for a while before Daddy yelled again, and Matt gave up and gave me the phone back.

BLACK.

Now we are sitting at the dinner table. Mom had made some summer squash and Dad grilled some deer steaks in his homemade marinade. Everyone was talking about their day and laughing. Matt was talking about dreading the upcoming cross country season, mostly because he didn't train all summer. I turned around because my phone had just dinged. I was hoping for a text from a boy I like at school. He wasn't really bright but he was a farmer and part of the school farming program. He asked me about something we had coming up and asked if he could text me later. So I was on pins and needles waiting. My phone went off. I opened it up and on the screen was a Deader!

I jerked awake as I fell off the top step and bumped my head on the next one. I hated when I remembered my dreams. It always made me miss my family. It was really dark, I had no idea how long I slept. I should've never fallen asleep, that was irresponsible. Daddy would have never let me live that down. I walked back to the top and looked out and to see if I could see anything. It was too dark with no moon to help me out. Even the man in the moon was against me. The one man that kept me company most nights and seemed to be looking down checking on just me was nowhere to be found. Stupid moon cycles. There was no telltale glow of these creatures, that might be a plus. Their glow was faint at best, but with it this dark I might've been able to see them from a decent distance to stay safe.

I slowly walked back down the hundred and fifty steps. I always thought it was easier going down, that was before a long run and an awkward nap. My legs were like springs that just wanted to wobble, it was hard to control my descent. My knees were weak from fatigue and my feet were screaming at me. I had trouble with a couple of steps and slipped from one to the other. *Wouldn't that have been great?* Fall down the steps, scream and break my neck. Just to stay alive long enough for the Deaders to come and drain my energy. Or worse no one comes and I die just to rise again as one of these things. That wouldn't have been a good ending. I slowed down, took stock of myself and descended the remaining stairs without that fatal trip. At the bottom I poked my head out to listen for anything moving then looked to see if I could see anything at all. My vision was good in the dark so I could see trees and rocks, an old busted car that was left in the parking lot. But nothing other than that.

I started back to the bunker. I was really worried because I had been gone a lot longer than I should've been. Andromeda worried when I left. Especially, when I was gone a long time. I couldn't blame her, I felt the same way when we were apart. You think about everything that could've gone wrong. I had told her I wouldn't be gone long, that I just needed some air and to enjoy the warmer weather. As I was heading back I couldn't shake that dream I had about my family, it was just sticking with me. Probably because of the worry about Andromeda. I couldn't help it, sometimes I just wanted them back and the world to stop sucking.

Even though I didn't want to, I started to cry, I missed my family. They had been all that was really important in my life. They were always there and always knew what I needed. *Crying sucks.* It was cold and I started sniffling, I couldn't see and it made it harder to hear anything else. If I kept carrying on like that I would likely run directly into a Deader. I slowed myself and got everything under control. Did what Daddy taught me, make very little noise, control my breathing and let my hearing warn me when something wasn't right.

It was a slow process making my way back to the bunker, partly because it was so freaking dark I couldn't see anything. The other part was because I didn't walk straight back, just in case. I avoided the paved roadways and stuck to the deer and animal trails. I ran when I had a clear path, walked when I didn't. At one point I knew I was close because I ran straight into a chain-link fence that was topped with barbed wire.

Yeah yeah, very funny crying girl running through the forest alone at night runs into a fence. Hilarious right?

If it wasn't me I would probably laugh. Well, it was me and I did laugh at myself a little. If you can't laugh at yourself who could you laugh at? I know I told you I could see things in the dark, but have you ever tried to look at a fence in the pitch black? Large shapes are easy, this not so much. After I stopped cursing myself for making so much noise, I realized where I was. This fence surrounded an area that used to be used for the University of Delaware. Not sure what they had tested here, but I really didn't want to ask anyone either. U of D was always working in the area around Lewes. Testing environmental changes and trying to grow plants. But after the incident and the world started dying, only to have been reborn, they took on new experiments. They wrapped the fences in barbed wire to keep people out, or in I wasn't sure. I think they were looking for cures, but that was all rumor mill and speculation on my part. Whatever they were looking for, they never found it. There hasn't been anyone here in a long time and obviously,no cure for us.

Now that I had my bearings I found that I had gone so circuitous that I went past my bunker without even seeing it. It was covered in sand and trees, not really easy to see. These bunkers were made below the dunes and hills to hide the entrances from enemy forces. It made them perfect for what I needed. I stopped when I stood across the road from the entrance, looking at the 18 ft. doors and wondering if I had left the one ajar or not. One door was open just enough for a body to get inside. I know the Deaders couldn't open doors, just like I know they don't swim or climb trees. I didn't remember doing it and Andromeda couldn't do that on her own, the doors were too heavy. There could have always been a transient in the area, or a group working from somewhere else and expanding their territory, it's not like these were kept secret before the Fall. A lot of people knew about these. If they looked around, this might have been the only one without a heavy lock on the outside anymore. It would have been an easy place to stay for the night. It was out of the way, it would have been pure dumb luck for someone to stumble upon my bunker among all of the others. My imagination may have been getting away from me again, the odds of this are so far from reality that there has to have been some other reason.

Unless, of course, they had been watching me for a while and waited for a time we were separated to make their move. Did they truly think they could just move in and take what's mine? If that happened, what did they do to Andromeda? Were they still there, did they move on? Panic was really setting in. Eventually I figured that the only thing I could do was go in and see for myself, sitting there was only allowing my imagination to go wild. My Dad always said I had a great imagination, in this world that was a curse, not a blessing.

Darkness was all I saw when I went up to the open door. Well, I guess open was an exaggeration, it was slightly ajar and I had to pull it farther open for me to get inside. I may have lost weight during the apocalypse but bone structure was still bone structure. No way that I could fit through without moving it, which was no easy feat as tired as I was. Remember WWII was a long time ago and no one has kept the maintenance up on these for many years. It did settle my mind a bit because if there was someone here, they either pulled the door closed behind them, or pushed it shut after they left.

But why would you do that?

If you came in and took what you wanted, wouldn't you just leave the door open when you were done? This pointed to them still being there. Pulling it closed would have warned them that I was back, that would have given them time to get ready for me.

No more delays. I had to know what had happened here in my absence. I eased the door open a little farther, as it let out a jarring screech, then I was in. No flashlight, no bow... *Wow was I unprepared.* I should have listened to Matthew more and stayed prepared for anything. He was a Boy Scout, his whole life. He loved it and lived it every day. He finally made Eagle Scout just after his 17th birthday, which made Mom and Dad so proud.

When I got into the bunker, I noticed was that it was completely dark. That could have been a good thing. If people were still here, wouldn't they have lights on? Unless they were sleeping I guess. I still didn't know what time it was. The next thing I noticed was that there were no sounds from anywhere. Even someone sleeping, or multiple someone's, there should have been noise of some sort. But they would have been quiet if they were lying in wait for me to get back. Especially after that loud metal band of a door announced my presence. There should also have been some sign if Andromeda was still here. I crept a little farther in, letting my thoughts drift from one bad scenario to the next. One bad thought made the next one worse.

Suddenly, my left foot slipped in something wet, making the concrete slippery. I couldn't tell what it was just that it wasn't a good sign. My mind instantly went to blood. The next thought was that I would be tripping over Andromeda's limp and dead body. I thought of her body lying in a pool of blood and the people that did it waiting just behind the next corner, or behind my chair. My mind was reeling. I couldn't control it, it was just too much. My eyesight adjusted a little more, although I didn't think I would be able to see much more. Perfect darkness was still perfect darkness. In times like these it was great to always have a phone to use as a flashlight.

I knelt down and touched the slippery substance. It didn't smell like blood, and I was not tasting it. The consistency was thick and slimy. I really couldn't tell what it was. The next instant I heard a low growl and something jumped from the darkness and bowled me to the ground. I fought to get a hold of whatever it was that had me. I was so scared that I couldn't think. The only thing I could do was react. There was a massive weight on my chest and hot breath in my face. I rolled to the side and pushed with everything I had and threw this thing to the ground. I struggled to get up and it was on me again. Standing over me, face to face. I was so scared I couldn't do anything. Whatever it was had me at a disadvantage and could do what it wanted. I was thinking that this was when I was going to die.

Then I felt a rough substance on my face. Starting at my chin and running up to my eyebrows. I got myself together and laughed despite myself. It was Andromeda, ok after all. I got back to a sitting position and felt around her ribcage and legs. I didn't feel any blood and my pushing hadn't caused her to stir, nothing seemed to be wrong with her. I pushed her off of me and got to the table to turn on a light.

I must have left the door ajar when I left. Trying to air out the place or something. I kinda remembered that after I thought about it some more. I could see that everything was fine and I didn't have to make a quick exit, I ran to the door to pull it shut before the light drew something that made my nightmares seem tame.

Ok, Ok, I'm guessing you have a new question.

Why was Andromeda growling and licking my face? Well, she was an 80 pound Chesapeake Bay retriever. She has been my best friend for as long as I could remember. She and her canine skills were part of the reason I had been able to outrun and outsmart the Deaders this long. She has a great sense of smell and hearing. She knows what to look for and what wasn't right. So I was kinda like Will Smith in that movie I am Legend. Badass dog that saves my life and grants me companionship. I was not trying to heal these things. Thinking about that movie though it's antagonist was a lot closer to these things than I realized before. Maybe Hollywood could get things right.

For those that don't know, Chesapeake Bay Retrievers are a water dog breed that was mainly used for duck and goose hunting. After the hunter would shoot the bird, they would jump into the freezing water, or run along the land to retrieve the bird and bring it back to the hunter. They have very strong bodies and an angled breast bone to break ice, if needed. They could track the bird from sight, smell and hear it if it was still moving. She and I used those skills to stay alive. Chesapeake's are mistaken for Labrador retrievers and have a similar build, but they are all brown and have oily kinky hair instead of the straight hair of a lab. They go from a very light tan to almost black in color. Andromeda was about as dark as a Chessie could get, which was part of the reason I couldn't see her before she jumped me. She has some sixth sense when

Deaders are near and knows how to avoid them. I guess a lot of animals do.

Once I found a flashlight, I could see that I slipped in a puddle of dog drool. She must have been sitting there waiting for me to come home for the longest time. Of course, she had to pant, she always pants. I was sure she went to the water bowl several times for a drink then returned right back to the same spot to wait. I hated to make her worry like that. Dogs didn't have the same sense of time as humans do, time could pass very fast or very slow for them. It really depended I guess. To make it up to her, I went in search of anything for her to eat, she must have been starving. Actually starving this time, usually she will pretend to be starving 5 minutes after eating, trying to beg some of my food. But I think she may really be hungry this time, since she missed dinner. I was ravenous too. I located some dried deer meat, pulled it apart for her and took a couple of bites, while I heated up some beans on the little burner I had. It was so good to be back with Andromeda, but I had to think about our next step. It wasn't going to work out this way forever, today was a perfect example of that.

While I ate the beans I thought about our options.

1. We stay in the park and continue to keep a low profile and hope these creatures didn't return in droves. Being on a peninsula and at the point of that peninsula meant there was not a lot of real estate to run around to stay away from them. Over 5,000 acres may seem like a lot, but not when you could only run north and south. There was also no real reason for them to come here. These two may have been a fluke today, but as I have said before, I have seen an increase in activity. There couldn't have been much for them to feed on around here. I have been trying to hunt for a while and was lucky to take down the deer I did.

2. We run, take everything we could carry and get out of this area. Not much of a plan but better than feeling trapped. But was it really any better? This was known. I would not know what I would encounter out on the road, especially with no real destination in mind.

As I finished my part of the beans and fed the rest to Andromeda I thought about which option was best. Stay or go? Known or unknown? I wished I could have been like my Mom and let eenie-meenie-miney-mo choose for me. I always was more like my Dad.

My heart wanted to stay and forget tonight's events. To just mark it as a fluke and move on the way things had been going. But my mind knew that the increase had to have something to do with the warmer weather. The animals in the area are one thing, but are the Deaders migratory? People were before they settled into cities and made homes to keep them warm in the winter. Natives always moved around to find food. Birds and other animals are migratory too. Weren't these things just basic animals? So this made sense. So that meant that as it warmed up, these things would head back to other areas, or come out of hiding.

Option 2 seemed the only viable option. Not only because of the Deaders, but because of resources. Food was scarce and getting harder to find. I wouldn't be able to go out on raids too much anymore if these things were running around again. Eventually, we would be found or we would run out of food. I was in a corner and there weren't too many ways to go. I needed to move, I thought that maybe I had stayed too long here as it was and these guys were just the reminder that I needed to get my butt in gear.

I could only head north to get off the Delmarva Peninsula. Both bay bridges were blown up by the military or some militant group, the truth was debated, trying to keep us safe from the infection. There were no international airports here to bring in the contamination and they had shut down the three regional airports before. Supposedly, they thought it would keep us safe from the plague. Now there was only one way off this place and that was to head north. Once I reached Pennsylvania I would have to figure out where to go from there. There was about 100 miles from here to there, that was a long time to think about what to do next. Moving and staying alive was always a good option. If I waited I could get caught with no food. Waiting until then to try to make a run for it would be impossible.

The best way up the coast was, literally, up the coast. Stay to the beaches and meander up that way. Keep away from any people that may still be out there. And keep most of the dangers to one side. No way to get turned around, keep the water on your right. Not hard.

I guess I had made my decision without even realizing it. The only thing left to do was get some sleep and pack up in the morning. I needed to make sure I had everything I needed to keep the two of us alive on the trek north with a little extra luck.Andromeda knew that something was amiss and that there was a change in the air. She always seemed to know what I was thinking even when I didn't say it out loud. She looked at me and then went to her bed and curled up. She wasn't one of those dogs that turned around three times before laying down, she would just plop down and be fast asleep in seconds. It always amazed me what she could ignore. I guess being a dog was a privilege sometimes.

Sleep

Real sleep this time. I could rest knowing that Andromeda and I were safe, for the moment. The doors were locked from the inside and there was no other way in. The Deaders couldn't see or hear me while I was in here. I could relax and take the time that I needed to think through this new course of action. Once I woke up with a clear head I could make better plans for the days to follow. I had to get to sleep first, I had a little bed area set up, no real mattress, just a bunch of scrounged blankets and my sleeping bag on top. It gave me more comfort than sleeping on the concrete floor.

As I laid there looking at the candle flickering in the moving air, I looked up at the graffiti art painted on the walls and ceiling in the times gone by. Some were just tags to let people know they were here, or to deface others' property. There was some real art painted too. You could tell when the world started to end people tagged notes about safe areas, about lost loved ones and where they were heading if they made it out of here.

I had read most of them in my time here, no TV or Snapchat to keep me entertained. But knowing it was my last night here, I wanted to let it all in, to let it wash over me. That bunker had seen so much over the years. Would it see anything more? Or when I shut the doors the following day would they never open again? Was the world that lost?

I started to drift off listening to the regular breathing of Andromeda, and occasional snore, at the foot of my makeshift bed. Thinking about things I tried not to think about all day every day. I thought about the days I was always warm, safe and happy. Sometimes it seemed like I was remembering someone else's life and not something just a couple of years ago. I had a big day ahead making plans and figuring out where we would go and how to get the supplies to get there.

It's kind of funny that when you are a kid you take the love and safety you get for granted. I had a lot of each, so much that I was surprised I could transition to this life as easily as I have. But then maybe having all that love and safety has stayed with me. It gave me something to hope for, to fight for. Not everyone was as lucky as me, but I didn't see it then. Like any kid, I hated that my parents were overly involved in my life. I wanted my privacy and to be left alone most of the time.

Now, I was on my own I had nothing but privacy, and I hated it. I would love to hear my brother's voice, see my Mom's loving face and have my Dad yelling at me for something I did wrong. It would all let me know everything was alright and normal in the world. I hated when I got in a loop thinking about my family. I tried not to think about them, to keep it at bay so I was not so sad. Losing them was the hardest thing in my life, even harder than living without them. Now I just moved around in a fog that kept me from thinking about them and what life was like before. I think that's why I like living here in the bunker and at the state park. It was old, before my time, yet none of it has aged much over the long time it has been here. It has always seemed like it defied time. The longer I stay here the longer I could put off how bad life has gotten in the real world.

I mean, I know how bad things have gotten but I could kid myself there. It was almost like I was just camping. When I leave the park I will just head home and everything will have been normal. My phone never had a signal here, so maybe it will have some back when I get back to Lewes and I will have hundreds of texts and voicemails from my family looking for me. Snaps from my friends showing the fun they have had all winter long without me.

These were the last thoughts I had as I drifted off to sleep. The only state that I could truly relax. At least for tonight, it will change in the days to come.

I was walking through the woods looking for firewood. My family and I were camping at Lums Pond State Park in northern Delaware. I loved this park. There was good fishing and I could take my paddleboard out on the pond to get out into the middle and just sit there listening to nature. I was planning on doing that later today after we got breakfast cooked.

I was looking for firewood. Mom was scrambling eggs and cutting scrapple. My Dad was self-congratulating himself for getting the fire started with nothing but flint and steel again. The fire was going and building up to a good cooking fire. We just needed some smaller wood to make coals a little faster to even out the heat.

I was kind of daydreaming as I walked until I saw something out of the corner of my eye. It was a fawn slowly walking out of the woods onto the trail. I stopped and tried not to move until she moved away. I didn't want to spook her. She looked right at me from about 40 yards away. Not scared, not knowing enough to be scared of man. She slowly walked off until I couldn't see her anymore. At this point, I could hear my Dad yelling for me to hurry up, so I grabbed another stick or two and hurried back to the campsite.

After breakfast was done and Matt and I cleaned up, we started to talk about what we were going to do that day. I wanted to head out onto the water, but Matt wanted to do Go Ape!, a high treetop course with three different zip lines out over the water. It would take most of the day due to some safety training and the length of the course. The three of us decided to do this and Mom decided that she would stay behind by the fire and read a book.

Glimpses of jumping from the zip lines to the different obstacles run through my mind. It was a great day......

I was in the woods again. This time I was sent out with five other teenagers to look for some food. The world ended about nine months ago. We were still getting used to the idea of the new way of life, and still hoping it would all end soon. Hoping that the government and the military would fix everything. Even though I had already lost my Dad and brother, my Mom and I were staying hopeful. We buried Dad, and feared Matt was dead, but his body was never found.

We have huddled tightly as a community as we lost contact with the outside world. We lived out in the country in a very small development. just outside the town of Lewes. Woods and fields surrounded us, there was even a small river to one side. Not a bad spot to hunker down.

We were laughing and joking as we came to the edge of the woods. John was in the lead and looked very concerned as he reached the edge. He stopped us and knelt down. We all stop laughing and were concerned. There was supposed to have been a sentry in the shed outside of the development. There was no fence, but we had people set at different spots to watch out for people or the dead. If no one was there, then it could mean bad news.

That's when we heard the first scream. John and the other boys dropped their bags and reached for the pistols strapped to their thighs. With a quick look back at us, the three of them took off at a sprint towards the screams. The other girl, Josephine, and I gathered their bags together and headed to the closest house, which happened to be my house. We stayed low but ran as fast as possible to get to cover. There were not many guns in our neighborhood, only three families actually had any guns at all. Most of them were long guns. So all we had were long hunting knives and one machete. There was a lot more screaming coming from a couple of houses down. We couldn't see anything else from where we were though.

Then we heard it, the cry from a Deader. It was known and unforgettable. They were there and they had found someone.

Gunfire. Over and over.

We reached the house and rushed inside as quickly as possible. Mom should have been there. I ran through the house screaming her name. Getting more and more scared as we moved through the rooms. My house was not big so she should have heard me as I walked in the door.

Then I heard movement in the back bedroom. Someone walking towards me. I slowly opened the door to see who it was. I was relieved to see Andromeda coming to me. But if she was there, Mom wasn't here. Andromeda knew that she shouldn't be in Mom's room. Josephine was scared for her family and wanted to go check on them. I threw some stuff in a bag along with the food that we found. I grabbed what I thought would be important for later. I knew that even if we found my Mom, there was no staying here.

We grabbed the bags and headed out the door and out the back. We needed to see if we could find Jo's family. But as we got out of the door and turned right, we heard a scream right behind us! A Deader scream. We were just seen by it. Then I heard another scream, it sounded like my mother. I hesitated, but just for a second. If she screamed she was caught, she was gone. We had to run to the woods, run away from the rest of the people to get some distance. Andromeda was in a low crouch and growling in the direction of the scream. Jo was screaming and trying to run to her house. She ran around the corner and straight into another Deader coming around that corner. They must have seen us go into the house. We thought we were careful, but we brought them straight to us.

Jo went down. I couldn't help her. So much happening, so much noise and confusion. I called for Andromeda and we ran towards the woods. Tears streamed down my face so bad I couldn't see where I was going. I could only see my dog as a brown blur, so I just followed her. She kept her pace so I could keep up, looking behind us every chance she got. When my vision cleared I looked up and saw we were not being followed. Jo screamed once, and only once. I knew she was gone.

We broke into the woods and stopped about 20 yards in. I slowed and tried to listen. I needed to know what was going on. The gunfire had stopped while I was entering the woods. I stayed quiet for what felt like forever, but was probably like 5 minutes. No more screams, no gunfire. No sound. I grabbed my knife and wanted to go back out there to see if anyone was still alive. As I tried to walk back out, Andromeda stood in my way. I moved past her and she grabbed my pant leg. She knew I couldn't go back. I knew it too. I huddled down to wait.

Time went by and no human was seen. The Deaders *moved into the homes and around the backsides of the houses. I couldn't see them any longer. I thought that it may have been safe to see what happened. To see if there were any survivors. But as I approached the edge of the woods I saw a Deader come around the edge of a house, looking towards the woods. Apparently, everyone else was gone and I was the only thing left in the area for them to eat.*

I could hear them communicating and see them coming my way, in my head. I couldn't stay there. If I did I would die like the rest. So against what I wanted to do, I grabbed our gear and ran. There was a sound in the woods, like a rustling and a whistle. It was just a bird scared out of its nest by me running through. Andromeda turned and looked, but she had always been interested in birds. She was a retriever. I whistled to her and kept looking forward. I ran and ran until I didn't even know where I was.

I jumped awake. I was still as scared as I was that day. Still crying from knowing I just lost my mother, my life and everything I ever knew. All except Andromeda, she was all I had left. At least with Dad we were able to mourn. We were able to say goodbye and bury him. I couldn't say the same about the rest of my family. They were lost to me. I still hoped that they got away, that they are looking for me. But how would they ever find me? I run from the slightest sound and keep hidden away far from anywhere people would look.

I grabbed Andromeda and cried into her fur for what felt like an hour. She didn't move, she knew what I needed and was always there when I woke like this. As I started to calm down she looked at me and licked my face. It gave me a small chuckle.

Well, we were up. No better time to get up and get started.

Planning

The beginning of the plan was pretty easy. North, I had to go north. When the sickness started spreading from around all of the airports in the area (BWI, Philadelphia International, Dulles and Reagan International in D.C) the locals thought we could keep it out by blowing every bridge. Basically trying to make the Delmarva Peninsula an island to itself. They blew part of the Virginia Bay Bridge-Tunnel collapsing part of the closest tunnel and making travel impossible. Other military groups also blew part of the Chesapeake Bay Bridge to Maryland. Obviously, this happened when we still had some sort of communication. I didn't hear about any of the northern bridges being blown, but I assumed they were too. The waterways are navigable without a big boat and I could see the other side, so I didn't need any navigation experience. That was good because I didn't have any idea how to navigate when it came to the water. I didn't think I could see moss on the north side of a tree in the middle of the bay.

So that was that. I decided to start heading north along the coastline. I would have to go inland at times to get around some of the bigger creeks and get some supplies. No water to drink from the ocean. Before the radio stations went down, there were rumors that the Deaders were not good in the cold. It was simply explained that their metabolism speeds up to keep their bodies warm in the cold temperatures. They are not dumb, but don't understand clothing and how to keep warm. I doubt they could build a fire. They would find and go to shelters when scared or hurt, but that was a basic animal instinct. If their metabolism ran at a higher rate in the cold they would need to feed more. Their basic instinct would keep them from the cold and moving to warmer temperatures. Basically they acted like cold-blooded animals. At least that was my theory. So maybe I needed to try to make it to New England, where the winters were longer. I thought that I could get us there without much problem. Well, geographically speaking, no problem. There would very well be a lot of problems along the way. Trips like this tended to bring problems with them in post-apocalyptic days.

It was a very long way with no transportation and no guarantee of food or shelter. I was sure I would run into at least one or two small pockets of the remaining humans too. That was always scary and you could never know what that might bring. There was nothing that could have been done about it. I couldn't plan against the unknown, I just had to be able to adjust as things came and be vigilant as we traveled. My dad taught me to hunt, and I had done well finding food over the last couple of months. I felt like I had the skills to put me on the right path.

I planned the food that I would take, I couldn't take too much, because it would only slow me down. All the cans got very heavy, very quickly. I did have some dried meat and some lighter packs of chips that I had saved. I just had to take what I could and get the rest along the way.

As I was taking stock of the food I had, I made a big breakfast for Andromeda and myself. No point in leaving food just to rot. Andromeda loved this idea of course, she would eat all day every day and get obese if I let her.

Do I take the baked beans or the green beans?

Corn in a can was good, but cream corn was all I had left, it just didn't cook right without salt and pepper. So I decided to leave all of that behind. I didn't realize I had accumulated so many cans over the past months. I knew I had some good hauls, but not this much. I've got some spam, some carrots and kidney beans. I didn't really like the kidney beans by themselves, but they were a good natural supplement. I packed up what I could carry and then returned to my breakfast.

As we ate I also packed up my only possessions left from before. My phone (dead of course), a family picture showing the four of us, my sleeping bag, backpack, the hunting knife I had the day my Mom was killed and a bow with six arrows I found while scavenging in Lewes. Not much in possessions, but it would keep us moving fast and wouldn't weigh us down. My biggest worry was water because I couldn't carry too much and couldn't guarantee I would be able to find some when I needed it, so I decided to take more water than I thought was prudent. As I drink it the weight would subside, I could make it work. Its times like this that I wished Andromeda was a horse, not a dog. But I still wouldn't want to do this without her.

All packed up. Nothing left to keep me from moving to the door and getting started. Nope. Nothing. Still not moving. Apprehension kept me rooted in place. Andromeda sensed this and started whining to go out. She knew we had to move, she sensed it too. So I got up off my laurels and pushed myself to the door. I opened it just a bit to look out and see if there was anything there. I then opened it a bit more to let Andromeda out to have her own look around.

As Andromeda sniffed around she seemed to be completely at ease. I did one final look around and took stock of our supplies one more time. I would have to go long times between drinking and eating to stretch what I had as long as possible. But I felt like I had at least a weeks' worth of food and water. That could get me quite a ways. The average person could walk 20 miles per day. So that was 140 miles in 7 days. That was very unlikely with the terrain and looking for food and shelter. But even half that was over 70 miles in that week. That should put me out of Delaware at the least. I had delayed long enough. The morning was moving along without me. I pulled up my pack and tightened the straps. Andromeda and I looked at each other, I took a deep breath and took the first step on our long journey.

And with that first step, I tripped on a stick and fell face-first to the pavement. I hit my face and saw stars.

I checked my chin and my teeth. Nothing bleeding just a bit hurt. Not a great first step on this journey. Andromeda sat there looking at me with her goofy grin, almost like she was laughing at me. Chesapeake's do this thing where they look like they are grinning, I have always called it the Chessie grin. Thought it was always cute, now it looks like she was making fun of me.

Stupid dog!

I picked myself up and planned on making my second step a little bit better. I couldn't help but think how history would've looked back at the moon landing if Neal Armstrong had gone to take that first monumental step and face planted on the moon.

That would have been classic.

Can you imagine the news headlines? Americans land on the moon to plant a flag, but face plants instead. The Russians and Chinese would have loved that. Would he have bounced back up to his feet, or slid for 20 feet along the moon's surface? All of this ran through my head as I sat there, trying to get back up. I guess this was another way for me to delay the journey. Andromeda just stood there and looked at me, wondering why I was still on the ground. I stopped daydreaming and wallowing in self-pity and got to my feet.

Now I looked at where my feet were going and started off on the path to take us to the fishing pier. This part of the trip took very little thinking. I had made this trip several times over the last couple of months. On my way through, I picked up the fishing pole I had been using. It broke down in half so it was a little easier to carry. In an hour I would be up to Lewes beach, then I would be out of the area that I knew so well and would have to be more careful of my chosen path.

Walking

There were a lot of romantic movies that had couples walking on the beach at sunset. Meeting on the beach at sunrise. It was a great feeling and solidified the relationship in those movies. I had always loved being at the beach, which was probably why that was where I ended up when everything went wrong. Scientists used to say that the smell of the beach, the saltwater, was calming and would help de-stress you. I always believed this was true. I always felt calmer on the beach or in the water. I would spend hours on a paddleboard or just hanging on the beach and fishing, always keeping my mind occupied, while letting my muscle memory run my actions and letting my subconscious work through my problems.

This was not the case on this day. I was taking in all that I could. I was worried about what was around the next corner and what was to come. I couldn't know the outcome or what was outside of Lewes. I had not been there in a long time. What had changed? Had the world fallen further apart, or had the human capacity for change allowed them to fight back and take back some of what was ours? Did more people move into the area in search of food and shelter since the last time I had been there? All questions I had, although the answers would only reveal themselves in time.

Andromeda walked beside me at the water's edge sniffing the air and running ahead at times. She saw birds, seagulls and Pipers, running along the sand. She ran after them at times, but never too far. She never barked or drew unneeded attention, she was just having fun. She was also wary, I could see it in her stance when she stopped and looked at the dunes. She sensed something, but nothing quite defined enough to stop her, or cause her concern. So I paid no attention to it myself. She was always more apt to sense something before I was. Guess it helped to have a greater sense of smell and hearing than humans.

We walked out towards the ferry terminal. This place was always busy before the Fall. It always had people going to and from New Jersey on the large ferries. Today there were no ferries, no cars, and no people. As we walked towards this old landmark, I looked at our surroundings and thought about the past.

It was the dead of winter, just before Christmas. My parents, brother and I were driving down King's Highway towards Cape Henlopen state park. We were going to look at the lights at Cape's Winter Wonderfest. They put lights up around the park and you drove through at your own pace and looked. This was better than the lights at Ocean City, MD because you could stay warm in your car. The plus of that was that you got to ride on a train around and see their lights. The downfall was that you had to wait for hours in the cold because it was always very busy. Then the train was a kiddy train that was open to the weather. At Cape we were warm inside our car and brought our own hot chocolate, or coffee in Daddy's case. Momma liked coffee but always got hot chocolate with us.

After visiting the lights, we talked about what we saw and what we liked as we headed to the ferry terminal. They have a carnival set up, you could ice skate, walk through Santa's Village and enjoy some carnival rides. I liked to ice skate even though I was not very good at it. It was hard to learn here in Sussex County, since we didn't have any ice rinks and it wasn't cold enough in the winter for ponds to freeze.

We walked around for a while and my brother and I skated. It was better than last year because it is actual ice. Last year was the first year and they had sprayed some water on plywood to make it slippery. It worked, but it wasn't very good. As we were walking it started to snow. Not hard, no wind, just a light falling of precipitation. Enough to make it feel like Christmas, even though it was still 13 days off. My family just stopped and we all held hands. Daddy's arm around Momma, looking up at the falling flakes, Christmas lights on and music playing in the background. Just a perfect night.

That was just a year or two before The Fall. We never made it back to see those lights together after that. I guess it was too perfect. My brother was older and had to work or hang out with his girlfriend. I got busy with my friends and we just never got around to it. There never seemed to be a push to have to. We didn't go every year just when we had time all together to enjoy. Thinking about it still brought a smile to my face.

As we approach the ferry terminal, it looked nothing like it did that night. It was burnt and run down. It looked like there had been a fire. I didn't know if people tried to get on the last ferry off this island, and when they couldn't they set fire to the place in frustration, or if the government saw this as a way off or on the peninsula and burnt it down, like they blew all the bridges. Either way, there was nothing here. I had been through it once before and found nothing of use, I wasn't going to waste my time again.

Andromeda and I kept walking up the beach to Lewes Beach. I came here with my great grandmother a lot when I was young. My father grew up on this beach with her and my grandmother. It was small and there wasn't much to it, but it was great for parents or grandparents with little kids. There were hardly any waves because the bay was usually calm, only disturbed by winds and heavy storms. In between the dunes was a flat open beach, you could see everything going on all at once. They could let the kids play and not worry about something bad happening.

It was no different on this day. There was no wind and no storm system, just a large placid body of water. It would have been a great day to get my paddleboard out and see how far out I could go. Just me, the wind and the water, enjoying the relaxation and the sun. Letting it melt away all of the bad and just refocus on the good and the steady. But that was no more. Now I had to concentrate on moving north and getting as much distance each day as possible. All the while keeping my attention around me for dangers.

You could see all the way to downtown from the parking lot of the beach. You could stop at the Dairy Queen on the corner, if there had been ice cream in the world at that time. That was one of my first stops on my first foray into town. It was a great disappointment, no ice cream left in the freezers and no food left in the whole place. I didn't know what I had expected, but it didn't pan out. *Oh well.*

Dairy Queen was not the only reason that I looked down this opening. There could have been danger there. It was very wide open, as I had said, and we were exposed. Not much I could do to hide along this 200 foot stretch of beach. Just had to be calm and get to the other dune as fast as possible. It seemed safe and Andromeda didn't seem to sense anything, so we just kept walking.

As we walked I had to think about what I would do as we got to the yacht club. There was no walking over the channel at that point. There was no bridge or land to get across. I could go inland before I got there or see if there was a boat and row across. Worst case I could swim but it was still cool outside and the water was frigid. There was no way I could continue if I jumped in the water and swam. I would have to stop and get warm and dry again before I would be able to carry on. I would lose a day at the least. I was in no rush but there was no reason to throw away a day if I did not have to.

I decided to keep walking towards the yacht club in hopes that I could find some kind of boat to cross. Anything else would take me into more populated areas, or what used to have been more populated. There was more chance that someone was still there, or that I would run into them. The area north of the beach had a lot more houses looking out to the water I was hoping these were the first abandoned and that no one was there.

Nothing seemed to be out of place as we made our way up the beach. I didn't see any curtains moving or any signs of life at all in the homes. With the chill still in the air you would think that if someone lived in the area you would see the smoke of a fire so they could stay warm. With that being the case we made it to the yacht club with no interruptions. I started looking around the marina for a boat of some kind, but didn't see anything of use, while Andromeda was sniffing around looking for anything out of place. Too bad she couldn't smell a boat for us.

There was nothing in the sheds or the marina. We looked for about 30 minutes and couldn't find anything that would help. I thought that this was the wrong choice and that we needed to head back down to the beach to find somewhere inland to get past the canal. Just as I was about to give up I saw a shed behind the house next to the marina.

Now, who would live next to a marina and not own a boat?

I walked over to check it out, but as we approached, Andromeda started growling and looked towards the shed. Shit! Why was she growling? I started backing away slowly, keeping my eyes open and trying to get Andromeda's attention to back away with me. She was so set on what was in front of her that she wasn't paying me any mind. I yelled for her again in a hushed whisper, but still nothing.

She had stopped growling but was still very intent on the shed.

Out of nowhere, she bolted to the shed at full speed. We were only about 50 yards from the shed, so she covered it instantly. Just as she approached the shed, there was a burst of movement out of the bushes. A form came flying out from the side of the shed and bolted away from Andromeda!?

I screamed at Andromeda to run. To get away. I couldn't lose her too. We were too close! We had to find a way to get away from them!

Away? The form was running away from us. Not attacking.

Then as my fear settled from my brain I realized the form was a small deer. It ran off before Andromeda could catch it. She only chased it for another hundred yards or so before she turned and walked slowly back towards me.

"Dammit Andromeda! You scared the shit out of me! Don't do that again!" I yelled at her. More in fear than in anger.

She walked back and hung her head. So I apologized and petted her head. She was just looking for food and maybe a way to burn some pent-up energy. I am sure she had picked up a lot of nervous energy from me all day. I laughed at myself and the irrational fear that had hit me. If I had been thinking I could have gotten a shot off with my bow and maybe got some fresh meat. Oh well, maybe next time.

Now that was over, I walked back to the shed, sweating bullets that anything else may jump out at me. My heart still racing at the could haves and would haves. All I heard was my heart trying to beat out of my rib cage. I stopped to steady myself and got everything under control. I breathed in then out, controlled my breathing to calm myself. I never did yoga, when that was a thing but I did read about it on blogs and on social media. The only thing that had really stuck with me was the breathing. The way to calm myself when things got out of control. It really helped with anxiety attacks too.

I reached the shed and checked the door, unlocked. I slowly opened the door and peeked inside. There was a two-person metal canoe sitting right in the middle of the shed. It was covered in dust and full of things that seemed to have been thrown around the shed in the haste to get out of the area. I checked the canoe and it seemed to be in working order, no holes or rust. I couldn't believe my luck.

I looked some more, but couldn't find any oars. That was fine because I could make something to move us across. With a little more looking I found a tennis racket in the junk and a couple of plastic bags. I used the bags to cover the racket. It would not be the best, but it would be functional. I took my backpack and bow off my back and threw them inside the canoe. It would take a bit of effort to drag the canoe down to the water by myself. In the end it still saved me a lot of time walking back inland. As I put the canoe in the water I tried to get Andromeda to understand that she had to get in the boat. She didn't like the idea herself, so I picked her up, even though she weighed half of what I did, and dropped her in the boat.

I jumped in and pushed us off the shore, before she could change her mind and jump back out. Even so she didn't make it easy, she was moving around and looking over the sides. I spent more time keeping us out of the water than paddling us forward. It was slow going, but we made it almost to the shore without tipping over. It felt good to move forward while being able to rest my back and legs. Taking that extra water may have been good in the end, but at the beginning, it was killing me.

Maybe the winter made me a bit lazy too. But we will go with the extra weight.

As I was enjoying just drifting across the water and thinking that maybe it would have been better to boat up the coast so I didn't have to keep walking, Andromeda hunkered down and went stock still looking at the shoreline. She wasn't growling, but she was very intent. I took stock of my surroundings a little better, the sun was starting to go down. Not yet sunset, but getting close. I guess it took me longer to walk there and look around than I had thought. I could have sworn it was only 1 or 2, but it must have been closer to 4. The weather had started to warm, but it was still early March so it was pitch black by 6 o'clock. The buildings around the shoreline are very dark inside, they didn't have many windows and the doorways were wide open.

Andromeda was still looking intently, so I decided to pull my racket in and let the boat drift as I got as low as I could. Just as I looked up again, I saw what she could already sense. It was one of the dead standing just inside the door of the building to the left, an old Coast Guard station. I needed to stay low and move farther up the canal. I didn't know if I could risk being anywhere near where this thing could see me, and I was a sitting duck on the water with no cover.

I was working through all my options in my mind as we floated by. There were several other buildings up ahead but I couldn't see if they had closed doors, or more Deaders. In my experience, Deaders wouldn't, or couldn't open doors, so if the building was closed up it was usually safe from them. Unless they had been trapped inside.

Unexpectedly, the deader came out of the doorway and into the daylight. He must have seen me. Then suddenly he was calling out to the others in the area. It was not a voice like you would think, and not like any animal call you would ever hear. The human voice box was not made to make noises such as these it was high-pitched and barely audible. Andromeda may have been able to hear these ranges, which was why she might know they are near before any human would. I took a second and looked at this creature. He barely looked human any longer. He was bent, decayed and his movements were jerky. For it to be out in the full sun, he must have been desperately hungry, or rabid.

Can these creatures get rabies? Possibly I guess they were still biologically human. Could you imagine this getting bit by a crazy, mouth foaming raccoon?

It didn't look right though. Maybe if they don't feed the body's natural decay starts to take effect? Maybe they could die of natural causes, after they died of natural causes.

I did know that I needed to disappear. But how, when I was out in the water in a metal boat. No bushes, no trees, no concrete bunker to save me today. He was above me so even ducking down would allow him to see me and Andromeda. Then it hit me, I was in a metal boat. Metal blocks electrical signals, or could at least mask them. If it was in as bad of shape as it looked, it may not have been able to see well. I quickly pulled on my bow and backpack and grabbed ahold of Andromeda so she didn't panic. Then I did the last thing that I wanted to do. I took a quick breath, then another to steady myself. Then.I capsized the canoe!

The water was as cold as I thought it would be. Andromeda started pulling away from me and started trying to swim. I held onto her and surfaced under the canoe. Luckily there were bars across the canoe that I could hold onto. The weight of my backpack and holding onto Andromeda threatened to pull me back under.

The cold took away my breath and made me start to panic. It was murky water that did not allow much light in, add to that being under the boat, it was dark and hard to see.

I could still hear the Deader calling around. It must have been confused to have lost its prey so quickly. It worked, my guess was right. I just had to stay there and slowly push the boat further up the channel to get away from them. All while holding my dog, bag and trying not to drown in the process.

I passed where the Deader should be and pulled the canoe to the shoreline. This way I could rest under the canoe, but have my body on the land, until it was safe to come out again. I had thought this area would be safe. Now I had to wait them out. Luckily, Andromeda wasn't a normal dog, she trusted me. As long as I held her she wouldn't fight or try to swim away. I just had to stay strong enough for the both of us. I had to keep us safe.

Just as I had that thought, something scraped along the front of the canoe. I could see shadows moving along around the outside of the canoe. With the sharp angle of the nose on this type of canoe the sides didn't fully sit on the ground, especially at the hard angle of the shoreline that I had pulled up to.

It meandered around the area but seemed lost and confused. Some of that was the canoe, the other I think was the loss of cognitive function from the deterioration. The brain would probably deteriorate faster than the body. I had to stay quiet and still to not show any more open areas than absolutely necessary. I pushed farther back from the nose of the canoe and back into a little bit deeper water. Maybe with the water and the metal I could mask any signals this thing was looking for. I grabbed ahold of Andromeda harder and made sure she knew that I had her safe.

Fear crept in with the cold.

Cold

The cold sank in and I had lost feeling in my hands and feet. I had no idea how long I had been in the water. I knelt to take the weight off my arms and put Andromeda down so she could stand on her own. But we had stayed under the metal canoe to stay out of sight. We hadn't heard anything in a while before it got dark. I tipped the boat ever so slightly out of the water on one side to let Andromeda out. She was better at seeing and not being seen than I. I heard her shake off and start sniffing around, and waited for her to search. I was not sure how much longer I could stay in the water.

It seemed like forever, but was only a couple of minutes until I heard Andromeda scratching on the canoe. She wasn't whimpering or growling, so the coast should have been clear. I rolled the canoe off of me and tried to stand. My legs couldn't take the weight and I fell. I was in rough shape, being in the cold water for that long meant I was probably getting hypothermia. I had to move, I had to get inside, somewhere to lock myself in. Somewhere to get warm, before I died.

After several tries, I got to my feet and walk/hobbled to the nearest building. Before I went in, I saw the door was already open. Couldn't choose that one, I moved to the next. This was a large building, it used to be a research and recovery facility for ocean life. I hoped there were warm supplies in there still. Everything I owned was soaked.

Andromeda walked beside me and kept her eyes and nose out for danger. I was using all my focus just to stay on my feet, just to keep moving. We moved to the door, and it was closed. Good. As I turned the handle I found that it was locked. Not good. I was way too tired and unstable to be able to knock the door in. My hands were shaking, so I couldn't pick the lock even if I knew how. I looked up and down the other sides and didn't see another door. That might have made it safe, but it was safe even from me. I saw a window to the side and decided to check to see if it was open.

I approached the window and pushed up on the glass. It moved! The window was open. I told Andromeda to stay by the door and left my pack there too. There was no way to get them up there in my condition. I pulled myself up to the window. Luckily, it was a normal 1ˢᵗ floor window and nothing higher. I didn't think I could have made anything else. I tried to pull myself over the edge and put my feet down, but my body didn't cooperate. I ended up falling on my shoulder and left side. I kept from hitting my head, but only barely.

My parents didn't name me Grace for a reason.

I moved as fast as I could, which was close to a snail moving through peanut butter. Andromeda won't leave me now and she is out there by herself. If they see her we are both in danger. As I moved to the door I tried to take in what I could about this place. There was not much to see. It looked like a warehouse but it had big water tanks in random spots. It seemed that this must have been a holding center for some of the aquatic animals. I had pictured something more along the lines of Dolphin tale, not a lab setting. But in real life, I guess this made more sense.

I got to the front door. I tried to open the deadbolt, but my hands wouldn't cooperate. I noticed that my fingers were blue and my hands wouldn't close properly. It was getting very hard to stand and I couldn't feel my feet at all, my insides wouldn't stop shaking, I couldn't breathe and my head was spinning. I focused and tried again. The second time I was able to get the lock to open. I opened the door to let Andromeda in and got my pack. Andromeda was happy to see me as always, she was no worse for wear from the cold, Chesapeakes were made to survive cold water. I closed and locked the door, then assessed my priorities. First, I had to get warm.

I shuffled to the back of the facility to where the supplies would be. There are go bags below what used to have been cubbies. They had been ransacked and the supplies were thrown about. Everything worth anything is probably taken. Just as I felt all was lost a glint of a small bag caught my eye. It was sticking out of an inside pocket of an open bag. "Emergency Blanket" was on the package. I had heard of these, they were supposed to be great at keeping all body heat in. They were made of mylar and were similar to the heat shielding used on the space shuttles. Or was, when we had those. As I opened the package I see that it is just a thin metal sheet, like aluminum foil, only more pliable. I am not sure what this thing can do, but was better than nothing. I grab the blanket and wrap myself in it. After several minutes I started to feel a bit better. Not good mind you, just better. I decided to search the other bags around us.

I found five more blankets still in their packaging, a couple of small hand towels, some hand sanitizer and a flint and steel kit. All things that others would think nothing about. I slowly and deliberately focus and get two of the blankets open. They are undamaged and whole.

I moved to a small office that was sparse with furniture but had a carpeted floor. I undress to get out of my cold wet clothes and get Andromeda to lay down on the floor. She is mostly dry at this point but I used one of the towels to dry her off a little bit more. I was getting very sleepy, but I knew I needed to stay awake and get this done. I used the other towel to dry me off. Mostly my hair.

I wrapped myself around Andromeda while wrapping one of the blankets around my back. I rip a piece of the other blanket off and lay it on the floor, then dump the bottle of hand sanitizer on it in front of me. I tried to get my hands to cooperate once more. It took three or four times to get the flint and steel to spark. On the fifth time, I finally got a spark and it ignited the very flammable alcohol in the sanitizer. This wouldn't burn long, but it would burn hot. I used the last of the second blanket as a heat shield to direct the heat towards us. I teepee the two together over my head with an office chair. The kind that is in every child's room and every office in America. Then I laid down on the carpet. I could instantly feel the heat from Andromeda and the flame warming me.

This made me even sleepier and my head started drooping. This would have been a very bad thing at that point, if the alcohol from the hand sanitizer hit the carpet we would die from the fire. Wouldn't that have been ironic? Trying not to die from cold water and end up dying from the fire meant to keep me warm?

I'd rather not.

I was able to keep myself awake long enough to let the fire burn itself out. Then I pulled the second blanket down around me and pulled it in tight. I had started getting feeling back in my extremities and my insides had stopped shaking for the most part. But, now I had to pee. I guess my insides were thawing and the function was returning. Good thing, yes, but I was not about to get up and find somewhere to pee. I was just getting warm. So I pushed this to the back of my mind and concentrated. I could now let myself sleep, just for a bit, not too long.

I could see my dad. Different images through time. Him sitting at a game of mine. Him throwing the softball to me. Pitching to me so I could bat, then practice catching.

The glimpses were coming so fast. So many memories of his face and what we did together. The others were there too, but the focus was my dad.

The scene shifts. I knew this place, it was my house. The house I grew up in. Usually, I would have loved to remember this house. To remember the things that happened in this house. But not this day. I recognized this day and I try to wake myself up. I was a third party to the events that I knew all too well. Events that ended my world and ended the way things had always been in my life.

This was the day that my father was killed and my mother and I went on the run. The day we left Matt behind to never be seen again. The worst day of my entire life, I couldn't stop the events from turning, from becoming what I knew they would become. I screamed at the top of my lungs for them to run, for the images to stop. But in the end, I just looked on in resignation of the end and hoped that I would wake up before the gruesome finale.

My Dad was cutting vegetables in the kitchen. We had started growing them after the fall of society. He had built our own little greenhouse in the backyard. We never had green thumbs, but we could get things to grow. Especially, when you needed them to grow for basic survival.

We got meat when my Dad and others would go on hunting forays into the surrounding woods. We lived in a small ranch style house and shared a small development with 20 other families. Dad and about four other men in the area had guns and knew how to hunt.

We came together as a community, everyone growing and sharing food. Making large meals for everyone to eat to save the resources we still had. We had lost power about three months ago and we're still adjusting to the way things were. Some thought the government would get everything back up and running, others hoped they wouldn't. We had heard about bad things happening overseas and in some of the big cities in the US, but nothing of the report had happened close to us. Radio broadcasts in the last three months had been spotty at best and offered no real information about what was happening.

Recently we had seen bright flashes in the distance and heard muffled explosions that seemed to have been from far away. So we thought nothing about it. We kept moving on and doing things the best we could. Luckily, our family had done a lot of camping over our life, so we had sleeping bags and tents, camping utensils and camp stoves. We had always loved our backyard fires, so we had a huge backyard fire pit, that was now our kitchen.

My Dad was a survivor. He knew how to camp, hunt, fish and live in the outdoors. He had loved the outdoors so much that we had all learned most of these traits. Mom didn't hunt or fish, but liked the outdoors. Even luckier for her, she could still sleep indoors during this extended camping trip.

I think we had the dinner shift tonight, so we were making meat stew. You couldn't call it beef stew, rabbit stew or even venison stew. Mostly because it had all of these. We used what meat we had that hadn't gone bad. It was February but luckily it wasn't a very cold winter in Delaware. The big community pot was on the fire. Mostly, these meals were very bland but food is food and you ate what you got.

I went out to check on Mom, who was tending the water and making sure the fire stayed hot. This was when the first scream split the air. It was a high-pitched scream and it ended very abruptly. At this point everything just stopped. Mom was looking through the house. Dad was running out the front door, shotgun in hand and pistol on his hip. We could hear several others yelling for help as they ran towards the scream.

It had come from the Anderson house at the front of the community. They kept to themselves and only came around when their help was needed. The next thing we heard will never leave my mind. I hear it in every dream. It was what I now know as the scream of a Deader.

There were several of these screams followed by a lot of shooting. Then the shooting stopped. The screams stopped and the world stopped.

Then another scream like the first, directly followed by Deader screams split the air.

Dad came barreling around the house as fast as he could run.

He was yelling at us to get in the house and close the doors. Directly behind him was the scariest thing I had ever seen. It was a woman running behind him, bleeding from what looked like a lot of bullet holes in her chest and even one from her head. The only thought in my head was; How could someone survive with a hole in their head? Then Dad was yelling again. He saw Mom and I hesitate, he grabbed us by the arms and threw us inside.

"Get in the big closet! Close all the doors you go through. Keep your heads down and wait until I come to get you!" he said "I love you both. Tell Matt I love him too!"

Then he turned and fired into the woman again. She stopped but didn't fall. The next thing I knew we were inside running for the bedroom. Mom closed every door on the way, leaving them unlocked for Dad. Just as she went to close the last door I screamed for Andromeda. She came running from my room and into my arms. I hurried her into the closet and shut the door behind us.

We sat there in the dark, listening. We heard more yelling, especially Dad's voice. Telling others what to do and where to go to keep the women and children safe. More of the ungodly screams. Then a couple of last gunshots. Then only silence. We waited for Dad, waited for something.

The longer we waited the more certain we became that Dad wouldn't be coming to get us. The more certain he had just given his life so we could live. Only once did we hear a noise that sounded like it was inside the house. It was near the beginning but Mom and I stayed quiet and huddled closer. There was no call out just a door opening and footsteps, hesitant footsteps. We thought we were done, goners, trapped in the closet with no weapons and nowhere to run. But as quickly as they came, the footsteps were gone out the same door they had come in. Maybe it was left open a bit and not shut correctly. That's how they got in. We didn't remember to look when we ran inside.

Hours later we decided we had waited long enough. Mom told me to stay put while she went out and looked. I didn't like this idea but she wouldn't relent. So to stop the arguing I sent Andromeda with her. They walked back to where we had last seen Dad. When they did not see immediate danger Mom called to me to join them.

The fire was out in the pit. Pieces were thrown everywhere and the pot was knocked over. But nothing of him. We looked and looked around the house. There were several bodies, many people we knew. Some we didn't. The ones we didn't were either decapitated or had knives in the back of their necks. They must have been the attackers. As we went between our two cars in the driveway I saw his boots. Both were covered in blood and he was laying on the ground. Mom and I ran to him, one on each side, holding his hands, begging him to be ok. But as we looked at him and held him, we knew that he was gone. No real marks, the blood on his boots was not even his. But he was no longer with the living, no longer with us.

I woke with a start. Bolted upright so fast that I got tangled in the emergency blankets that I was wrapped in. It took me several moments to remember where I was and what had happened. It felt like that day had happened again and I was just that scared little girl holding my Dad's hand.

Andromeda looked at me from where she was across the room. Looking at the door. She had that worried look again. I got up and wrapped the single blanket tighter around me again. I started to pick up my clothes but felt that they were still damp from before.

How long had I slept? I felt confused, groggy and lost but my hands and feet had returned to normal color and I had decent mobility back in them. I looked out the door and could see that it was daylight outside. I had slept the entire night and part of the day. I pulled the door open and let Andromeda outside to pee and then pulled the stuff out of my bag to let things dry as I got food for us to eat. I made sure to drink a lot of water to let my body heal.

"Nothing heals the body like a regular intake of water" Dad used to say.

After I let Andromeda back in she walked through the warehouse as I gathered a couple of things, like paper and cardboard, to start a small fire. The place was big enough and the floor was concrete, so if I started a small fire to dry out my clothes and cook a meal, it wouldn't fill the area with smoke. Since the building had concrete walls I was safe from the dead too. Not a bad place to finish up the day.

After eating and having the fire burning, I moved my sleeping bag and my clothes close to dry out. I spent the rest of the day wrapped in the emergency blanket, which was quite annoying because it made a lot of noise when I moved just a tiny bit. But it was warm and I was not walking around naked. I went back through the bags by the cubbies, making sure there was nothing else of use in them. There really wasn't, but it was worth the check. I then went through the rest of the building. It had been checked over good in the past so it didn't hold any treasures for us to keep.

By this time everything was dry, I put out the fire and headed back to the office I had slept in the night before. After getting dressed and wrapped back in my emergency blanket, I thought about what had gone wrong and what I needed to do in the future to be better.

First thing; I would not be going back into the water. It was faster and more relaxing, but also very deadly if things went wrong. So I would stick to land from now on. With the rest of the trip I had planned, it really wouldn't be that hard.

Second thing; I should keep my clothes in a plastic bag to keep them dry in weather or another water issue. I would have to be on the lookout for plastic bags when I could.

Third; I now felt very ill-prepared for this journey and didn't know if I can do this alone.

I kept this thought for only a second. I couldn't let it get in my head. I had Andromeda and she would help me through this. She was the one that alerted me to the Deader to begin with. It was a hard night, but I was a Washington and we didn't give ground easily. Tomorrow would be better. I would be better prepared and know more than I did yesterday.

Andromeda and I ate a small meal again and laid down for another night's sleep. Day 3 would go better than Day 1. It really had to because that was a disaster and I didn't get very far.

Fishing

It was the crack of dawn, but I didn't do much but sleep for the past 24 hours, so I was going to take an hour and do some fishing. I could use the meat and this was a perfect spot for flounder. Since it was spring, the worms and other creepy crawlies were moving around enough for me to get some bait. I really didn't want to use any of my food for bait at this point, and none of it had spoiled yet.

After about five minutes of digging, I found a couple of worms and a roly-poly, enough to get some fish, I hoped. I walked to the pier and cast my rod. Of course, Andromeda was with me and she was keeping a keen ear out for trouble. The deader from the other day was nowhere to be found. I had heard him calling for his pack, but I never saw another. Hopefully, it was alone.

As I sat there waiting for a fish to take the bait, I started thinking about how bad a shape that deader had been in. It was like, Walking Dead zombie from season 8 bad. Barely moving and decayed so badly you couldn't tell the sex. I wondered what could make that thing look that way. In the past, they all looked normal. They didn't seem to decay and look like zombies. They had weird jerky movements to them, different than a normal human would make, then you had the weird glowing eye trick too. But other than that they could move and looked like I do.

Well, maybe not as pretty as me. But you get the picture.

This made me wonder how much I really knew about these creatures. Not much at all from what I was seeing. Hopefully enough to stay alive for a while longer though. Suddenly, my rod bumped and I was reeling in a small flounder. It may not meet the game warden limits imposed a few years ago but I think getting arrested and fined by a game warden was the least of my worries. I stuck it in the bucket and tried again.About 30 minutes later I had three new fish to add to my bucket and I was all out of worms. It was amazing how the wildlife had grown over the past two years.

The sun was up so I decided to gather up Andromeda and head back inside. I started a fire again in the warehouse on the concrete floor, with actual fuels this time. Less smoke and more consistent heat from wood over cardboard. I started with paper that I found and worked my way up to boards and office furniture that I was able to break down into smaller pieces. I rigged up something to let me cook the fish over the fire after I gutted and cleaned them. They tasted amazing. Andromeda seemed to like hers too, you could never really tell though since she would eat just about anything.

There was no time to relish and procrastinate. I got everything packed back up and got ready to hit the road. Well, not the actual road. I wanted to avoid that. It was just a saying my parents used to use.

We walked back to the boat that I beached a day ago. I know I said I wouldn't go back on the water, but we are in the middle of a marsh and I needed to get over to the other side of the canal to get anywhere north of here. We loaded up and I used my makeshift paddle to get us the rest of the way across. Andromeda was even more leery this time.

I guess getting dumped unceremoniously into the water will do that.

Nothing out of the ordinary happened and we got across safely. We then headed up the beach towards Broadkill. There were a lot of beach houses and cottages in that area. Some of them could still be intact and useful to us. The sun was midway up in the sky when we ditched the boat on a sand dune. We had lost half the morning. I really didn't have a timetable or anywhere to be, so I tried to enjoy the walk.

It really was the little things you learn to enjoy in a post-apocalyptic world. The sounds of birds chirping all around, the water and its little bit of movement along the beach. The smell of saltwater. My aunt used to tell me that a day at the beach would relax away all of your stress. She would swear it was a scientific fact. I think she just made it up to excuse sitting at the beach and doing nothing all day while drinking wine coolers with my mom. But maybe that was the stress reduction she needed. Andromeda and I walked for an hour or so before we started seeing houses on our left. Most of these were not in tip-top shape before The Fall, so you could imagine what they looked like now.

We slowed our pace and walked closer to the dunes to keep an eye on the houses for any movement we could see. We kept this up until we were past the houses and what used to be the beach store. We had seen nothing to spook us or spark our interest in these homes, we just kept moving. It was past lunchtime, but the breakfast we had was still sticking with me. The area north of the store had a lot more homes and potentially a lot more danger. We moved along to this area with bated breath.

Since I had eaten fish, my breath may have smelled like bait too!

As we got a couple of streets farther north, I thought about doing some recon in the houses to see if there were supplies we could use.

Note* When searching homes that have been closed up for months or years, with no electricity under no circumstances do you open the fridge. People in movies do this all the time. If you do, the smell will make you retch. There was not going to be anything good in there for you to eat. Just don't do it. *

It was around September when the world started going to shit, most of these homes would have been closed up for the year already. It was winter when the US closed down and we really ended up in the storm. So there really shouldn't be much here. Nothing worth the time to go through the houses anyway. So we kept walking, past noon and into the sunset. We left Broadkill Beach in our wake, along with the Prime Hook wildlife refuge. We were coming up on Slaughter Beach, an area that had more full-time residents, just after the sunset. Most of these people would have fled before the bridges were blown if they could. Or moved towards the inland with friends or family, since there was nowhere to grow food along the beach edge. The soil was not good for growing anything but beach grass, or the glorious areas that had beach plums.

For those that don't know what a beach plum is, you don't know what you are missing. It was a small berry about the size of blueberries, but they were a plum. They had a very tart outside skin and a very sweet and succulent taste inside. They were unexplainable in taste really. They grew on the beaches and sandy areas.

This area was a good place to look for supplies. Anything north of here was desolate for at least another 10-12 miles. I couldn't make it there before nightfall, I used the last bit of light to check for a safe place to stop for the night. We made our way off the beach and onto the streets of Slaughter Beach. I hate the fact that I decided to walk around and check for zombie-like creatures and weird pockets of people in an area called Slaughter Beach. It felt like an omen in a bad horror flick. You know the type of movie where you're yelling at the television and telling the stupid white girl not to go into the basement. Just before she breaks a heel that she was wearing with her string bikini, and falls down the steps injuring her ankle. But I really didn't think Broadkill was any better.

What was up with these people and the town names? Seriously!

We walked down the streets and took in the sights. You know, the sights of the apocalypse, homes that are falling apart, doors busted out, cars left anywhere in the street and nature growing out of every pore and crack in the concrete. We looked carefully in a couple of houses but didn't find anything of use. Most of the homes had doors that were broken or missing completely. They wouldn't be safe to stay in overnight.

I was getting tired by this time. The weeks spent in Cape and not traveling had made me soft, I guess. That or I hadn't completely recovered from my bout with hypothermia. Either way, I had to find a place to rest for the night. Andromeda as usual was ready to keep moving all night if she had to. But dark was upon us and we needed to find shelter. At the very north end of the beach area, there was a house that looked like no one had been in for years. It was a moderate one-story home with painted shutters to match the front door. It was all peeling and nasty looking now, but the door was still on the hinges and intact. It had a large driveway that had to have held a boat at one time. Knowing the area it was probably a fairly large one too.

This may have been how the people escaped. There were a lot of people that thought living on the water in their boats would keep them safe from harm. And it may have, except other people thought this too and became modern-day pirates. Those that the pirates didn't loot and kill, had to contend with lack of supplies and the ocean itself. She could become very angry during storms and many people were lost. You could find the wreckage all up and down the coast. I had seen a couple myself on the ocean side of Cape.

The front and rear doors were intact and the layer of dust over everything inside would show if anything, human, or otherwise, had been inside. The front door was even locked. So I discreetly let myself and Andromeda in for the night.

By discreetly, I mean I broke the window in the door and reached in to unlock the deadbolt. But now it's semantics.

The place was in good order. Whoever left it had obviously taken care of it. The fact that it was located as far north as you could get in Slaughter, without being in the marshland, had kept out the looters. There was nothing of use here though, it looked as if everything of value was taken when the people left and locked up after themselves. That led me to believe these were people that thought their boat could save them. Maybe it did, maybe it didn't. Most likely no one will ever know the truth. It felt safe for the night. So we settled in.

We ate a small portion of our rations and laid down on the king-size bed to rest. Even though I didn't mean to, I fell asleep almost instantly. Good thing Andromeda was a good watchdog because I didn't remember anything until the next morning.

When I woke, I thought about our supply concerns and what needed to happen next. As I said the next 10-12 miles was a very desolate area, so I wouldn't find anything to help me there. Milford was probably the biggest town I would be near until I hit Dover. It was on the border between Sussex and Kent counties only 6 or 7 miles inland from where I was staying. I know I wanted to stay towards the coast, but I needed supplies. I was running out of clean water a lot faster than I thought. I still had some, but I needed to replenish when I could. I was drinking more throughout the day than I thought I would.

Dad always said I didn't drink enough water.

The body could go without food for a week, but only a couple of days without water. Days without water would slow me down and not allow me to move as I should. I needed to get some and Milford was my best bet. There used to be a lot of stores in that area, people and houses too. So I really needed to be on my toes.

We packed up our things and started the trek down Rt 36 to Milford. Rt. 36 was an old paved road. It was in bad condition and had nature taking back over in every crack and edge of the road. But it was still better to walk on than the sand. My shins and calves appreciated the change in pace. As we walked I couldn't help but admire nature. This was a kind of major route in Delaware before The Fall, it had a lot of farms along this stretch which made it easier for nature to rule the roost and take back the area that the asphalt had taken from it before. Nature always has a way to push back on man-made things.

I stayed away from the big farmhouses and tried to stay out of sight. These people were the ones that were prepared for The Fall. Some preppers waited for the end of the world and swear they predicted it. Others were just really good at canning and making their own food. I knew a friend of mine's family that had a years' worth of rations in the cellar between pickles and jellies their grandma and mom made each year. These people could still be in the area, hiding in their farmhouses and making sure no one came to take anything from them. They could have been more dangerous than the Deaders, they were definitely more unpredictable.

The fields should have been cultivated right now and getting ready for the spring planting. Sweet potatoes, corn, wheat and beans in this area. But it was all just natural growth. I thought about walking some of the fields with my bow and trying to get some rabbit, but it would've probably taken more time than it would have been worth. The grasses were waist high with shoots even taller. It made me feel safer than if it were short but it would've been very hard to hunt in with no shooting lanes and low visibility. We walked on and kept the sun to our backs until it got too high in the sky to be behind us anymore.

Now I didn't remember Milford very well, I went in and out with my parents but only from major routes. I never paid much attention to the smaller roads or the ones that were residential only. We didn't spend much time here, so I would have to do the best I could. I knew there was a grocery store of some kind out near the police department. But those were always the first hit and the worst to go back to.

Do you remember the scene in Zombieland in the grocery store? I stick with the rule to stay away from them.

I didn't have the rules that the main character had in Zombieland, like buckle up and double-tap. But everyone needs their rules. Before the Fall there were a lot of rules made for us. Laws and moral codes that were widely accepted. Not too many of those anymore, so you had to make your own and stick to them yourself.

If society is to be brought back, rules have to be made.

There was a school near the end of Rt 36. I just had to work my way around to find it. There should still have been some signs up in the city to help me. People went to these as shelters after they lost power, but the natives got restless with no form of government or police, so the strong took what they wanted and made the weak work. Typical dystopian story. Mad Max and the like. It didn't take people too long to learn to stay away from the shelters

A lot of people left quickly after the shelters turned dark. They left quietly in the night and couldn't take everything with them. There might have been some stuff still stashed in places, I might have been able to find some new clothes while I was there too.

As I entered the town the amount of debris and cars in the roadway increased greatly. Made sense because there were more people. A lot of the surrounding area had nothing to offer so people tried to make it here only to find roads blocked and the area no better than where they left. I walked the streets, keeping my eyes on the houses and windows. I was not only worried about Deaders, but people too. There would be more people still here than there were along the beaches and in the south.

There were a couple of roads blocked so I took an alleyway. I kept trying to remember where the school was and how to find it. I walked peacefully until the cars seemed to have been placed to make you walk in a certain direction. It came upon me slowly, just a couple of cars at an intersection, making one way easier to go than others. Then the feeling became more pronounced, ore cars at a corner made it near impossible to go in one direction. There were more coverings over the house windows and doors, making it hard to see inside them.

I felt like I was being pushed in a single direction, and I didn't like it. I didn't see anything else out of the ordinary or see any signs that Andromeda felt out of place. This wasn't the type of thing that a Deader would do, so it had to have been humans. Was it drawing me towards something or away? They could have been pushing me away from where they were staying to keep themselves safe. Or they could have been drawing someone unsuspecting into a trap. A trap seemed more likely as it started out kind of subtle, not a glaring go-away sign.

So we did the only logical thing that I could think of, we got off the path. I looked for a fence to a backyard to get off the streets. I found one with a gate that was not locked and entered there. I didn't want to get caught in someone else's game, I did want to see what was happening in this area. Maybe there were good people here. Maybe there wasn't, but I had to know. I kept the streets in sight and followed the man-made detour to its end from back yards and alleyways.

If these people were no longer around, they could have left a lot of things for me to pick over. I had not seen any movement in the windows or heard anything out of place. Andromeda hadn't even blinked or slowed down during the whole walk, I still needed to be cautious though.

I stopped and went into a couple of houses on the way. Ones that are not so blocked up, and had a second story so I could get a better look at the route. It was kind of winding and circled back on itself throughout the streets. I was guessing this gave whoever, plenty of time to see people or creatures coming from a while out. You would think that if this was a trap, the road to it would've been much quicker. Like a dead end, not a maze. A maze was meant to keep people or objects safe. It was good too. Not overly obvious, just simple enough to make you want to go the way they wanted you to. All the time taking you to the Minotaur at the center.

You know what the Minotaur was right?

It was a half-breed character in Greek Mythology. He had the body of a man and the head of a bull, big old horns and everything. He lived at the center of a labyrinth created by an artisan to house the monster. Every year or so many kids were sent into the maze to become tributes to the beast.

See my connection here?

From the second story of one particular house, I could see that I was close to the end. The maze led to a small little sub development inside the town limits. All the houses faced each other and had a cul de sac in the middle of them. I couldn't detect any movement anywhere and all of the front doors were closed. This had to have been a community that was serviced after The Fall. But were there people still here? Andromeda didn't seem to be upset or looking at any particular home, though it could still be dangerous. If they had to leave quickly, or if they were all dead from something else, there might have been a lot of supplies in this area. Better than at the school.

I decided I would try to look into a couple of the houses, but bug out if something felt off. A lot of time had passed since The Fall, people that had gathered together fell apart and moved on or passed away. I noticed this a lot in Lewes as I went through the town in the past year. Maybe it was the same here.

I worked my way around the outside of the little village. That's what I was calling it in my mind. A death village surrounded by a Minotaur maze. I saw no life anywhere. I checked the back door to one of the houses, it was locked. That at least meant there were no Deaders inside, unless they were reanimated in there and were never able to leave. But would they still have been mobile? Or would they have looked like the one that I saw near the canal? I wished I had known more about their anatomy and how they worked.

It would have made too much noise to break in, so I moved on to the next house. That door was unlocked and swung in silently. I pulled my bow and knocked an arrow, my knife was on my hip to be easily drawn. I got Andromeda to stay and keep watch at the door as I walked inside the house, which I hoped didn't have a Minotaur.

I really wished that I had never made that connection so it wasn't in my head every second.

I walked the house and saw that it was organized and clean, besides the dust. This helped show that no one had been in the house in a while as none of it seemed to have been disturbed. I checked the whole house and found no one. I didn't check for supplies yet because I wanted to clear the other houses first. There were five houses on the block in this village. All but the first house with the locked back door were exactly like the house that I had cleared originally. Neat orderly, almost clean and no one home. My footprints were the first there in a long time.

Since all the other houses were clear I figured I could check the first house through the front door. As I walked up the front walk I could see the back door through the window. It was not just locked, it was barred from the inside. Good thing I didn't try to break it down, that would have hurt. Have you ever tried to put your shoulder into a door to bust it open? Don't! The doors didn't give like you think they might. Not well-constructed ones anyway.

The front door was locked too, so I wondered if it was also barred. I couldn't see it from any of the windows. But I did see a couple of turned-over glasses on the front living room table, nothing else out of place. I went to one of the bedroom windows on the first floor. It was partially covered with plywood that had started to rot in the weather. The plywood was fastened on the outside, almost like keeping someone in, not out. That started to get my mind working on the Minotaur again.

What if this was the center of the maze?

I still didn't see any movement and didn't hear a bull inside. Would a bull be loud? I've heard the term a bull in a china shop, but that is more big and clumsy than loud. I pulled the board off and jumped inside the window anyway. As soon as I did the smell hit me hard. It smelled so much like death and decomposition that I could hardly stand it. I made Andromeda wait outside. Something or many things died in there some time ago. If it had been at the Fall there wouldn't have been as much smell. The home being closed up had kept the smell in, but this death seemed recent. Weeks or months not really sure, going back to the "science was not really my thing" quote from earlier. It was definitely not years.

I don't know why I pushed on into the house, morbid curiosity maybe. I kept moving forward, careful for Deaders. What I found upstairs was more disturbing than even my imagination could have conjured. There were bodies everywhere in one large bonus room. All in different levels of decay. It looked as if the people didn't kill their prey from the maze, but injured them and brought them here to die. There was no blood anywhere else in the house, but there was a lot in this room.

It was so bad. Bodies maimed and bloodied like a dog got to them and ate on them after they had been killed. I couldn't take it any longer, so I headed back downstairs. I needed to check the rest of the house in spite of my find. If this was the main home for this village, the food may also have been stored here. I went back to the empty glasses on the table in the living room. Some had been turned over, others still on coasters, and all had some congealed liquid in them. Some kind of juice. I was not sure what this meant other than the fact that someone had not cleaned this room after they got together. There must have been no one left to care.

I found a basement door. If this house had the layout I thought it did, then this shouldn't have a full basement, just a cellar for food and storage. As I opened the door I could tell I was right. It was not big and open as a full basement would be. It was small and I barely had enough head room to get down the stairs. I slowly headed down. My bow was on my back, my knife was in my hand. This close I would never get the bow pulled back in time if I was attacked. I didn't have a flashlight and it was dark as Hades down there.

Got that Greek mythology in my head again. Uhh!!

I let my eyes adjust as much as possible and started down the rest of the steps. When I turned the corner I heard movement. Not shuffling on concrete, more like something swinging. No groans, just air movement. The sound you make when you are swinging and just loving the feel of the air on your face. There was also a squeaking, very light, but like a boat at the docks. I was not sure what could be causing that sound in a basement. I stopped trying to figure it out, I just needed to concentrate and get out as soon as I could. I needed to endure to make sure there wasn't anything there for me.

I was looking for canned goods or jars of jellied fruits. These might still be good and would keep for a bit longer. I came around a shelf unit into bodies, arms, and legs, all reaching out to me in their death. I couldn't see how many there were or how they had snuck up on me. I didn't hear anything shuffling on the ground, nothing that would have made me think there was anything in here with me. The basement door was not open, so how would they have gotten in. But there they were. Their hands were in my hair and trying to grab me to drag me closer to them. I jumped back so fast I almost dropped my knife. I then remembered the knife and swung at them as hard as I could. Trying to create distance between us. Maybe I would be able to run up the stairs and get away. I tripped as I swung my arms around my head. The only reason I didn't fall was because I backed up into the shelf unit. My heart was beating out of my chest.

Stupid, pushed too far. I made a mistake and it was going to cost me my life. I couldn't get through the shelf. I had lost which direction the exit was in relation to where I was. Then I realize they weren't moving towards me. As I moved back they stayed where they were. The squeaking noise had ramped up and was the only thing I really heard. They also only had hands in my hair. Nothing on my arms or shoulders.

I realized that they were very tall, taller than any human should be. How? What were they?

Then it clicked and I could see it all a little clearer. There were Deaders swinging from the rafters. All of them had nooses around their necks and they were all reaching out to me. But they couldn't hurt me as long as I kept my distance. They couldn't move, their feet were not touching the ground. The ropes around the rafters were the squeaking noise I had heard. I never really thought of anyone killing themselves since The Fall. I thought everything was about survival. I figured everyone that was still alive would fight to keep it that way. I guess depression or hopelessness finally got to these people. It caught me off guard, that won't happen again.

As my eyes adjusted I could see that eight people were hanging there. All eight must have hung themselves together. That's probably why the glasses were on the table. One last drink together before mass suicide to end it all? I knew I wouldn't drink the Kool-Aid in this house if there was any. Although I would have loved some grape sometime.

We had heard about the end of days types before I lost my family. All getting together and going into the afterlife on their terms. I guessed these guys didn't get the memo that any death made you come back. You just entered a new hell on Earth. One that you couldn't get yourself out of. They looked almost as bad as the bodies upstairs that were dead and decomposing. When they didn't get to feed as Deaders they started to decompose, I guess. Interesting. I mean these guys were barely moving even with me in the room. Hopefully, soon they would die again and be out of their misery.

Before I got any more heeby-jeeby's, I headed upstairs to get away from them. When I got back upstairs I found Andromeda, she was sitting at the bottom of the stairs looking up at the bonus room door on the second floor. It was like she didn't care about the ones in the basement, something was more interesting upstairs. She looked at me quizzically and then went back to the upstairs door, not whining but was very intent. I didn't see anything up there when I was there before, but she seemed to think that I missed something.

Then I heard a bump. Very slight and I probably wouldn't have heard it had I been moving around at all. I heard it again. It couldn't have been the Deaders downstairs. There was nothing for them to bump against. I gripped my knife again and headed back upstairs.

Why? This village was the best chance I had of getting supplies again, so I needed to be able to check the houses that the Jonestown-esque suicide didn't happen in. But to do that thoroughly I needed to make sure there was nothing here that could harm me. To make sure there was not something that may come out when I least expected it. Also, my adrenaline was still coursing through my veins. It was a proven fact that this made you make bad decisions.

Well not proven, again-Science.

It was probably an animal in the room feeding on the bodies. An opossum or raccoon that I hadn't seen or had scared into hiding. As I walked back around the wall to the room, I braced myself for the smell. It didn't help, it was still overpowering. I walked as close to the bodies as I dared, looking for the raccoon or opossum that made the noise. Then I saw the chain connected to the wall. It was a heavy chain with a heavy ring bolted into the studs. I wasn't sure why I didn't see this the first time.

I followed the chain with my eyes, I was not getting close to that. Then I saw it around the neck of what used to be a young child, about 11-12. As I was taking this in the thing lifted its head ever so slightly then fell to the floor. It didn't have enough energy to lift its head and the thick chain. It was so decomposed I couldn't tell the difference between it and the other bodies.

Then the thought occurred to me, there was a Deader chained to the wall. It had blood all around its mouth and face. It was only at this point that I looked around the room. It was not just a large bonus room. It was a child's playroom. It had toys everywhere. Most of them were thrown around and covered in blood. The only ones close to the thing were battery-operated cars and trucks. Presumably for it to drain the power from them when it needed to feed. That's why all these other people were injured and brought here. It was to feed their child. All of these people in this village must have been family. They must have been trapping people and hurting them to feed their Deader child. If you kept it fed, it would continue to look human, just act sick. It would just act hungry and have glowing blue eyes. People could ignore this I guess.

No wonder these people finally gave in and killed themselves. They must have figured it was never going to be little Johnny again and the guilt of what they had done to these innocent people weighed on them so much they couldn't take it any longer. OMG! I felt sick to my stomach and it was not from the smell any longer. What these people had done. I knew people did things, odd things brought on from fear, but I couldn't wrap my head around this.

This thing was looking at me and trying to crawl towards me. I slowly backed towards the door, as Andromeda whined and backed away with me. I didn't know what to do. On one hand, this was an abomination and should not have been allowed to live. On the other, I wasn't sure how to kill this thing. Since it was chained to the wall, which had held this long, it wasn't really a danger to anyone. There was no one to bring it "food" so it would only get weaker like the ones in the basement. Best to keep my distance and just let it be.

As it slithered along the ground, the chain slowly pulled taught. It tried to reach me as I slowly backed away towards the door. It was pushing bones and gore out of the way as it moved. When it could no longer move forward it started opening its mouth as to yell at me. It tried to lift parts and pieces of the bodies and throw them in my direction. Its eyes stayed locked on me.

I had to get out of this house.

I ran down the steps and flung open the front door. I couldn't get enough air. I couldn't get the image out of my head. I imagined what these people did to others to feed that abomination. I mean you see this kind of thing in the movies, you read it in books, but you never think it could really happen. Feeding people to your sick Deader child? It made me cry with fear, loathing and anger simultaneously. I broke down in the middle of the street then I vomited, trying to purge it all.

A couple of minutes later I got myself together. Andromeda was by my side again and looking at me to see if I was ok. When I could think again, I thought about how to get supplies. Was this place safe enough to take the time to walk through the rest of these houses? These people left their homes and took great care to make them neat. They couldn't have left them empty. There had to be stuff that was usable in them. These people had functioned as a family for months after The Fall. They had to have been resourceful. I mean they made the decision to kill other people to feed this thing. But they had the energy and the mental capacity to do this and then to end their own lives to stop what they had started.

Maybe it was because they were out of food and not because of their conscience. But it was nearing dark now anyway and I needed to see if I could resupply.

I went through each of the other four houses. I was very careful and came out with exactly five things worth keeping. The first was a high-powered flashlight. It didn't run on batteries! You had to hand crank it. This wouldn't attract any unwanted attention from the Deaders. This would have been handy in the creepy house basement.

Shooting

Shooting.

It was a warm summer morning. My dad and I had stopped and picked up a couple of scrapple sandwiches from a small country store on our way to the shooting range. It wasn't too far, but we had a little bit of a ride. It was just enough to eat our sandwiches and drink our coffee, well him his coffee and me a juice. I really didn't like coffee much.

We were meeting my brother at the range so he could get some shooting time in too, he had to work afterward so he drove separately. I thought this was great because he didn't get a scrapple sandwich with Dad. When we pulled up the place was pretty busy. We had only been here once before, it was a small range, but the people were nice. We headed inside to pay for an hour of range time and grab a target or two. My Dad was just going to go over some basic techniques with us and get us more familiar with shooting the pistols. I had only shot the pistol once before and my brother had never shot it. He had to work the last time we came. Most of the time would be going over safety and just how to hold and sight properly, my Dad had said. I had just turned 15. I was really excited today because with my brother being here I would get to shoot more while he had to get the safety lessons from Dad.

I liked shooting and spending time with these two. Mom was at home doing her crafty things, she didn't mind guns but really didn't enjoy shooting the way we did. Not like there was ever going to be an apocalyptic event where you had to rely on a gun.

There were a lot of odd conversations going on about some meteor hitting down in Russia or Europe somewhere, I really didn't pay attention to much of it. Old guys talk about a lot of boring stuff at the gun ranges. As my brother pulled up I started helping my Dad unload the guns and putting in my hearing protection. This stopped the odd conversations for me as I had to struggle to even hear my Dad's directions. We went about our hour and Dad taught us safety lessons and let us shoot until we were consistently hitting our targets. Not a very good grouping, but we hit the bottle target every time we shot.

"That is all you are trying to do. Put the target down when you aim," Dad was saying.

"More practice will bring better groupings," "We will work on that more next time."

After that my brother had to go to work, so we said our goodbyes and headed home. We didn't have anything planned that day since I wasn't working. Mom had been called into work. So it was just Dad and me for the day. Of course, the first hour home was breaking down and cleaning the guns. But after that, we turned on a movie and vegged out for the day.

When Mom came in the door after work she started talking about the same meteor that crashed landed in some Koala peninsula in Russia. I had never heard about it and really didn't care, tuned her out. The only thing I heard was blue dust and a very big rock.

I was zoned out on my social media pages. People were talking about this thing on there too. Then I found out that Jenna broke up with Brandon because Brandon kissed Julia and I lost every train of thought about my parent's conversation. I mean Julia, really?!

The next thing I knew I was in a black room. All I could hear was my Dad going over the safety of handguns. How they operate. What the difference is between a semi-auto and a revolver. I couldn't see anything. He was talking about squeezing the trigger and not yanking. About being surprised when the gun went off so you aren't anticipating. Then, I could hear squeaking, sounds like a swing set that needed to be oiled. But a lot of them. The sound started coming from all around me. It was getting louder.

I can't hear my Dad any longer, the area around me started getting a bit lighter. The sound of squeaking was getting louder, maybe ropes on a boat? I couldn't smell saltwater or hear the waves. It was getting louder. I could start to see shapes. I could see that they looked like the targets we took shooting. They looked like bottles. But they were moving. Swinging. Back and forth. Back and forth. Left to right then back left.

No..No..NOOOO! I could then see it all clearly. The ropes and the swinging were the dead from the village. The mass suicide of the Jones town people. But now they were all looking like Minotaur's, not bottles anymore. My hand was hurting from gripping something, a gun. The gun I found in their houses. I looked around for Andromeda. She was not here, I called out. Still nothing. The only thing I could hear was those damn ropes. The squeaking of them the air moving as the bodies swing. More bodies than I could count. They seemed to be multiplying. I could hear my Dad again. Breathe out when you pull the trigger. Steady your breathing. See your target, not the sights.

But I didn't want to see these targets. I just wanted to run, to close my eyes and make them go away! I needed to find Andromeda. They were all around me. So I pulled the gun up and set in the isosceles stance like I was taught. I targeted the first one. Breathed out and waited for the target to swing into my path. I pulled the trigger and it disappeared in a cloud of dust. I then turned to the next and the next. All of them went down with a single pull of my trigger. Dust was everywhere. I could taste it and it was burning my eyes, making it harder to get on target. Harder to make these things, these creatures disappear. To get them out of my head.

There were way more than 7 of them. But as I pulled my trigger the gun kept firing. It went off and one of these things disappeared. So I just kept on shooting. Shooting until there is nothing but dust and silence.

When they were all gone so was the gun. It disappeared out of my hands and the room lit up. I could see.

I was back on the couch with my brother talking about our day on the range. At some point during that nightmare, he must have gotten home from work. He was saying something about the weaver stance being better than the isosceles. But as he was talking I could hear the faint rustle of a chain, followed by a bump. Bump. Bump. Oh No! The deader kid? In my house?! I jumped up looking for my gun. I couldn't find it.

Even though I was running around, my brother kept talking like I was sitting next to him like normal. Why wasn't he helping? Couldn't he hear this creature? Suddenly the creature reared up from behind the couch, going after my brother. I could do nothing but watch. Then a crack and it turns to dust too. I looked around and my Dad was standing in his bedroom doorway with a gun that was still smoking from the barrel. As the dust settled I felt water on my face. But there should have been dust.

Then I felt it again and a scratch on my stomach. I was confused. I started to walk back to the couch...

I woke up with Andromeda pawing at me and licking my face. I must have been squirming and yelling in my sleep for her to wake me up. It was still dark outside, it wasn't time for her to eat yet. She was worried about me. That dream hung with me. That village must have messed with me more than I thought. Man, I hate having a vivid imagination in a post-apocalyptic world like this one. One where people kill themselves and feed others to their Deader children.

I had only walked about 2 miles away before I had to rest and see if I could get those images out of my head. I stayed in a house off the side of the road, that I had cleared. I sat down to read a happy children's book that I found in a small kid's bedroom. I guess I fell asleep while reading. I never was a reader, really. I liked history and learning, I just never really had time to read for fun. I had to keep up with my social media, I guess the term was FOMO, fear of missing out. My Dad just called it an addiction.

Man that was a messed-up dream. Hope that cleared it all out of my head. I won't be able to rest if I keep having dreams like that. I cranked up my new flashlight and looked through my pack for some breakfast. I stumbled upon the picture of my family and I remembered the good part of that dream. I needed to remember those parts and hang on to the good things from before.

I was not going back to sleep after that dream so I figured I might as well eat something. Of course, Andromeda liked that idea, because that meant she would get some too. As the morning sun broke the horizon Andromeda and I were already back on the road. I was still a little flustered from the dream and needed to get on the road to clear my head. The farther I got from that place the more I could put it behind me.

Maybe.

The weather was a bit chilly that morning, but that was spring in Delaware for you. The day would warm up and I would take my jacket off by noon. The roads were paved here, but I was still being vigilant and careful of what roads I took. I stayed to the shoulders and ditches so I could be quick if I had the need to hide. We were making good time, Andromeda seemed to be enjoying herself. She took to running off a little to burn the extra energy that dogs always seemed to have. Especially retrievers.

Then just after noon, Andromeda started limping. At first, I could barely tell, then she started whining and refused to put her back right paw down. I stopped her and looked at her paw. She had a small cut on her pad. Nothing too bad that wouldn't heal, but I couldn't tell if anything was in it. She must have cut it in the last field she went running in. She had seen a rabbit as we got out of the town proper and went running off for about 20 minutes. She did bring the rabbit back dead, but what did it cost now? I wrapped her foot to help keep the bleeding down. I couldn't carry her very far, so we had to find shelter for the rest of the day and let her heal. The Walmart was just up ahead, she would have to make it that far.

I really didn't like heading onto the main road like this. We were stuck between two of three main throughways in Delaware, Rt1 and Rt 113. Just north of here they merged and became one of the two main roads. A lot of people had tried to get out of Sussex County this way. A lot of traffic got backed up and a lot of cars were left on the road. If you looked past the dust and rust on these cars it looked like a Sunday afternoon in the summer. Thousands of people heading back to their homes in the north. Ready to leave us alone for the next four days, until they got back in and headed back for another weekend at the beach.

I stopped often and looked through the windshields and windows to see if there was any movement. It seemed like everyone cleared out of here a long time ago. The slower pace was helping Andromeda and it wasn't like we had any place to be at any particular time. I looked for any supplies we might use, I wouldn't have minded finding a tent or something to sleep in besides the vacant homes of people past. I didn't mind it until that house had set me on edge. Now I felt like some good old outdoor camping might have been the right strategy. If I covered the walls in the emergency blankets that I found, it might just hide our signal from the Deaders.

It was a risk, but it might keep me sane.

After a short time, the center came into view. As I thought about it more, I guessed now that Andromeda was hurt I really needed some supplies. Hopefully, there were still some bandages in there too. Some antibiotic cream to keep the infection down maybe. It seemed odd in the 21st century to worry about dying from a small infection but, this was a real fear in the world that I now inhabited.

I came up to the back of the building. There weren't many cars in the parking lot. Not much shopping was being done before the end of the world, everyone was just trying to get off the peninsula before it became an island. Everything was quiet, I swear though if something squeaked like a rope I was getting out of here in a hurry, even if I had to carry Andromeda.

I found the rear door next to the loading dock unlocked. As I said before Deaders couldn't seem to open doors, so this was a good sign on their front. But people can open doors, and then shut them behind themselves, so there was still a risk. The door being unlocked led me to believe that no one was inside. If they had tried to live here and didn't want anyone else around, why leave it open? Unless it was a trap to capture, maim and otherwise kill the unwitting.

Stupid imagination!

As I walked in, the first thing that hit me was the smell. Not sure what it was a mixture of, but it meant this place hadn't been aired out in a long while. Good sign? I was just trying to find what I needed and avoid people at all costs, dead or alive.

Or would it be undead or alive?

The sights were the next thing I registered, the place was a wreck. You couldn't step anywhere without stepping on something, most of it was unrecognizable. Looks like people were grabbing and running out the door not caring what was dropped in the process. But from what I could see there was nothing that I could use here. Everything was dirty from people stepping on it, spilling on it, and then the time since that had allowed things to grow on it.

I looked to Andromeda and she didn't seem to care about anything but her foot hurting. She was sitting down leaning to the side of her good paw. I had never seen her hurt before. So with her in pain, I didn't know how reliable she would have been for danger. I had to trust that danger would override her pain.

As I walked out of the loading area I learned that the smell and the sights didn't change. There hadn't been anyone here for a very long time. This was probably ransacked near The Fall and people had been scared to come back since, or there had been no one around to come back. There was no one living here, no tent city inside the Walmart, although that may not have been a bad idea if you stayed away from the huge glass windows at the front. I had not seen any signs of people on my way into town. None of the cars looked like they had been touched, there was dust everywhere that lay undisturbed, no footprints or scuffs that I had seen. Maybe this town was deserted.

I slowly made my way to the pharmacy aisle. Hoping they had some gauze and sterile pads. Hoping beyond hope that there was some iodine or triple antibiotic ointment left. I did learn a little about animal husbandry in the FFA in high school, I should've been able to bandage her up easily with the right supplies.

The pharmacy aisle was as bad as the rest. I took some time and rifled through the stuff. I found a couple of things that would work for the situation we were in. Some of the things were dropped and stomped on, so there wasn't much left that was usable, but anything was better than nothing. I called Andromeda to me and proceed to add some salve to her wounds and then bandaged it up. It seemed to help because she licked my face before she walked away. Keeping a little more pressure on her right paw. It seemed to have a pain reliever in it, acting like a local anesthetic.

With that done, I stuck the rest of the supplies in my bag. Depending on the weather and road conditions I would have to change these out a couple of times a day. I headed back to the grocery area and hoped there was something left that was still in good condition. As I walked past the toy section, I swore I saw something move out of the corner of my eye. Andromeda didn't seem to see it, so I guessed it may have been a shadow or something. Most likely my imagination getting the best of me. I made sure to keep an eye out though as we got closer to the food. We hit the old freezer and refrigerator section first. None of this was going to be any good, and it smelled so much worse than the rest of the store. At some point, one of the doors got opened and was stuck that way. Otherwise, maybe the smell would have stayed in the freezers.

I missed ice cream.

Mint chocolate chip was my favorite, but I would eat anything but plain vanilla. My dad's favorite was always rocky road and mom's was anything with chocolate in it.

Further in I see a Hawaiian frozen pizza wasting away. That was one of my favorites. I know most people thought pineapple didn't belong on pizza, but that's how I was raised. My family was mostly Hawaiian, you know. I say that, but the pineapple on pizza was actually a Canadian invention., hence the Canadian bacon with the pineapple.

Did you know that?

As this dribble ran through my head, I swore I heard a footfall. Just some small sound, like a foot hitting the floor. No squeak, thank god, but a sound nonetheless. I didn't think that I was alone any longer. I thought about pulling the pistol for protection, but I haven't shot in a long time. If there was more than one person, it would draw the others. If I missed they would have the drop on me. If it was a Deader, it wouldn't do anything anyway. I hadn't found a way to kill those things yet.

So as this thought goes through my head, my mind wanders just a bit to an old song. I didn't know if it was the words *Ain't found a way to kill me yet,* or the situation felt like walking through a jungle. But Rooster started bouncing in my head. My Dad loved this song and I was partial to it myself. In a situation like this, I needed to concentrate and my brain came up with a song about war.

Wow! Thanks, brain.

I looked at Andromeda and she was completely calm. Nothing different in her demeanor, except the limp. So maybe it was nothing. Just as I thought that and started to walk further towards the food aisle, Andromeda perked up. She was not looking in the direction of the sound that I heard, she was looking in the direction of the big plate windows and the entrance door.

Then all of a sudden a huge yell from someone in the front of the store.

"Awe. Man Son of a Bitch!! It smells rotten in here. Can't we go somewhere else Pa!" says person 1.

"No, we need to see if there was anything left in here. Shut the hell up and stop your complaining!" says the person I assumed was Pa.

"George take Stevie here and go back to the food aisle and see if there was anything that didn't go bad!" says Pa.

Ok, so now I knew there were at least 3 of them. And that they were headed back to me. I had to find a place to hide. I had no idea who these people were and what they were capable of. I called Andromeda and we headed quickly and quietly to the back of the store, past the food I was looking for and into the baby section. These guys should not have a reason to go back there. I found a set of shelves that had fallen over and had clothes thrown all on top of them. This should be a good place to hide.

I heard the people yelling back and forth through the store. It seemed like they were not making their way closer to me and had just stopped for the food aisle. Great minds think alike, I guess. They were yelling about some cans they found and how disgusting the freezer section was.

That I could agree with them on.

Then I heard gunshots. Multiple. Too many to count as it caught me off guard. What could they have been shooting at? They were nowhere near Andromeda and me. Then I heard them laughing.

"Ha ha ha! Stevie just about pissed himself pa," George, I think.

"It was a damn rat! Damn thing jumped up in my face when I picked up a box of Cap'n crunch!" Said, Stevie. "It was the crunch berry kind too."

"Knock your stuff off and gather what we need," Pa said, "I gotta see if I can find diapers for Meredith."

Oh no! Diapers were in the aisle that I was hiding in. From the sound of Pa's voice, he wasn't far enough away from me to risk moving to another location. I had to hope he found what he needed before he found me. Just then Andromeda started a low growl in her throat. Just enough for me to hear. That meant this guy was very close. I got her to quiet down before he heard. Obviously, these guys shoot quickly and don't ask many questions. All of a sudden I could see him through the shadows. He was an average guy. Looked like he was in his 50's. Good shape and carrying a very large shotgun. He had a duffle bag thrown over his shoulder for carrying his finds.

I could see all of this so well because he was just 10 feet away from me and walking right towards my aisle. He walked cautiously but confidently. He had been through a lot, probably a lot before The Fall by the looks of him, and all of this shows in how he moved. All of a sudden he stopped. He was not looking at me but maybe sensed something. He stopped moving towards me and walked off to the left. Out of my line of sight. Maybe he saw what he needed for Meredith. Maybe he saw something else.

A minute or two goes by and I started to relax. George and Stevie said they found all they could. Only one bag of stuff and they were heading back to the front of the store. Pa didn't respond to them, I hadn't heard him respond since he disappeared from my sight.

Then I quickly learned why! "Get up slowly and control your animal. Dog is as good of eatin' as any other animal," Pa said.

Crap, he had somehow seen me and snuck up in my blind spot. He was behind me and probably had his gun pointed straight at me. I grabbed ahold of Andromeda's neck by the scruff so she wouldn't try and jump and slowly lead us out of the hiding spot. As I stood up and turned around I could see that his beard was all white and he had a very bedraggled look to him. But what I also saw was another person with him, a woman. Meredith maybe? She was about 5'9" easily as tall as Pa and stick thin. She must have been behind me and alerted Pa to me being there.

Pa let out a long whistle and yelled for the other two.

As we waited for them to join us, Pa looked me up and down and then at Andromeda.

"What do we have here?" he said "Where did you two come from?"

"Just passing through," I said "Just stopped to look for food, just like you. I ain't no trouble though. I'll just go on my way."

Just then we heard a yell and a crash. Sounded like the building was coming down.

"Pa! Pa! There is someone here! They stabbed George in the leg," Stevie said.

"I got one here! They must have been together!" Pa yelled. "Susie get ahold of her and the dog. We need to find the other one!"

Susie, not Meredith, smiled and rushed over to me with rope in hand. She put a piece of rope over Andromeda's mouth to keep her from biting and then around her neck. She tied the rope to a shelf unit so Andromeda couldn't move more than 6 inches away from it. She then grabbed me by the shoulder and turned me around roughly. She tied my hands behind my back.

Meanwhile, I kept pleading with them to stop. That I didn't know anyone else. That I didn't know there was anyone else out there.

Susie said "Shut up!" as she tied a bandana around my mouth to shut me up.

With this done, Pa ran off down the aisle to help the other two find the one who stabbed George. Susie just took a seat on the edge of a broken cabinet and watched me while flicking the edge of a blade with her thumb. As I looked at her I could see that she had 5-6 knives on her at least. I bet there were some more hidden other places. She didn't really seem too concerned with what was happening in other places in the store. She just sat there watching Andromeda and me while flicking her knife.

I tried to keep Andromeda calm and get her to lay down, but she hated having her mouth tied up. She was using her paws to try and get it off. I didn't think she would try and hurt these people, but they may hurt her if she got her mouth free. This Susie doesn't look entirely stable. There was some yelling and rustling and then more yelling coming from the front of the store. A lot of cussing and what sounded like shelves falling over. Then silence.

I had no idea what was happening and what had gone so wrong. I knew better than to come to stores and areas where people were heavily populated before The Fall. I went against my better judgment and landed us in this mess. I thought that maybe people had moved on. But really thinking on it, where would they have gone. Everywhere fell, everywhere was just as screwed as the Delmarva Peninsula. I was so scared and mad at myself that I was shaking. I couldn't control it and I even started to cry. We may not make it out of this. These people didn't really seem like the forgiving and nice type. They may even think that I was in with whomever just stabbed George. Susie started looking like she wanted to know what was going on instead of babysitting my dog and me. She started pacing and patting her knives to make sure they are there. More than 5 minutes go by with hardly a sound from the rest of the store.

She kept looking at me like I was to blame for this mess, like I was the one who stabbed George. She didn't look stable and being gagged there was no way to try and talk to her. There was more than a little crazy behind her eyes. That crazy wanted to come out.

All of a sudden the place erupted into a cacophony of sounds!

Yes I know big words too!

It was so loud. Banging and yelling and screams of a little girl. Andromeda was whimpering, I held my ears. Susie's eyes lit up with the sound, looking for a fight. But just as fast as it came, it was gone.

"Susie! We are good. Found the other one!" Pa said. "Bring those two and we will get out of here. George needs some help getting out and we need to get him stitched up back at base."

"10-4!" Susie yelled back in confirmation. Then pulled me to my feet and untied Andromeda from the rack. She handed me her rope and pushed me in the direction of the noise, flipping her blade in her hand as an incentive. Andromeda and I shuffled to the front of the store. I wasn't in a hurry because they had already made up their mind that I was with this other girl. That wasn't good for us. Susie had other ideas and kept pricking me with her knife in the back to keep me moving at her pace. I think maybe she was worried about this George. Maybe there was a little something to her? I really hoped I was not around long enough to find out.

As we approached the front of the store I could see George, Pa, and Stevie. George must have been the one with the bleeding leg wrapped in some nasty-looking sheet. That thing was dirty before he bled all over it.

That was going to lead to an infection. Ewww!

He was tall and a little overweight, which was hard to do in this day and age. Gotta figure how big he was before all of this. Stevie must have been the short one in the front. He was pale, about 5'6" and 100 lbs. soaking wet. He was probably a track runner before, he was at least built like it. He was holding another person in front of him. A small girl, maybe 14-15. She stood 5' if she was wearing tall shoes and was probably 85 lbs. She looked like she has been through hell. If she was here all by herself, then she had. I didn't know what I would've done after we lost Mom and Matthew if Andromeda hadn't been with me.

Once Pa and the others saw us, he smiled and they turned and walked out of the store. As Susie pushed me through the doors I could see them as they threw the small girl in an Amish looking wagon. This wagon was all black on the outside and could probably hold six people inside. There was no outside perch for the driver to sit. The doors were open as they grabbed me and threw me inside too. After I got myself up off my face I could tell the whole inside of the wagon was lined with metal plating.

They helped George inside and moved the three of us out of the way as Pa got inside and behind a seat in the front. It seemed odd because there were two handles and no reins for a horse. There were no horses either, come to think about it. How were they going to move this thing? Just as I thought this I knew the answer. I heard someone outside pull starting the two-stroke engine. Pretty smart, this type of engine didn't attract the Deaders when it was off because it didn't have a battery. Basically, they turned this thing into a big go-kart. It probably wasn't fast, but it was better than walking and shouldn't attract the Deaders. That was why the inside was lined with metal, so the electrical signals from the people inside didn't attract them either.

Smart.

For people I considered dumb, they were proving me wrong. Very, very wrong. Now if only I could prove them wrong and convince them that I was not with this person and get them to let me go.

The last two climbed in and Pa pushed the gas and got us moving. On the way home I guessed, where ever that was. I looked over at the stern-faced little girl and could tell that she was terrified of all of us. She was shaking so bad she might actually hurt herself. I found myself moving towards her to try and comfort her. Even though this would make it look like we knew each other, I couldn't let her suffer like this alone. I had a thing for people that needed help, I always had. I was raised to help people that needed it. No matter what the cost may be to you.

Backward

Now, I was going backward. I couldn't see much from the small windows in this contraption but I did see a road sign for Rt 1 south. I guess these hillbillies had a place south of Milford. Of course that in itself didn't mean much and the distance was hard to gauge since I couldn't see enough to get an idea of how fast this pieced together piece of junk was going.

So I just sat back, uncomfortably I might add, while this crazy woman went through my bag. She pulled out all of my food and handed it to the boys riding with us. They added it to their pile from the take. Of course, they found my newly acquired gun. She threw my foil blankets and flashlight back in the bag. Then she and the others had a hearty laugh at the fact that I still carried around my phone. Luckily, they threw that back in the bag too. She took my fishing pole and my bow and arrows too.

Susie's eyes lit up when she found my buck knife on my side. She looked it over like it was the last piece of meat on Earth. Then she put it in her belt! There was no way she was taking that from me. That was my Dad's hunting knife. It was the only thing besides the family picture I had left of him. I started to struggle against my bonds. They had removed my gag when they put us in the wagon, for some reason, so I took this opportunity to say my piece.

"Put that back you bitch!" I say. "That's not yours to take!"

That got me a backhand to the mouth.

"I'll take what I want, and you have nothing to say about it," Susie said. "I own all of your stuff, up to and including your life at this point," she continued.

I sat back rejected knowing that I could only make things worse. I decided to shut up and wait until I had a chance, then I would get my stuff and get even with these people. If I lived that long, that was. At this point, they might've just been inviting us over for dinner, or to be dinner. The end of the world had changed people and not in a good way.

I sat back and thought about how all of this was going wrong. How I had failed myself and Andromeda. As I thought about her, I looked at my dog, my best friend, her hurt paw and the rope around her muzzle. She was being a really good dog to this point. She had always liked going for car rides, she hated the rope around her muzzle but otherwise seemed unfazed. She didn't blame me for what we were about to get into, or so it seemed.

That's unconditional love.

Maybe I should've been more like her and took each moment as it came. It was hard to look to the future in a world like this. I then turned my thoughts to the new girl. She had not spoken at all since we got in the carriage. I took my time and looked over her. I had no idea what her name was so I decided that in my head I was going to call her Giggles. Why? I didn't know, but I felt that everything and everyone needed a name. If I didn't know their name I tended to make one up.

As I noticed before, she was very slight of frame, she was terrified, but she had stopped shaking at this point. She was sitting there, stiff and refusing to look at anyone in the carriage. She almost seemed to be set for an inevitable end and was no longer scared to face it. She was tied up just as I was and I could see blood on her left hand. That told me that she was left-handed since that was the strong hand she used to stab George in the leg.

She has been on her own for a while and she hadn't eaten well. You could see malnutrition in her face. She was pale and her eyes were a bit sunken and there were dark rings around both of her eyes. She had a very haunted look. Her ethnicity was a little in question. She was so dirty and dusty that it was hard to see more than just that. Her hair was so dark it was black and her eyes were brown, but that could mean just about anything.

It was kind of funny that this was something I was still looking at. In all reality, what did it matter where her heritage hailed from? Would that change her, or my opinion of her? I guess it was just something we noticed here since we had so many different heritages in America.

I guess I was staring. Trying to figure her out because all of a sudden she turned and looked at me. I tried a slight smile, but she just turned her head away and looked at her feet. This was when I noticed she didn't even have shoes. We were just coming out of winter and it looked like she hadn't had anything to cover her feet in a while. You could tell the damage they had taken. That must have been why she was in the store. To find things she needed, she was desperately trying to survive. If we made it through this, I thought, I needed to help this girl. It was what I was taught to do.

It was hard to see exactly where we were going, but I could see road signs every now and then. We were heading south and they were sticking with the route 1 corridor. I had walked through here the previous day.

Damn!

Then all of a sudden we took a turn and headed east again. A couple of minutes later, we turned down a broken driveway. I could see a small sign at the edge that said Home of the Brave. I remembered this place. My Dad was in the military so he had spoken of it. This was a place that helped homeless veterans. It used to keep them off the street and help them get back on their feet. If I remembered correctly there were two buildings, each with a couple of bedrooms and living space. One place was for women and one for men. Even when the world ran, it was off the beaten path, and surrounded by farmland.

It made sense someone would have taken up here after the world fell. It should have been stocked and ready to live in. If you covered the windows and were careful, it might not have been bad. Looking at the group that picked us up, they didn't look related. They may all have been veterans that were staying at the place when it all fell. But maybe not. They seemed to follow orders well, but I could've been wrong.

Suddenly, we stopped and Pa yelled something to a person outside of the carriage. I lifted up a bit to see better and got a smack to the head by Susie for it. Before she got me to sit back down, I saw a fence erected around the perimeter of the homes. I would have guessed they went all the way around, but I could only see the gate.

This fence had to have taken some material because it was completely solid metal, just like the carriage we are traveling in. There were several different types and sizes that were all tied in together. Even the guard tower seemed to be completely closed off, it must have had a small window to see through. When Pa called out the gate opened with no hesitation. As we rolled through we took a hard right and the engine stopped. Then suddenly before I could even register what was happening, the back doors were yanked open and Susie grabbed my arms and threw me out of the back onto the ground. I hit awkwardly and cried out. Then I looked up at the doors and had to roll out of the way quickly, because

Giggles and Andromeda were being thrown out right behind me. Both crying out as they hit too.

Susie thought this was funny, but Stevie just rolled his eyes as he helped George out of the carriage.

"We need a medic over here!" cried Stevie.

He didn't wait and started carrying George himself to the closest door. I sat up and looked around and tried to clarify what I saw. I was expecting something rundown. A tent campground or a military-style setup. Something along those lines, especially after I put the veteran piece together. But this was just wrong. I couldn't believe anything I was seeing. From the look on Giggle's face, she couldn't either. The sight just was not what anyone would have expected. It was hard to believe that something like this still existed. It was...

It was a Paradise.

Gardens blocked the view from where we sat. You could see the buildings over the leaves, but I couldn't take my eyes off the fresh fruits and vegetables. It was just now spring, but they had gardens and gardens in full bloom all around us.

I couldn't believe it. But just as I started wrapping my mind around it, I was roughly dragged to my feet and drug into a building on the other side from where Stevie took George.

Giggles was not brought with me but was taken along to the building with George. To my horror Andromeda was being taken away from me too. That was more than I could take. I stomped down on Susie's foot with all of my might and drove my shoulder into her chest. This caused her to drop my bag and she lost her handle on me. I started screaming:

"Andromeda! You can't take her! You can't! She has to stay with me!"

Then a sharp pain in the back of my skull and everything went black.

As I was passing out, I thought that everything was going wrong. Everything was backward now.

Backward is right. The next thing I knew I was seven years old. I was standing in my old house with my family around me. My dad was asking if there was something that I had always wanted. Something that I had never had to this point.

I was so confused. It was not my birthday, nor was it Christmas. It was June 15th to be exact. It was always fun this time of year. School got out, father's day was around the corner and my great-grandmother's birthday was today. We didn't see her much, but her birthday was just after mine and my brothers and just before Daddy's. I had no idea what my Dad was asking me about. Why would I be getting a present this time of year?

"Well?" he asked again.

"I don't know, a lot of things I guess," I said

"What is the biggest thing you have always said you wanted?"

"A pet, but you always said we couldn't have anything but fish."

"What kind of pet have you always wanted?" he asked

"A dog, a dog like Grammy's" I squealed.

I got excited because I remembered that my grandmother's dog had just had puppies about two months before. She wanted to keep one of the puppies to show. My Grandmother always showed dogs in breed and obedience. I went with her several times to help watch the dogs.

"Am I getting a puppy?!?" I exclaimed

"Yes" my Dad stated with a big grin

So a couple of minutes or hours later. I am not really sure because all I could think about was what I would name my puppy. Then all of the wonderful things we would do together. How she would go with me to college and move in with me to my first apartment, just the two of us living on our own. It was going to be glorious.

As we pulled onto my grandmother's road I could barely stay in my seat. I looked over at my brother to see if he was as excited as I was, but he was asleep leaning against the window with his forgotten Gameboy DS in his hand. He was drooling on the window, Gross!

As soon as Dad stopped the car, I tore off my seatbelt and practically flew to my grandmother's kennel where she was keeping the puppies. I knew she would be down there and not at the house. And really I didn't care because my future best friend was down there and just ready to go home with me today.

Then I stopped dead in my tracks. It hit me. Which one would I pick? I had been down here several times and there were eight puppies total. Six girls and two boys. I knew I didn't want a boy and neither did my grandmother so that left 6 to pick from. There were too many. How would I pick the right one?

"What's the matter?" my dad asks as he catches up to me. "You couldn't wait to get here and now you're stopped five feet from the door?

"How could I pick one?" I said in a whisper more to me than him.

"What was that Ava?"

"How do you expect me to pick one of the six girls?" I asked "they are all so cute and each already has their own personality. How could I choose just one of the bunch?"

"You are only getting one so you better choose wisely" he chides.

This made it even worse. What if I chose wrong? What if we never got along and she wasn't my best friend in the world? What if she liked my brother more? I almost asked Dad these exact questions but just as I did my grandmother opened the door to the puppy pen.

"Hello, release the hounds!" my grandmother yells.

All paws and ears, the puppies came running towards me. I could see there are only 6, she must have only let the girls out.

"Sold the two boys today and one of the girls online. The people come to pick them up next week," she says. "I hear your Dad is letting you get one of these today."

I just stared at her. She sold one of the girls before I could pick one. I know she sells them, I had been here with the previous litters to know as much. But how could she sell one without me getting the choice first?

"Which girl did you sell?" I asked

"None, in particular, you get the first choice, Ava." she says "they will come pick theirs when they show up next week."

I almost cried I was so happy, for just a second though. Then the fear crept back in on making the wrong choice. I guess my grandmother knew this was my problem because she came over to me and whispered in my ear.

"Just look with your heart. You know these pups and all of their personalities. Which one will be the best for you?"

Then, just as if she was called for, the biggest girl in the litter walked over and sat down right next to me. She was always one of the less playful puppies. They all play, but this one was usually mellower than the others. The first to the food, but not to hog it all. She took her food and then moved away when she was done. She seemed to always be watching the others and making sure they were ok. I had caught her sitting with me before, watching the others play just as I was.

I guess she made the decision for me, not the other way around. As easy as that pick came, so did her name. I remember an old show my parents used to watch. It was a Sci-Fi show about some guy in the future on a spaceship. They had a small crew that was like family and an android/hologram/voice that was the ship's artificial intelligence. She watched over the crew every day and made sure they were safe. She talked to them and helped when hurt or sad. This is what I felt this dog was to be, a protector and a healer.

Her name was Andromeda.

As that memory faded away, so many more came up. Playing ball in the back yard. Her first snowball fight and how she loved jumping into the snow piles. How she would chase us around and just keep running when we fell in the snow. But then turn around and make sure we were ok. The years she would sit behind home plate on a leash next to my parents and watch me play softball. How we would just sit in the back yard and I would tell her about my day. Years and years of these just flicked through my memories, even faster than I could comprehend.

She became my true protector after the Fall. I thought about how she would warn the family if something was off or someone was near. How she would stay up at night while we slept to make sure everything stayed as it should be. How she was all I had after I lost my Dad, my brother and even my Mom to these creatures. How she would just stay there as I screamed and yelled and completely went insane about how unfair it was until I fell into an uneasy sleep at night. How she looked at me when I would awaken in the morning all puffy-eyed from crying the night before. No judgment. Just happy I woke up and wondering if we would eat that day.

After this menagerie of memories flooded through me, I seemed to fall into a dreamless sleep for an undetermined amount of time. Nothing but black and a pulsing throb coming from somewhere in the back of my mind. I knew Andromeda was ok, she always was, and she would find her way back to me, back to this place that I was, but couldn't remember. Where was I again?

Paradise

That was the first word that rose to the front of my mind as I woke up. The second word quickly followed though and that word was, pain. The pain was so intense it made my stomach queasy. It made me shut my eyes so tight that I needed the world to go away again. Slowly, the events leading up to my intense stomach-altering headache came back. Getting captured and thrown from the carriage. Them taking Andromeda and Giggles. Me getting knocked out cold.

That bitch was going to get it when I saw her again.

As this came back to me I started wondering where I was. I was sitting on a bed in a room with a very high window. One that could let in light, but not let you see out of it. There were four walls and a toilet in the room. Very much like a jail cell in the movies. The door was a regular door though and not a barred door like in a prison. So I decided to try it out and see where I was. Standing up was not an option at this point, so I decided to crawl to the door. The handle turned and the door released and moved in towards me. I was hopeful that it would be that easy. But as the door opened I could only see bars.

So this was a jail cell, only one with privacy? I could see one other door like this, but the inner door was shut, so I didn't know if it was occupied or not. The hallway was empty and not very long. It led to a set of stairs to the left and a blank wall to the right. They must not have much use for these cells too often, I guess only for people that stomp on their feet and try to run away?

What I didn't understand was why they took us to begin with. Why bring me here to keep me in a jail cell. All I would do was deplete whatever resources they had, whatever they gained from the run to Wal-Mart. They would lose by keeping the three of us here against our will. I guess they could have been cannibals. Keep us long enough to kill us and eat us. Maybe I was the second course and they had already killed the girl, maybe they had already killed Andromeda!

At this point, I came to a real quick conclusion. I wouldn't eat anything they bring to me that had meat in it. At least until I saw them both alive. I had seen the Walking Dead, good society with gardens and everyone working together, only to turnout to be cannibals and eating anyone that showed up.

God! I needed to see them both alive.

I realized that I was still on the floor with my face pressed against the metal bars, I decided to crawl back to the bunk and get some sleep. I had to get my wits about me before they came to kill me, or whatever it was that they were going to do. I got back in the bunk and tried to think, but this damn headache was stopping every thought before it could form. So I stopped trying to fight it and let sleep take me again. The next thing I knew I heard a door open. And someone walking down the steps.

I was awake but pretended to be asleep to see if maybe they would open the door and I could rush past them. I stayed in the same position and tried to not react to the noises as they approached. Now that I was listening for them, there were two distinct footfalls on the steps. I could also tell that my headache had lessened, at least in this position, because I could get thoughts straight in my head.

"She has been up," says one of the people. "The inner door is already open."

"Be careful," the other one was Susie. "She is a feisty one. Damn near broke my foot."

"Well if you had not been so rough with them, maybe we could have explained things better," speaker one says

"They stabbed George! What was I supposed to do? I was angry about that."

"And they fought back because you didn't explain. "

"You weren't there. You wouldn't know Dr. Sal," says Susie.

"Alright calm down. Since the door was open, we know she can move. Although probably with a killer headache after the hit you gave her"

"Humph," Susie grunted.

I heard a key being put in the lock.

"Just be quick Doc."

The metal door opened, but I couldn't move to the door and try to fight my way out. I just sat there and waited.

"Hello, young lady," Doc Sal says to me. "I need to check you for a concussion. You took a very hard hit to the back of your head. I know you're awake I can tell by your breathing."

I turned over to look at the doctor. He was a tall man, over 6 feet tall. White hair and beard he looked and talked like he was a kind man. Would he have been working with cannibals? With Killers? I tried to sit up and Doc Sal shushed me and placed a hand on my chest holding me in a laying position. He took out a couple of implements from his bag and sat on the edge of the bed. He then started examining me, as my family doctor did before.

"I am Doctor Sal Wagner. I am the doctor here. I need to check you out and make sure you are ok," he says.

"Where is here?" I croaked from a dry throat. I didn't realize I was thirsty until I tried to speak.

"Shush now, don't talk. You have been out a couple of days now. I have stopped in and tried to give you fluids, but we don't have a working IV, so it has been difficult. Could you sit up?" he asks.

I nodded yes and tried to get into a sitting position. He helped when I struggled. He seemed genuinely good, which seemed odd for a place like this.

"How do you feel? Does your head hurt at all?" he asks

"A bit, but not as bad as the last time I woke up."

"How long ago was that?"

"I don't know. But it was light out," I say as I looked at the window and realized it was pitch black outside. How long was I out?

"Well that may have not been too long ago, we are not long into the night now. Take these and drink this whole bottle of water. But drink it in small sips, be easy with it," he instructs.

I pulled back from him. Even though he was nice, I didn't trust that he was not drugging me. But my body was so thirsty, I just kind of whimpered as I backed away.

"Now child, I didn't nurse you back to health to harm you. I will take a drink of the water first to show you it is nothing harmful," he says as he drank a sip.

I took the medicine and the water and drank as fast as possible. It felt so good on my parched throat. I didn't think I had ever been that thirsty in my life.

"Easy, I said drink it slow," he said as he laughed.

I put the bottle down and burped. Like a real lady. Mom would be proud.

"Now rest again and I will be back to check on you in the morning. Do you think you could eat something? It has been a couple of days."

I nodded my head yes and he smiled and walked away.

Susie closed the metal door.

"Get her some food, she needs her strength," Doc said to Susie.

"Whatever!"

Then they both headed up the stairs and everything was quiet again. Although with that visit and the fact they didn't even look in on the door down from me. I felt that I was the only one here. They weren't keeping any other prisoners with me. So where was the other girl? And my dog?

A little while later I heard the door upstairs open again. I had been able to sit up since the doc left. I still hadn't stood up yet, not ready to try that. My head still hurt a bit, but mostly like a bruise, not the raging puke-inducing sickness that I had before. The footsteps were lighter this time. It couldn't have been Doc or Susie, it seemed like a small person. I risked standing up and almost fell back onto the bunk. But after the first wave of dizziness and blackness around my vision cleared, I could stay standing. I wouldn't be running anywhere anytime soon, but I should be able to walk to the door.

I looked down the hallway and saw a small girl walking down the steps with a tray. I guess they have her bringing me my food. Another small girl was here. That may mean that my small friend and my dog are ok. I guess it showed on my face because I was beaming as she stopped in front of my door. She gave me an odd look and handed the tray through a slot in the door.

"Have you seen my dog?"

"Yes, she is fine. They are keeping her in a kennel upstairs. She went a little crazy when they took you away. But she is better now. "

"When was that? How long have I been in here?"

"Two days," she said to my astonishment.

"What is going on here? What is this place?"

"I have to go. This place is nice. You will learn that. Please eat and be nice to them when they come for you. They don't want to hurt you. They never hurt me."

Then she was gone.

The food looked good. My stomach was rumbling before I even heard the door shut upstairs. So I took the tray to my bunk and sat down to eat. I still stayed away from the meat, but there was rice and green beans and even a nice fresh apple. It had been a while since I had fresh food, I didn't know how to react.

There were a couple of problems here. One was that I was being held prisoner, but she said it was because of my actions. Which were a bit aggressive. My people skills were never the best in rough situations like that. Next, they brought me nice fresh food. I had not had this many fresh vegetables in a long time. It seemed they wanted me to feel better. So I didn't know what to think. I guess I would just have to wait and see. I would bide my time and get a better read on things here.

The next morning I awoke to the girl bringing me breakfast. She was tapping on the bars trying to get my attention. Without even thinking of the fact that I have barely talked to this girl I blurted out. "Good Morning. What do we have for breakfast?"

"Oatmeal of some sort. Not bad, but not good either"

"Well thank you anyway. We shall make do with what we have."

The small girl said nothing as she walked away. I closed my door, listening to her walk away. It sounded like she stopped at another door before she went up the stairs. I thought that maybe she was just taking a break and thought no more of it.

When the girl brought lunch, I asked her if I was the only one down here. She didn't answer me, but looked to her right, towards where she seemed to stop earlier that morning.

"I am not allowed to talk to you anymore. Susie says," then she quickly turned and went down the hall.

I quickly got up and tried to see where she went. I couldn't see much but I saw her stop at a door and try to peak in. I guess the inner door was closed because she just moved on and back up the stairs.

"Anyone there?" I yelled. "Hello?!?"

I didn't get a response. But I tried again every couple of minutes. I was not sleeping all the time by this time, so the day dragged on.

After dinner on that same day, Doc and Susie came back and he checked me out again.

"You're healing well. I don't believe there will be any permanent damage. If you feel strange let someone know though. Ok?"

"How would I do that? There is no one down here to hear me?" I asked

He pointed to a camera mounted on the wall. "There is always someone watching you. To make sure you're ok. That is why you're underground, so the creatures can't detect the electrical signal. The monitor is upstairs but heavily shielded, to not draw attention."

He then got up and left again.

I was left staring at the camera. So were they watching me to monitor my health or to see how I was acting? The camera was outside of my door so I could shut them out.

I got up to do just that.

Each day was the same thing. I just began a running conversation with myself. I had seen Doc and Susie go in another door once in the past couple of days and the girl did bring two trays of food down for breakfast the previous day. Or at least I think it was breakfast. I was so bored that everything was running together.

There were no more doctors' visits so I only had meal time to look forward to. I did try to get up and walk around the room as much as I could. Tried to get my strength back, to not be lethargic. I did pushups and sit-ups. I got up to 4-minute planks and 100 burpees a day. When I got my chance to get out of there I was going to be ready. I couldn't fall back and be lazy because I couldn't believe that these people had my best interests at heart. If I got my chance to find Andromeda and get the hell out of there, I needed to be ready to take it.

While working out, eating or just laying down, I was having long-winded conversations with myself and the walls. No one ever said anything back and I never heard a noise from the other room. This went on for a week. A frustratingly long week, all without a sign or a noise.

Then suddenly after lunch one day. Day fourteen of my forced imprisonment, as my brother would say, I heard something.

"Do you like to hear yourself talk?"

"What did you say?" I asked wondering if I have gone insane.

"Do you like to hear yourself talk? You have been doing it an awful lot and it was very painful to hear sometimes," she said

"Giggles is that you?"

"What did you call me?" she asked

"Sorry, I don't know your name so I made up a nickname in my head for you. That wasn't supposed to have been said out loud. You are the girl they brought in with me, right? The one that stabbed George?"

"Yes, and I don't want to remember that too much. It wasn't my fault. I was scared. Why Giggles?"

"An ironic name because you were so serious in the carriage. You wouldn't speak to anyone. Sorry if it offended you"

"No, not really just caught me off guard. My name is Jordan. But I really don't care if you call me Giggles." There was a long pause and then she said "But you will not hear me giggle."

"Understood. Nice to meet you Jordan. My name is Ava. "

That was all that she would say that day. I stopped running a dialogue each day so she didn't have to listen to me. I was just happy to know she was ok and that there was someone there. I wasn't going insane.

Well, at least not yet.

As the days drug on, we talked more and more. All light things like our favorite foods and the movies we used to like. She would talk only for a couple of minutes at first, but it grew to a couple of hours a day. All the while I kept up my training and made sure I stayed in good shape. Shoot, I was probably in better shape now than before I was put in there. I also had more reason to be in shape to fight and not just run.

One thing I would give her though. No matter what we talked about, no matter what was said. I never once, in all that time, heard her giggle.

Giggles

I still used that name with her. More as we became almost friends. We talked about many things, but she always avoided my questions about our captures and the place that we were in. I had been so long in this hole that I had lost count of the days. I didn't know how long this had all been going on. I wondered if they were ever going to let me out of this cage, there didn't seem to be an end in sight.

I couldn't even remember the last time the door to my cage had been opened. I guess it was just the last time the Doc had been here to check me out. How long had that been? One week? Two?

I was a person that liked to know a lot about people around me. So I felt that I needed to find out more about Jordan if only just to get her side of the story. I had to know what brought her to Wal-Mart on that fateful day. The day that ruined everything and separated me from Andromeda. I had told her most of my story, just to fill the time and connect with another human. It had been a long time since I had done that. It felt good. I think she may have needed the same thing. I had to get her to talk to me about it.

"So what is your story Jordan?"

"Wow, you must be serious to use my real name."

"Just curious."

"My story isn't a fun one. It isn't something I like to talk about."

"None of us do, but you know mine. We have talked about me losing everybody I love, except Andromeda. It helped me. It helped us connect. I just want to know why you were at Wal-Mart that day too."

"Well, my story really isn't all that different from yours. Except for the fact that I lost everyone at the same time. They were all taken from me on the same day. Also, I had no one to help me through it. I didn't have an Andromeda to cry into each night. I just had myself."

"That must have been awful, I don't know if I could have done it. How did you lose your parents?"

So then hesitantly she started to speak, and she told me her story.

Jordan Davis hailed from a small town in Maryland, just this side of the bridge, called Grasonville. She lived in a higher-end community called Windward Cove. This was one of those places where every other house had a pool and every house had a boat dock to the creek outback. This creek lead directly to Eastern bay, which led to the Chesapeake Bay.

Jordan grew up with money. Her dad was a lawyer in Washington D.C. and her mom sold real estate in the Bay Bridge area. She lived a very happy spoiled life. She pretty much had everything that ever came out that she wanted. Always had the new iPhone as soon as she turned 9 yrs. old. She had all of Barbie's accessories. More than Barbie knew she had I think. She had the lifestyle that most kids dreamed about. There were a lot of kids in that community that lived just like her, so she thought it was normal. Even in school, she thought kids like me were poor and were to be pitied. Although she said this she still didn't feel she had a spoiled life. I mean she didn't get an allowance and she was once told she couldn't go to a friend's party because both of her parents had to work that weekend.

I mean how rough!

All was good until The Fall of course. Then money and power meant nothing. If you had no survival skills you were out of luck. This was where the farmers and hunters of the world that were scoffed for being trash and animals, thrived. She knew nothing about guns, except that they were bad because the media said so. She knew nothing of growing food, I mean where do ham sandwiches grow and was there a special plant for no crust?

I think this was a little more than she said, but I decided to ad-lib a little.

When The Fall came she and her parents were completely unprepared. She was only 13 years old at the time. When the news started talking about the disease and the creatures, her parents locked the doors and kept the windows shut. There were a lot of families heading out of town and trying to get to other family members' houses in the country. The media told everyone to stay inside and stay safe, so that was what they tried to do. They wore their masks and stayed the required distance from others. With them being pretty well off, they had plenty of food in the pantry and multiple refrigerators and freezers.

Unfortunately, this food still only lasts so long. The prognosis for the country got worse and the power went out, everything was going wrong. They had to change something and try to get somewhere so they wouldn't starve. They knew there were some farms just outside of town, so they packed up some meager belongings and headed out.

Everything went well for the Davis family on their trip. They got to the farms pretty quickly considering they had to walk and none of them were accustomed to hiking in the wilderness. With their limited knowledge, they camped outside at night, no tent or sleeping bags, just blankets and pillows that they had carried with them. Not the best idea, but they made it through to the next day. The first farm they came to had room and was willing to let them stay there as long as they helped out.

This was where they stayed for a couple of months. None of them had ever seen a Deader, they had only heard rumors from others passing through and the media before that went down. They lived in this denial of reality for a while and actually started to enjoy living in the country and learning to raise cows and grow their own food. Then came early spring last year. The plants were in and everything was going well, just like it had all of her life. But that was going to end real soon.

The farmer's wife became really sick, no one knew why. They were an older couple and it may have just been ailing health with the stress of everything through the winter. It may have just been a spring flu that came through. Since no one really knew anything, they did what they could, but her condition worsened. A week or so later the old lady died. The farmer was a disaster and laid her out in the barn so they could have a proper funeral the next day. As we now know, she only stayed dead for a little while. Longer than most it seemed, but time to a 14-year old that just went through the first tragedy in her life wasn't a real priority. They laid her out in the barn and went back inside to mourn before they dug her grave.

As they came back out of the house to get the shovels, the old lady was walking back towards the house. They must have been mistaken, they thought. Maybe her heart rate just dropped too low for them to recognize. They all thought that they had almost buried the woman alive. The farmer took off running towards his wife. The tears in his eyes blinded him to the truth. As the old woman looked up her eyes glowed with an eerie blue. They didn't look right, and neither did her walk. She had always walked with a limp and now she was walking better than a spry 20-year-old.

Jordan's dad called out to the old farmer to get him to stop to see what was different. The farmer either didn't hear or just ignored him completely and embraced his wife. He then held her at arm's length to get a good look at her. He suddenly stiffened as if seeing the change for the first time. He tried to break away at that point, but wasn't fast enough. She turned on him and took him to the ground.

Jordan skipped the details at this point, but to say the least it stuck with her. She wasn't sure if she had smiled since that day. It was so horrific and all they could do was stand there and watch it happen.

When she finished with the old man she screamed some shrill cry and looked at the living. Jordan's family all ran to the house and locked the door. They made it just ahead of the helpful old lady. The lady that had died right here in the kitchen they were standing in.

Needless to say, the Deader couldn't open the door, and they were safe as long as they stayed inside. But her mom had remembered hearing that the Deaders could call for each other. It was one of the first things they had heard on the news. They did not know if there were any others in this area, as they had never seen one before today, but it was not worth taking the chance. They packed up a few small things and some food as fast as they could and ran out of the other door and away from the farm. The door just happened to point east, so they headed in that direction.

Although they were all together, they were scared for their lives and totally clueless about what to do next. The next week or so was a blur to Jordan. All she really remembered was walking, being wet and being hungry. They didn't have the skills to start a fire at night and were afraid of the things in the night they might attract. Soon they came across an old state park with cabins that used to be for rent, their luck had held.

The cabin they had found seemed secluded. The area seemed safe. When they went inside, the place had been fully stocked with gear and blankets. There was even some canned food in the cabinets. Their luck still held. Their mom called it the Davis luck. She always said that this family could never die because their line traced back to Jefferson Davis.

Although Jordan's mom was of Hispanic descent and her dad had a strain of American Indian in his bloodline, they still thought great things about their ancestor. Her mom would say things like "He did great things in an unfortunate time for our country." They felt that his history and his prowess lived on through them and that was what was helping them get through this difficult ordeal.

With the food and the supplies, her Dad thought that someone may be back for them. He thought that maybe this person was just out on a hunt. They sat on the front porch and waited for someone to return. When no one returned by dark, they moved inside but still stayed vigilant for the hunter to return. They did this for three days. No one ever came back.

They took this as a sign of good fortune and decided to make the place their own. If someone ever came back they would apologize and move on. But after another week this became a memory and they made the place fully their own. They felt comfortable to the point where they had planted some seeds that they had taken from the farm. It was a little late in the season, but they still might get something from them.

They stayed there for a long time. They were able to forage in the forest, which was mainly untouched by man, being a state forest and all. Subsidizing that with the supplies they had and the canned food in the cabinet, they were comfortable. The season turned and their plants did not come to fruition. Fall was settling in and the food supplies were very low. No one had a gun or a knife and they definitely didn't know how to set a snare to get animals. Jordan's parents went with less food and tried to make the supplies last. Her dad went on forays to the other cabins from time to time to see if any other had the supplies this one had. But to no avail. That was what the last tenant must have done to get all of the supplies that were here when they moved in.

By November the first freeze came and they were in bad shape. They had waited too long to strike out again to search for a new area, to try for a new lucky find. They were all too weak and had pretty much come to the conclusion that they wouldn't last the winter. Death came quicker than any of them would have thought. In the second week of November Jordan's mother died in her sleep, she had been sick and coughing for days. The sickness and lack of food had gotten to her and there was nothing they could've done. Everyone had been waiting to see if she got better, but they all knew that she wouldn't.

The problem with dying in her sleep was that she shared a bed with Jordan's Dad. He was sickly too, so he slept hard when he slept. He actually slept better for a few minutes because her mom had stopped coughing, letting him fall into a deeper sleep.

This lasted less than 10 minutes though because the dead rise and when they do they are hungry. Jordan heard her dad scream from the other room before it was cut short. She ran to the room to see what had happened and saw her mother's eyes glowing blue as she fed on her father. Jordan spent no more time and ran out the door shutting it behind her as she ran.

This was probably what saved her life.

She ran for an unknown amount of time. Crying from fear and grief in equal measure. She had left with no supplies and no more clothes than what was on her back. Soon she found a ramshackle house falling apart but still mostly standing. She completed her night in this building.

The next morning she moved out again and tried to find a place to stay. She would not go into too much more at this point, except to tell me that she was on her own for the next few months. Eating when she could and freezing most of the time. She had found some shelter, but never stayed put for long. She kept going east and that was how she eventually ended up in Walmart in Milford with me on that fateful night a couple of weeks, or months, ago.

I was really having trouble processing what she had told me and how awful and terrifying that had to have been for her. She had never really known fear before and now that was all she ever lived with. After she was done telling me her story, she went quiet. I was so shocked by her telling, that I couldn't ask her anything more. I sat there for a long while trying to figure out how she even had the power to go on each day. Let alone how she had been strong enough to stab a guy in the leg after he got too close to her. It was almost like she had gone a little bit feral in her time alone in the wilderness. Maybe that was why she skimmed over that part so fast and why she sounded ashamed as she finished. I had to make sure she knew that this didn't change anything between us. That knowing this only made me want to help her more. To be her friend and help her through.

The next day after we had finished our grey gruel they call oatmeal we heard heavy footfalls coming down the stairs. I jumped up and looked at who was coming. It was Susie and Georgie, no way was this going to be good. They stopped at Jordan's door first and wrapped on the interior door to get her to open the door. They opened the outer cage door and started talking to her when she did. I could only pick up a word or two here and there. It was hushed tones but heated. It seemed that Georgie had healed ok, nothing in his movements gave away the injury he had sustained.

After several minutes of them talking, they stepped back and Georgie took Jordan's arm and started up the stairs.

"Hey," I said, "Where are you taking her!"

Susie walked down to my cell at that. "We will take her where we want to take her. If you shut up and listen you may be able to go too."

"I am not going anywhere with you," I spat.

"See that is what I had told them before I came down here. They just won't listen to me. They want me to see if we could make amends and get along."

"Just listen to her," Jordan said as she walks up the stairs.

"What do you have to say?" I asked.

"The uppers want to see if you have calmed down enough with your forced time here in this cell, to see if you would listen to reason and be a good member of our society. That is just what we were explaining to your friend there. That is why Georgie and I came down. We are the ones that had the trouble with you two, and they feel if you could bury the hatchet with us and vice versa, we could get you to get along with everyone else. You do want to see you're doggo right?"

"I do. What do you want from me?"

"I want you to rot down here, but that isn't good for our community. You are a drain on our resources and no good to anyone down here. You're strong, I have watched your workout routine. It is good. A little rudimentary, but not bad for a beginner. We could use your strength on the farms."

"Why would I listen to you and want to work for you here?"

"It's safe and we have a good thing here. We haven't been attacked by the things with the glowing eyes in..."

"Deaders" I chimed in

"What?" She asked startled

"I call them Deaders"

"Whatever you call them, we haven't seen them here since the winter came. We think we are safe here. You could be safe too."

"I thought I was safe at Cape, but they came for me there again. That's why I ran. You are never safe," I shivered just saying it.

"Well, we are a good group. I know we got off on the wrong foot, well you came down on my foot, but you know what I mean. Could we let you out and show you what you could have been part of?" She was actually very sincere.

"Are you cannibals?" I asked.

"What? Is that why you never ate the meat here? You think we eat people?"

"I watched the Walking Dead, I know how these places could be."

Susie actually laughed out loud. So hard in fact that tears came to her eyes.

When she finally came to her senses she just looked at me and reached her hand into her pocket. I grabbed the door ready to slam it in her face if she tried anything stupid. But when she took her hand out of her pocket it was a key in her hand. She looked at me and put the key in the lock and unlocked the door.

Now, this was something that I had imagined several hundred times over the last months. What would I do? It was just her and me. I could take her, I was in better shape than when I came here and she was not ready for me to fight. The door slowly opened. Time seemed to slow down. What would I do? What to do?

But as the door opened and Susie raised her hand out to me for a handshake, all of that left me. All of the fear and hatred drained in an instant. They were just trying to keep themselves safe. They were afraid and they thought I could help them. And I would, for now. I took her hand and then we walked up the stairs. The first freedom I had felt in a long time.

Freedom

Freedom could mean so many things to many people. I say freedom at this point because I was no longer in a cell. But was I free to leave? Was I free to stay? I guess time would tell.

Obviously, as soon as we opened the heavy metal door at the top of the stairs, one thought was on my mind. Andromeda. I think Susie could even tell because she said one word and pointed.

"There."

I broke off at a run. But even at this easy lope, I could tell that even though I was stronger from my workouts, my breathing came heavy and I was not ready to run quite yet. I slowed down to a trot until I hit the building she had indicated. When I opened the door I could instantly tell by the noise and the smells that this was being used as a barn. Smart, it seemed everything was insulated and kept in the animal's signatures as well as the sounds so the small compound was not awash in the mooing and squealing of the animals.

All thought of that went away as soon as I saw Andromeda curled up beneath one of the horses in a stall. It seemed she had run of the barn and was well taken care of. She lazily looked up and yawned before she recognized that it was me. Then she was up and to me in a matter of eye blinks. Jumping up and knocking me to the ground, again. Licking my face. Suffice to say I think she was as happy to see me as I was her.

We stayed there for what seemed like hours. I was just lost in my love for her and the fact that she was ok and we were back together. It was probably only minutes, but it was what I needed. I looked her over and saw that her paw was healed and she looked healthy and fed.

Maybe a little overfed to be honest.

I got up and we walked out of the barn and back into the sunlight of the day. With Andromeda at my side I could now focus on the world around me and the sights there were to behold. Well, focus may have been a bit of a stretch. I could get the basic gist of what was around me. My eyes have always been light sensitive and a bright sunny day has always made me wear sunglasses. That day was bright and sunny, and I didn't have any sunglasses. I was also kept in a basement jail cell for the last couple of weeks. Needless to say, I really couldn't see the details of anything. But the overall feel of the place was nice, tinged with an electric feel of fear. But maybe that was just me.

The first thing I saw was the plants, just like the day they brought us in. But this time I could focus more and see farther than I could then, as long as I used my hand as a shield and kept my eyes towards the ground. I saw the people, the buildings and the fence that protected it all. This place may have been safer than all the other places I had been, but it would never be safe. There were only three buildings including the barn I was just in. The prison building looked normal from here, with no hint to the basement cells that had been my home. It was two-story and had lots of windows, yet all of these were covered and probably insulated for safety of those on the second floor. The Deaders could see electrical fields for miles. The other building was similar in style but just a one story. This one seemed to have the kitchen because the chimneys had smoke pouring out of them and the smells from there made it clear they were cooking fires. There were also a couple of ramshackle covers that housed animals outside.

When I rounded the next building Susie was there with George and Jordan. Jordan seemed happy to see the sun and kept closing her eyes, looking up taking it in and enjoying the warmth. It was warm too, it took me a second to notice. Not the heat of summer, but definitely farther from winter than when I got there. Being locked up had taken away most of my spring but not quite all.

Susie and George took us on a quick tour of the grounds. Told us where things were and what was expected of the people that lived inside of these walls. Most people helped with the animals and the farming. This was what kept everyone fed and alive. There were people that took turns keeping watch but not like you would see in the movies, I wasn't sure what that meant, so she explained. The Deaders were called ED's (Energy Drainers) here, for obvious reasons. Since they could see electrical energy from the people on the wall at farther distances than up close walking on top of the wall would actually attract the creatures and not help warn them away. These people, Bravers they call themselves, had bulletproof glass that they were able to put into the metal fence to create windows. It was believed that since the window was so thick it let less electrical energy show through and made it possible to see but not be seen.

The thing I found odd, was that the guards didn't carry guns. They just had a chair and looked out of the glass. The glass had an opening on the side with a hinge that enabled them to drop a cut piece of the wall down, for shooting. This was where I would probably fit in best. Jordan wanted nothing to do with this detail and from her history, I couldn't blame her. I was a hunter. I had sat for long hours staring out into the woods or the fields looking for the slightest movement that may mean my prey was near (or in this case my predator).

Although I was not sure why I was thinking about where I would fit in. I was not staying here. This was fake security, a false sense of safety. This was what got more people killed. If not from the dead, from the living wanting what you have.

The two main buildings were the housing areas. When this was a veteran home the rooms usually held one or two people. The rooms and the living spaces had been modified to hold the growing number of people inside the fences. George told us that there were currently 50 people on property living in these housing units. The one had homes on both floors and the single-story was for cooking, food preparation and storage. Everything that was not eaten fresh was canned and pickled so it could last as long as possible.

Everything here was done well, very organized seeing as it started as a home for homeless veterans, it made sense. These were mostly people that had served in the United States military in some capacity. They were trained to be organized and have a leadership structure. In times as trying as these we stick to our core values in training as a lifeboat. The tour took us to Pa's office. Jordan was taken into the office first. As the door opened I could see he was sitting behind a big oak desk, he didn't look at ease or imposing as they say in books. He was just sitting there. A man behind a desk that had a few papers on it and not much else. As Jordan entered the room George motioned to a chair for me to sit in. I sat there for about an hour before the door opened I was motioned inside to join them.

"Thank you for joining me," he started "I wanted to talk to you about our oasis here in the desert of death."

"That's a gloomy term," Jordan said

"Well, Jordan it is a gloomy life out there on your own. One like you should know that, I would think,"

I started to say something in her defense but he held up his hand before I could.

"I mean no harm. I am just pointing out the history that I have heard about Jordan here. She did tell you her story?"

I nodded

"Then you know the heartbreaking life she has had these last couple of years."

"To start with, your incarceration in the cells was just a precaution. It was not punishment for what you may or may not have done to our people. There are a lot of diseases out there running rampant. The death virus is not something that you carry around or could contract.. It doesn't happen from a bite like in those old graphic novels, this we know. But we also know that a real virus as small as the flu could be deadly without the right treatments. We keep all people in quarantine for a time to see if they exhibit any symptoms of being sick," he continued.

"Months? That's a quarantine?" I yelled

"Month singular, and not usually, but Jordan here seemed sickly. She wouldn't eat and kept refusing to see even our doctor for a time. She kept her inner door closed and we couldn't monitor her progress. This made us wary. We kept you in there also since you came in together, we thought that maybe you had been traveling together and could have the same illness. Things like Ebola and mumps are a thing again. I wouldn't have been surprised if the fleas brought the black plague or a bat with Covid-19 came back. We had to be careful. But when she started talking to you and leaving her door open the monitoring started in earnest. We don't have the technology to scan the blood or any of the technological ways hospitals did before. We are back in the dark ages."

"So we were stuck down there because of me, for so long?" Jordan asked.

"Yes in a way, but we just had to be sure. To keep our community safe. I hope you understand."

I said nothing as I stood there fuming. A month lost, I could have been traveling out of danger, or maybe into more. It was farther into spring now, they may have been moving more than before. I could have been a lot farther north. I guess I could live with the explanation.

"Susie, George. That will be all from you for now. Please wait outside while I talk to our newly free guests here."

He waited for the two to leave and close the door.

"I know they won't go far. Probably just outside the door if I know them. But I wanted to take a few minutes and talk to you about what we have built here. Then possibly offer you a place here with us."

I started to speak again. And yet again he stopped me with his hand.

What was it with this guy?

"Before you speak Ms. Washington. I want you to hear me out. I want you to understand what we are trying to make here and why. After I have spoken my peace, you are able to make your own decisions at your leisure. But please hear me out first."

I let him speak, for now. However, it was going to be a waste of his breath.

Pa started with the basics.

First off his name was Paul. The others have such a southern accent that I thought they were saying Pa. The hierarchy here was pretty easy-going and not as rigid as a military would be. You had Paul and then George, Susie and Steve were the acting heads of the departments. Each had their own tasks. They had the doctor, Sal, which I had met too. Paul ran things, because he used to be an officer in the Army. He would assign us each a task, if we stayed. There was not a whole lot of free time but he didn't work the people like slaves. He wanted people to be happy under his command. He wanted it to feel safe and like a home.

He sent the team out on patrols for supplies weekly to see if there was anything left out in the world that they could use. Susie and George usually ran security. He didn't usually go on these raids himself that just happened to have been a fluke when we met them. Stevie was the brains of the operation when it came to the design of the carriage that brought us here and other safety features from the ED's. He was also the best with the horses.

Those four had been here when the ED's started walking around. Back then it was wide open to the farmland. Not too long after the Fall, they had met with other farmers from around the area and had a meeting. If they took everything they had, they could fortify this area and keep each other safe. Safer than any of them could in the individually isolated farmhouses. There was push back and some of the farmers went their own way and refused to join. Some moved on and others just barricaded themselves in their own homes. No one was really sure what happened to most of them anymore. But there were enough that came together to erect a small fence and join their supplies. It was a slow start, but a start nonetheless.

Over the last two years, their numbers have grown. They found people during their raids and offered them a place to stay in exchange for the use of their skills. They had expanded the fence a couple of times for more farming areas. They have spent most of the time growing their families and the food to keep them alive. They have welders, mechanics, blacksmiths and cooks in the community. They had even fortified the fences to make sure they are infallible.

I asked, "What about the Deaders? How do you keep them at bay? How do they keep them out? Once they see you they tell the others and nothing can stop them."

"Well, there is a way to stop them. If you separate their head from their body, they tend not to move again. They can't communicate with their friends and can't bring them here. We are careful too. In the beginning, there were more. There had been big groups of ED's coming through. Our spotters would see them and we would hide everyone below ground or in the insulated rooms and freezers. Anywhere that would hide the body signature. There were times when a couple of them got in the gates and some of us were killed."

He then explained how they had fortified and how they had changed their approach. If they see one ED they take it out long distance. They had a military issue .50 caliber rifle on property. One headshot from that and the thing never moved again. If there were any more though, they did all they could not to draw attention. Even trying to take them all out has had bad consequences.

"As you said it only takes one to know where we are. Then they leave and tell their friends. We usually let the large groups pass. Since we insulated the barn and the animals don't draw them, it is easier to hide," he stated. "We have it figured out, it is safe here."

"What about human raiders?" I asked

"We had some of them turn up a time or two. We try to speak to them from the top of the wall. If they don't want to join us or leave us, we do have some weapons to fight for our survival. We do have the upper hand, being enclosed in a wall and all," he explained.

When the conversation was complete, Paul called Susie and George back in. As he thought, they were standing just outside the door. They took us back to the front gate. They gave us the option right then and there. If we wanted to stay in the safety of their compound we had to contribute. No thefts, no fighting, no bullshit of any kind was tolerated. If we couldn't do the work that was assigned to us or refused to do that work, we would be out on our butts. If we felt that we couldn't or wouldn't conform to their rules we could walk out of the gate. There were two backpacks with supplies, one of which looked suspiciously like mine anyway. As I thought this Susie bent down and picked up my bag and handed it to me, roughly.

"All of your things that you came in here with are in there, plus more food and water that you would need to get through a couple days," Susie said.

"If you don't leave now you are agreeing to our terms. It's a good place," George said, "But we are not tolerant of the actions that you displayed on your entrance to our home."

I don't like ultimatums. I don't like being told what to do or told that my actions were not justified under the circumstances. But I looked at Jordan and she was terrified of going back outside the fence. She bought the whole safe aspect of their speech. She thought these walls would keep us all safe and we could get some piece of what it was like before The Fall. Andromeda seemed to think it was relaxing and nice here too, but she would go anywhere I went, no questions asked. Jordan would stay here no matter what I said or did. She refused to even take the backpack that was setup for her. She wanted to believe this so badly she would not even consider anything else.

At that instant, I knew I had to stay here and protect Jordan with all of my ability. I had lost almost everyone in my life, but she had lost everyone. She lost them in the worst possible way, she had seen them turned. She was not capable of thinking clearly on this and if things went bad, she would die. She would be so immobilized by fear that she might as well deliver herself on a silver platter. Maybe with me staying, I could help her when it happened.

Or I could be wrong about her. She had made it on her own for months.

I put the bag on my shoulders and tightened the straps. Susie started to open the gate to let me leave.

"I am not going anywhere. I will stay and I will listen to your rules," I declared, "But I am keeping my stuff, and you will not touch any of it again."

As I finished my statement I grabbed Jordan's hand, called to Andromeda and walked back towards the housing areas to find us a cot to sleep on. There were a lot of people in the gardens as we walked back, they were working on the plants, moving dirt in wheelbarrows and just milling about. Everyone seemed focused and paid no attention to the two new people in their midst. They had seen us when we went through the first time and I guess the second coming was of no consequence to them. Another set of hands to help, but another set of mouths to feed. Everyone just went about their day.

Everyone except one person standing next to the corn about 500 feet from where we walked. It was a woman standing there looking at me. She had dropped a basket that she was carrying, it lay forgotten in the path. She looked familiar, but I couldn't tell from this distance as to why that would be. As I stood there looking at this woman she started to walk towards me. As she got closer I could see a very peculiar expression on her face. It was a face that I should know, but my brain wouldn't allow me to remember. She walked with a very bad limp that seemed to pain her in every step. Andromeda became aware of the woman approaching me and looked at me with an odd look. She then stood up and whimpered as if to say something and sat down by my side. She very obviously wanted to go to this woman. Only her dedication to me overrode this need. Maybe this was who took care of her when I was locked away.

I looked up again and the amount of emotion that hit me at that second couldn't have been recalled. My eyes had finally adjusted to the sunlight that I had not seen in a while. The woman had also come close enough for me to see her clearly for the first time.

I broke into tears. The woman hobbling toward me was someone I never thought that I would see again. Someone I had lost to the Deaders, someone I had left behind.

My Mother.

Guilt

I had left her behind. I had assumed that she had died when the Deaders had attacked back at our home. That was over a year ago. I had left her, to save myself. What would she think of me? I stood there with Andromeda at my side watching this woman I had mourned. The woman I couldn't look at in the eyes because of the guilt that was stabbing me in the stomach. The woman that had always protected me and when the tables had turned I left her for dead.

I brought that memory back. Looked through everything again. I had heard her scream. It was her, I was so sure. It was a scream that only came to an abrupt end with death. I had heard that, hadn't I? But there she was. There was no mistaking now who she was.

She stopped short, taking in the sight of me. I was sure the look on my face stopped her. It was conflicted. The look on her face was one of pure happiness, pure joy at finding her lost daughter. What she must have been thinking. I was not running towards her, not jumping into her arms like I had done before, so many times.

I decided to act happy, to show her what she was showing me. I lunged forward the last two steps and took her in my arms. I buried my head in her chest and let the emotions that were roiling in my head spill out. I was happy to see her, I was just guilty for leaving her behind. Andromeda got up and walked over too. She shoved her head in-between the two of us until she got her head rubbed and got her lovin's too.

"Ava, I never thought I would see you again." She said in almost a whisper. "It's a miracle."

"I...I thought you were dead." I said shamefully.

"Anyone would have. I thought the same about you a couple of times too. When the night and loneliness would get to me. Sometimes it brought grief, but mostly it brought relief. This is such a hard world to live in, especially by yourself, all alone."

"But I was never alone. I always had Andromeda. But I left you. I left you to die and just ran off without helping. Without checking. I am so, so sorry momma."

"Shh, there is nothing to have been sorry about chica. You did as you were taught, as your father taught you. You survived. But where did you come from? How did you get here? After so long." She asked.

We moved out of the middle of the walk. There were a lot of people moving through and we were in their way. We found a small bench set by one of the flower gardens and sat down.

"What is wrong with your leg Momma?" I asked

"It was broken on the day you left. It never healed right and pains me to put weight on it to this day."

"I am so sorry, is there anything that could have been done."

"Before the Fall, yes. Today, no. it was never set correctly and I walked on it when it was broken. It will be this way until I die. It was a small price to pay. But enough about me for now. Tell me your story."

So I did. I started with that day. With the day I left my mother for dead, to defend herself with a broken leg and a broken heart. I told her about everything, even the time cowering in the bunker in the state park. I told her how I decided to run and how that led me back to her.

She obviously stopped me at times and asked questions or just to offer support in a decision that I had made, or something that had happened. The whole time I was talking she was petting Andromeda and the more it was clear that she was the reason that I was alive, the more she would love on her.

The story didn't take as long as I thought it would. The telling was full of detail, yet it still seemed like it was insignificant to the time it portrayed. I guess emotions charge things and change your perception of them through time. When I was done, we sat there in silence and just enjoyed the reunion.

After a time I finally asked. "Now it is your turn, how did you end up here?"

"Well, it is not nearly as exciting as your tale, let me tell you that. But there are some interesting parts I guess."

Then she told me her story.

She, like me, started her story on that fateful day. The day that was almost a year ago to the day. She started a little earlier in the day. When I had left with my friends to scavenge. She watched me go into the woods and then started her chores for the day. There was not a washing machine or a dishwasher anymore. It had reverted to the people to do that. So that was where she started. I was not completely sure why she included the chores in her part of the story, but mothers have their own strange way of thinking at times. Knowing that the laundry and dishes were done in the house before all hell broke loose seemed important to her.

So after I had gone into the woods and she had finished her chores, she took a small break and went outside to enjoy the day. She sat out back and enjoyed another cup of coffee, something she rarely had two of anymore since it was scarce. She felt rejuvenated and that it would have been a good day. (Well that went to hell in a hand-basket really quick.) But she enjoyed that last sip of the coffee and decided to walk around the neighborhood and enjoy some of the daily gossip that goes around a small community. She went to a friends about four houses down from ours and sat down on their back patio.

Although I didn't like to interrupt, I stopped her and asked her "Why was Andromeda in your bedroom at the house and not out with you? She loves the outside and would have enjoyed the day a lot too."

"She was acting agitated and odd. She kept trying to run off around the front of the house when I was enjoying my coffee. So I put her inside, but she kept scratching at the window, so I locked her in my room." She said. "Do you think she knew something was wrong?"

"Knowing what I know now about how she could find these things. Yes. I think she knew and was trying to tell you."

Momma looked down and petted Andromeda's head. "I should have taken the time to listen to you. I am so sorry Hunny."

Andromeda had the look of someone accepting an apology. She looked up at her and then at me. She then leaned further into my mother's leg to assure her that it was all fine.

"Please continue." I said.

She told me that she eyas at her friend's house when the first alarm went up. One of the sentries in the front of the community had seen movement. Not sure if it was alive or dead. It was more of a call for the other sentries to be on alert, than for a true alarm. But just a minute after that several other sentries called out the same movement. They were surrounding the community. All of the people started running for their homes, either to grab weapons and help or to hide with the young ones. Mom went running for the house but never made it back there. She was just leaving the front of her friend's house when the first Deader screamed.

That was the scream I heard from the woods.

Then the gunfire started. It was everywhere. She had nowhere to run, she had to get to cover, but she didn't know where I was. So she ran behind the houses to the woods. She knew that we were returning soon and wanted to stop us before we got to the community.

Little did she know that about the time she was hitting the back of the house down from ours, I had just entered our house and was finding Andromeda.

So she ran to the woods all the while looking for me and the others. When she reached the wood line she hid behind a bunch of brush that the community had cleared out earlier in the year. She stayed there hoping she could stay hidden and stop us.

She heard more gunfire and screams. Really trying to block it all out. She was not a fighter and never wanted to be the hero or in harm's way. She was best staying out of the way, she would only get herself and probably others killed.

She had her back to the community with the brush behind her, hiding her from the intruders. All the while wondering where I could have been.

Another scream, this one seeming to come from closer, the back of the homes. They had reached that far into the community. Not contained to the streets any longer. So she did what she knew to do. She hunkered down lower and tried to make the world go away, for her not to be seen.

A couple of minutes later she heard the brush rustle and what sounded like steps in the woods. They stopped well in from her, closer to the wood line. After a short bit, they stopped and she heard nothing. She was scared to move, and make any noise, even if it was one of the neighbors.

There was no noise for a while, she thought that maybe she had not heard it or that the person was injured and died where they sat. She was worried because even with all of the noise in the community, she had still not seen the kids return. They should have been back by now unless the things had gotten them too.

Just about the time that she thought it was clear to move, she heard movement again in the woods. Two sets of footsteps. No other noise. She started to peak her head around and get a look when the pace of the steps quickened and started to go deeper into the woods. She turned to see what was making the noise, thinking that the Deaders had found her and that this was the last day on earth for her along with so many of their community. But she saw me instead. She tried to call out, but the time in the panic state and her current fear keep the yell to a squeak, barely a whistle. It was enough that Andromeda stopped and turned. But she could see that I never slowed, that I didn't hear her. She tried to get her voice again while waving at Andromeda to come to her. But I whistled first and kept running, so Andromeda ran with me.

She tried to get up to follow me. To run after me and keep us together, but she was never an athlete, she never ran cross country and couldn't keep up with the fear pumping in my veins and the loss making me faster than I had ever been. She made it about 50 yards farther into the woods when she went down. Her leg caught a root and she fell onto a log. This fall was what caused her leg to break. She went down but didn't cry out. She knew at this point if I had heard her, I would come back and stay with her. That she would hold me back and we would both suffer for it. So she tried to get up on her own, but the pain was so bad she passed out and fell behind the fallen tree she had broken her leg on.

She does not know how long she laid there, but it was dark when she woke. The pain in her leg was unbearable. It was twisted at a wrong angle just below the knee. It wasn't a compound fracture, but it was bad. She laid there wondering what had woken her up besides the pain.

As she looked around she could see shadows moving in the woods. She wasn't sure, but she didn't see the glowing eyes, so she thought they were human. She called out. Again and again.

One of our neighbors finally called back and found her lying on the ground. It was one she barely knew but had seen before. She asked if anyone had survived. The neighbor replied that only six people had survived the slaughter. They had stayed in their homes and hunkered down for the last couple of hours. They then gathered up what they would need and set out. As quickly and quietly as they could. They had not seen any Deaders since the slaughter, but they were being cautious.

The other five joined him and my mother, then they fashioned a crutch for her to walk with. They took it slow and moved through the woods until they came to the open fields on the other side. After some talk and heated discussions, they decided to head north. There were more places to stay and hide, with the population being higher there before the fall.

For days they walked. They didn't encounter anything at all. They stopped often because of Mom's leg, but they made steady progress along the side roads. They moved during the day, at the best pace they could and hid at night. Only twice hearing the calls of the dead.

About a week after they had started their journey, fate and luck collided. They were in a dark portion of the woods on a very cloudy day that had been meant for a shortcut. But this would cut them short in the end. They ran into a single Deader walking through the woods. They saw it before it saw them, but that made no difference. With Mom not being able to run, they hid her behind a tree. The two men that were left tried to attack the deader and kill it. They only had knives as all the ammo for the guns had been used in the fight in the community. The others, all women, stayed with Mom and hid.

The plan went awry as they always do. One man dead in seconds, the other running for his life. He ran away from the women and the Deader followed. They waited there until night fell and never heard from the man or the Deader again. It seemed that he had died to save them that day.

The next morning the women got back on the road and stayed to the side of the roads and out of the woods. It was here that they found the body of their savior. Lying in the road, devoid of all life.

Two days later they were out of water and food. They were completely lost and mom's leg had gotten progressively worse and seemed to have been getting infected. She told the others to leave her to die and save themselves. They could move faster without her.

Hours of argument later and they decided to do just that. Cull the herd as they say. As they syere saying their goodbyes, they heard movement from behind them. It sounded like horses. They all sat there looking at the horses come around a turn and reveal that it was pulling a carriage. The very carriage that brought me to the Home of the Brave. The driver saw the women on the side of the road and stopped to render assistance. They had food and water. They offered the group refuge at their camp. The camp also happened to have a doctor on staff that could help my injured mother.

They were obviously in no condition to turn down any help that was offered. So they went with the guy, which turned out to have been Paul himself on this trip, and took the ride to the Home of the Brave.

When they arrived a small committee welcomed them and sent them to the jail rooms for quarantine. The doctor came and looked at my mom's leg. He wrapped it and casted it, but it had already started to heal in the wrong position. He had no way to re-break the leg without risking further injury and infection. So they left it and let it heal on its own knowing she would never walk without pain again. But this was a small price to pay to have actually survived something that most had not.

She then spent the last year at the Home of the Brave. Helping plant and harvest as best she could. She was happy here and loved the people that had and were still helping her. She would have never survived on her own, even without the broken leg hampering her movements.

"So I am the reason you broke your leg. The reason you almost died out there on the road." I said.

"No sweetheart. I had lost you before I had run after you. I was never going to catch you. I should have been able to call out to you to get you to stop. Long before I fell and broke my leg. You are the reason I kept going and didn't lie there and die that day. I knew you were safe and that fate would bring us back together sometime." she stated.

"But I should have heard you. Should have listened to Andromeda and turn to see what she was looking at. She knew and she tried to tell me."

"You had to learn that. Before that day you were a girl and her dog. A dog that was her best friend, but a dog that had an easy life and had never shown signs of greatness. You didn't know then that she would become what she is today. You had to learn that, just as she did. You trust her now and wouldn't make the same mistake again. We are together now, no matter what caused this, this is what is true and what matters."

We sat there for a long time after that. Sharing small stories and if we had run into anyone else that we knew. Gossiping about the happenings of the people in the new community. Reminiscing about the people we had lost and the things we had done. All the while petting Andromeda and just enjoying each other's company.

Long after everyone went to eat, Giggles brought my mother and me some food. She brought some for Andromeda too. The four of us sat there for another hour or so before we decided to move and get back to our rooms.

I obviously moved into my mother's room, even though it was tight for the three of us. I didn't want to be far from her at any time again. I had thought I had lost her and had for a year. I was not going to do that again.

Giggles moved into a room just down the hall. They were all sparsely furnished but comfortable for a room in this post-apocalyptic world.

Not long after getting to the rooms, we laid down on the floor and I fell asleep. A long peaceful sleep with no dreams or nightmares. Just the sleep of a person with no guilt, something that I had missed for a long time.

Shots

I am out shooting at the local range with my brother. Matt likes to go shooting when he can. He likes the pistols but he has never been a fan of long guns. I agree with the pistols but I like the rifles. I like to see at what distance I could put a hole in the paper center mass. Dad was always a fan of shotguns, that is what he grew up with, but he has never met a gun-type he didn't like.

Dad isn't with us today. He had to go to work, Matt and I had a weekday off together. We really aren't supposed to be here without an adult. Matt is just 17. But we have shot here forever and they know we are safe. There is always another guy here that could vouch for us if the cops ever showed up. Shoot, one of them is a cop that would vouch for us.

Today I am taking it easy and don't feel like walking far, so I just set up at 100 yards and brought my Ruger 450 Bushmaster. It is my hunting gun, season is just around the corner so I need to make sure my scope is on point. You can't hunt with long rifles in Delaware, they just opened up these for hunting this year.

My brother is shooting beside me and it seems there is someone else shooting near us, but I can't see them. I could hear shots every so often, but I thought the other guy had gone inside. I get up and walk to the stations on the other side of the shed when I hear a very loud, very close shot go off.

That was what pulled me from my deep sleep. It was still dark outside and Mom seemed to have been used to it because she didn't wake. I had heard some shooting when I was underground but it was so much louder here. I looked for Andromeda and saw her standing at attention at the window. She saw something she didn't like and let out a low growl. I dragged myself off the floor and went to the window too.

There was not much to see. There were no lights allowed at night that were above ground, especially in the second stories. I heard another shot and could tell it was coming from my right. I concentrated on that area and tried to get my eyes to adjust. There was no moon tonight, and clouds stopped all light from hitting the ground. It made it impossible to make out shapes or what they may have been shooting at. I was hoping it was just some human intruders coming too close to our camp. But the way Andromeda was acting I don't think this was the correct answer.

Just as I started to get dressed to see if there was anything I could do, the alarm inside the camp went off. Mom jumps up in bed and looks around for the first time. She sees me and her face softens just a bit. Then panic takes over again. She was up out of bed and limping towards the door. She turns to me and tells me to follow her.

"There are protocols. When the alarm sounds you drop what you are doing and get to your assigned shelter." she explains. "Ours is in the basement of this building. "

"I am going to help." I state. "They could use my help."

"This is not your fight anymore." She argued. "I just got you back. I can't worry about you tonight, if you get assigned to the wall then you will be included in their plans and reactions. You are not and you will only be in the way."

"You are right." I confessed. "Lead on."

We walked down the stairs to the basement. There were a lot of people there. This was the most used building for housing so it made sense I guess. These were the workers, the kitchen help, the growers and the cleaning staff. All the people that have to rely on others to keep them safe. These are not fighters and you could tell that by the way they were moving and worried. These were the people that make for fodder in a real fight. Or that get you killed by not reacting. They needed to have been better trained, not just sent to hiding when there was a problem. I made a decision to talk to Paul about this ASAP.

I couldn't hear a lot of the shooting or shouting while in the basement. It hid a lot of the sounds. But about 20 minutes after the alarm sounded Andromeda calmed down and actually laid at my feet relaxed. So I then relaxed and tried to fall back asleep. No one else in the basement relaxed for another 30 minutes when the all good alarm sounded and they went to go back to their rooms.

I watched them all shuffle out. The worries and stress were instantly relieved as the alarm sounded. No questions asked, no caution upon opening the doors and going back to their lives. This would have been ok if the attack was from the Deaders, but not if another group of humans was attacking. Any idiot would make a fake one night, learn the patterns, and then attack another night. They could have taken over and are sounding the alarm.

Ok. I know I was being a little paranoid. Everyone else was ok with this and Andromeda and Mom seemed ok too. I was not used to being with other people, and it didn't end well the last time.

Mom and I got back to the room. It was early but moving on to morning, so I just changed and got ready for the day. I was supposed to meet Paul today and learn where I was going to be assigned. I was hoping it was not washing dishes. I just may have walked out to the Deaders for the hell of it. As we got to the hallway, I realized I hadn't seen Jordan in the basement. I broke into a sweat and ran to her room. I knocked and heard slow movements inside. It seemed like an eternity before the door opened. It was Jordan looking like I had woken her up.

"Didn't you hear the alarm and the shooting?" I asked.

"What shooting? What alarm? What are you talking about?" She said quizzically

I took the time and explained the last hour to her. She had never heard anything. She wouldn't have known what to do even if she had. She didn't have a roommate or anyone to explain it to her. Something that I had not thought about in my sleep-addled state. So I explained to her what happened and how to respond. Giggles was a fighter, but not by choice. She would have been a good person to stay with the sheep in the basement and react if needed. I then told her about what I witnessed and my plan to talk to Paul.

"I wouldn't do that. There is probably a reason it is this way that you're not seeing." She says.

"I can't see a good reason for it."

"There are people out there that just can't fight. People that will never have the reaction that you have when they are stressed. They shut down. You can't make people like that into fighters, no matter what. They get in the way. That was probably why they send them to the basement. It is out of the way and prevents them from hindering the response teams. "She explained

"I never thought of it that way. Ok, I will let it be for now. I just wanted to make sure you were ok. Get dressed. We might as well start the day."

After she was dressed we headed down to get breakfast. Since there was no night shift to keep noise and lights off at night, breakfast was usually a very quick meal. I actually got more of a meal when I was being held captive. A quick grab and keep moving type of meal. It's early this morning so we still have time before I have my meeting with Paul. We take our food back to the room and sit down with Mom. I liked just being around her. Just the feeling of having her back. Of having someone again, besides Andromeda.

Sitting there with Mom back, I think about the day we lost both Matt and Dad. Dad was lost saving us and trying to help others. He didn't know how to kill those things or even what they really were at the time. It was only a couple of months after we started hearing bad rumors coming out of Europe. No one knew what we were dealing with.

Well in all reality I still didn't know.

Matt was another matter. We have no idea what happened to him. He went that day on a foray into town. He had a motorcycle that was old but still working so he could make longer runs than any of the rest of us. He was due back about the time the Deaders attacked. We always assumed he was killed or ran off, but we stayed in place for months after and he never returned. If he had been run off, wouldn't he have come back? We may never know the real story of what happened to him. I just wished that he thought we were all dead and moved on himself as we have done without him. That he was still out there and still safe.

I snapped back to reality and decided that Jordan and I should go. Just as Mom started to go out of the door, she stopped by a cabinet and opened it up to a mirror. She checked her hair and closed it. At this point, I came to the startling realization that I had not looked in a real mirror for over a year. My hair was always long, so I just cut it myself when it got too long, but it was long enough to cut without seeing my reflection. I used to be borderline vain when the world still worked. Well, maybe not so borderline. I would stop and look in every mirror or reflective surface I passed. I couldn't remember the last time I even thought about a mirror now. I decided it was long past time to see what everyone else around me saw. I stepped up to the cabinet and opened it.

What I saw surprised me a bit. My face was leaner than it used to be. That could have been from borderline starvation, I would think. My hair was still the bushy fuzzball that it had always been, yet it was several shades lighter, maybe from the sun. I have been in the sun a lot, but it could have been from malnutrition too.

The biggest difference was in my eyes. I knew that there was a difference in me from before I lost my Dad, my brother, thinking I had lost my mom. I had been in a continuous fight for my life, either from storybook monsters or death himself. But I didn't think that I had changed that much. My eyes were still brown, they didn't glow like the Deaders, but there was a deepness to them that I had never seen before. There was a haunted look that made me shy away quickly from the mirror. I have not aged physically all that much since I had seen a mirror, but apparently, I had changed a lot emotionally and it showed heavily in my eyes. Pain, fear and constant loss took a toll I guess. Who knew?

I moved away so quickly that Jordan actually jumped standing beside me.

"Wow, what has you all wrapped up like a snake?" She asked.

"Nothing, just...Nothing. Leave it be." I plead

"Ok, but you're not ugly, your own reflection shouldn't scare you." She joked.

"It wasn't that. Just wasn't expecting to see myself in a mirror today. Let's go."

Thankfully Jordan let it go and we left the room and that soul-crushing mirror behind. I called Andromeda and she followed me out of the room.

We went to see Paul to see where he would assign us. When we arrived at Paul's office again for the second time in two days, we knocked on the door and waited for him to invite us in. What I wasn't expecting was for Susie to open the door half a second after I knocked. It pushed me back into a defensive posture.

"Wanna fight again?" She said. "Didn't fare too well last time."

"You just scared me, hawking at the door like a crazy person." I jibbed back "But you won't fair the same next time we go."

Susie let that lie and waved us into the room. Jordan and I walked past her and up to the desk that Paul sat behind.

"Have a seat ladies." He said as he motioned to the chairs in front of the desk. "You too Susie I want you here for a while."

Susie sat on the beat-up couch in the corner. It was probably the only thing in this room that looked out of place and overly used. But I figured from the remnants and discord of the theme in the room it was all taken from somewhere at some point in time.

"So I have an idea on your places to work, but I would like your input on it before I make it official." Paul started. "Now I want you to know that I did listen in to several of your conversations over the last month." He put up his hand before I could even lean forward to speak. What was it with this guy?

"We started it to see what you were saying to profile you for potential candidacy for being a Braver. Then we took it farther to see where you might fit in if you decided to stay, which of course you did, so it will potentially save time and having to move you around to see where you fit."

"Now, Jordan you like to be alone and don't like to speak to others much, but you seem to be a caring and loving individual. I would like you to go to animal care. You wouldn't have to be a vet or anything like that. Just feed and water the animals and muck the areas as needed. You will report to George. Is that going to be a problem?"

"I like the job, I love animals, but I don't have much experience. Also isn't Mr. George going to be mad at me? You know for stabbing him and all? I don't want any trouble."

Just like that Susie breaks out laughing. "Mr. George" she says in a sarcastic tone. "Has never been mad at anyone for longer than 2 minutes. He can't hold a grudge more than you could hold a pig rubbed down in bacon grease."

"Just like Susie so eloquently put it. George is a kind soul and harbors no ill will for you. Also, he could be a great teacher. He will teach you what you need to know. If that seems to fit you…" Paul said

"Ok, I would like that." Jordan agreed.

Then Paul looked towards me. "You are a little tougher. You talk a big game and act like you like to fight. I am not so sure that is the full truth." "Ah ah ah. Before you talk let me finish."

The hand again!

"I would like Susie to take you out to the fields and see how you can shoot. I need more people on the rotation since we seem to be getting an unusually high number of ED's coming to our little neighborhood lately. Luckily in ones and twos. But still more frequent. Not sure if it was the weather or something else drawing them back out. But if you can shoot, I could use you there. I know you showed interest when you were there."

I didn't say anything at first I just looked over my shoulder at Susie. She was sitting on the couch like her stuff didn't stink. Loving the fact that she could make or break this opportunity for me. Or was it that she wanted to take me out there and have an "accident" on the shooting range. I was not sure I had the energy to deal with her right then.

"First I want you to know you'll be safe. Nothing will happen out there. Susie really is not as bad as she acts. Kind of like you." Paul says. "Take the time to go to the range and we will take it from there."

"Fine." I say. "Let me show her up there too."

Susie and Paul both smile, but I was betting for very different reasons.

With that taken care of we all stand and Susie shows us to the door. Jordan knew where the stables were and Susie told her where to find George to report to him.

Then she turned to me and smiled.

"Now we see if your mouth is backed up by your talent." She said.

I said nothing and we walked out of the building.

We walked for a bit through the camp until we got to the outskirts of the buildings.

"This is where the practice range is. It is still inside the camp so it is safe, but far enough that we won't risk anyone getting shot. Good thing the ED's aren't attracted to noise. We are bringing out the big ones today. Ever shot a .50 caliber?" she asked.

"No, I have not." I told her "But I should be fine."

"Always the hard-ass, huh?"

I said nothing and walked into the shed as she unlocked it. It was set up like a small armory. Racks of guns on one wall and ammo on another. There was a table and two chairs in the middle to work on and clean the guns.

There really wasn't much here. I would have thought there would have been more. Susie seemed to read my thoughts and responded.

"Used to have more, most of these have been with us a short time. The problem was this was a place for veterans before the Fall. It was a place of peace and rest for people to get straight and back on their feet. They didn't need guns for that. Just encouragement and help. All guns either came with people when they showed up or we found them on the raids. And unfortunately they break and we don't have the parts to fix them. We keep the ones that break a spring or something small, that may be replaced when another goes down for a bigger reason, but this was all we have for now."

We sat down and Susie showed me the functions of the two guns we were going to shoot that day. One was a basic hunting rifle and then the .50 caliber. After she was confident I knew how to hold the guns and keep them safe she picked up a couple of pieces of ammunition and we walked out of the shed.

"That's not many rounds." I stated.

"Well we don't have many to waste, so you better get it down quickly." Susie retorts.

We walked out back and I could see a truncated target range set up. It was not much, but it would work. I saw a table and chair that resembled the elementary and middle school desks, where they are connected. I sat there and started to set up. Andromeda sat to my right and then laid down, bored with the going-ons of humans.

I looked downrange and saw the targets. They were small.

"We don't have a lot of downrange so we compensate with smaller targets to force perspective. Aim small miss small. When you are aiming at the ED's you have to hit the neck straight on. Otherwise, they don't die. Then they run off and tell their friends." She said. "That is a loss of life waiting."

Susie wanted me to use the hunting rifle first. I set up on a target 50 yards out. About the size of an apple. I missed the first shot. Low, compensating for the recoil, rookie mistake. I didn't let Susie say anything. It had been two years since I had shot like this. I just loaded the next round and set again.

Breathe in, hold, and breathe out slowly as you pull the trigger. Center mass of the target.

"Lucky shot, do it again at 100" Susie says.

I reload and refocus. The target was now a lot smaller. But I aim small, center. Breathe out slowly and pull the trigger slowly.

BOOM! Center mass again.

"Good." She said. "Now we don't try to take shots any further out than that. Too much wind and other problems. If they are that far out, you may miss them and they us. No point in chancing it. Now let's try the .50. This will put you on your butt if you don't set right. Get set and try at 50 yards."

I switch guns and get reset with the larger caliber and more awkward gun. It was hard to get comfortable. Once set, I loaded the round.

"Now you are going to shoot the small metal target at 50 yards. It will show where you hit, not just that you hit it. We have to make good shots with these." Susie guided.

I took aim and got the rhythm. Breath in, breath out. In, hold, slowly out as I pulled the trigger. Then my shoulder erupted in pain, my ears were ringing and I couldn't seem to see straight.

"Holy hell that thing packs a punch." I yelled, when my senses started coming back.

Susie was laughing but pointed downrange. I had hit the target just a little low and left of the center mark. "Told you, but you got the shot. Now try the 100."

I gave myself a second to re-acclimate and get my sight back straight. I realize what happened besides the enormity of sound. I didn't keep my shoulder as tight as I could to the gun and I didn't lean into it. I was used to the easy hunting rifle and got lazy. Won't be doing that again. I looked down at Andromeda and she hadn't even flinched. Not sure how, but she didn't seem to care at all.

I get set and pop off at the 100. I hit it easily. Guess there wasn't too much rust on me after all.

Susie seemed satisfied so we went back to the shed. No more shooting today. Couldn't waste the ammunition when I was on target for those so quickly. Which was good to me because my shoulder was hurting like hell. She took the guns from me and said that she would clean them and put them back up. She told me to go to the medic to get something for my shoulder and go help in the kitchen until she could speak to Paul about rotation.

I did exactly as she asked, although I was hoping the medic could do more for me than I thought they could.

Medical

It was pretty much what I expected it to be. The office was just a room with some medical supplies lying around on desks. Dr. Sal didn't come in to see me, which was just fine. The nurse, if you could call her that, introduced herself but I forgot her name.

She looked at my shoulder and gave me some small pills for inflammation and pain. She then told me to go to the kitchen for some ice, because she didn't have any ice packs.

In the post-apocalyptic world that we live in, ice was not such a luxury as it was before the fall. I decided that my shoulder would heal on its own and I didn't bother the kitchen staff for something they may not even have.

As Andromeda and I were walking out of the medical office, Susie yelled to me from the street behind me.

"Hey, you go on watch this evening. Meet me at 8 pm at the south watch station. Forget about helping in the kitchen, you need to get some rest. "

I waved to indicate that I heard her and would do just that. Not the hand gesture I'd like to give her, but it was the one that was appropriate for the situation. I needed to calm down with her a bit I thought because she seemed to be the one making my work schedule now. I could get some good shifts and actually get to see people like my mom and Jordan, or I could work all the night shifts and hate life. Susie was in charge of that now. Maybe that was why she decided to take me on. That might not have been good.

Wonder if I could change my mind?

Since I didn't go on watch until later tonight, I decided to go to the kitchen anyway, but this time for food, not ice. Lunch was simple and Andromeda seemed to enjoy it. We walked as I ate and I threw some of my scraps to her as she walked behind me.

I decided the best course of action was to go to the room and rest as much as I could. The last 24 hours were a whirlwind and I needed to catch my breath.

As I walked into the room, I looked at the cabinet with the mirror. Nope, not doing that again today. I just kept moving and lay down on the bed. Andromeda knew better than to jump on Mom's bed so she laid down next to me on the floor. It's funny how something that small had stuck with her through all of the stuff we have been through. She never had a problem sleeping on my bed in the bunker. She was always there and would hog it if I let her but it was like she knew this was Mom's and reverted back to the rules from before.

I wonder if humans could be like that. I wonder if this disease, or whatever it was making people undead, was to disappear tomorrow could we fall back into our society's rules from before. Somehow I didn't think it would be that easy for us. Andromeda still trusted mom and me to do what was best for her but people in general have lost the ability to trust each other.

I didn't think that I would fall asleep, but just minutes after listening to Andromeda snore, I was out myself. I was woken up by Mom coming back to the room. As I come awake I hear others in the halls too. I guessed that the first shift was off and coming home.

Mom came in and smiled as she was prone to do. I was wild-haired and sleepy but smiled back. She told me about her day and I told her about the range and how I would be working on the front lines, starting that night.

Mom frowned a little at that but knew that this was what I wanted and what I was good at. I liked protecting people. I felt the need to protect her.

When I showed her my shoulder she frowned again and said that I should have gotten some ice, even if it wasn't much. The shoulder was a little sore from sleep, but nothing I couldn't work out now that I was awake.

Jordan came by a little later and we all went off to dinner together. This was the biggest meal and had to be eaten early for all of us to be together. We didn't have many lights and we couldn't run them at night or we would attract the Deaders. Most people would take an apple or a piece of dried meat with them after dinner for that hunger pain later in the night.

People didn't seem to sleep well and paced their rooms throughout the night. Even in a safe place like this PTSD from before was hard on everyone. No one slept deeply anymore. Well except for Andromeda.

As dinner was breaking up and most people were heading back to their rooms, there was a loud ruckus at the front gate. Some shouting and screaming. I left Andromeda with Mom and ran for the gate to see if I could help. As I ran down the line, I could see that no one was running for the armory so it couldn't have been a Deader running close.

When I got to the gate I could see the buggy coming in. A guy falling out of it as soon as it cleared the gate. Luckily medical was very close to the front gate. I ran up and help the people get him up off the ground. He could barely stand on his own. There was no blood and he looked fine physically, yet his eyes were sunken in and he seemed to have very little life left in him.

Paul ran up with Susie at his side. The guy that was driving the buggy told them that they were attacked by a group of ED's while on the road back to the camp. They were outside the buggy gathering supplies. There had been a few small trees that had started to bear fruit on the side of the road. After they had been out of the buggy for a couple of minutes and their hands were full was when they were jumped by the group. There were 5-6 of them. Came out of hiding and had them surrounded. Lucas, the guy that was hurt, went down under two of them.

The driver was able to scare them off with his machete and pistol, at least enough to get Lucas back in the buggy and to safety. Then they ran the motor for all it was worth speed-wise, which was not much, to get back to the camp.

When he said this Paul, Susie and I dropped our jaws and looked at him.

"So you led them back to us?" Paul shouts

The guy just stammered something about getting Lucas help. Another person and I grabbed Lucas and drug him to medical. As soon as he was down I was running back down the path towards the armory.

I was about 100 feet behind Susie and losing ground. Man was she fast. But we both had the same ideas. When she hit the armory she was yelling at an attendant to act as a runner and tell all the watchers that trouble was coming.

He was out the door just about the same time I was heading in. Susie just turned and looked at me.

"Guess you're starting a little early." She said.

I didn't respond, just started grabbing ammo and guns and throwing them in packs and bags as fast as possible. This could get bad quickly.

By the time we retrieved everything we had in the armory, we had decided to drop something off at every station and keep the big gun around the front gate. This group had seemed to lay in wait for the buggy team and attacked before nightfall. This was different and not in a good way.

Susie started off clockwise so I went counter. There weren't many guns, only two more long-range guns than I had already handled. But I equipped each station with what I could. I told them what happened quickly and told them to keep a closer eye out than usual.

When I got back to the front gate, Susie was already there and talking to Paul. They roused the other third of the watch staff and sent the last of the first shift to bed so they would be ready for rotations later in the night. We needed to be over vigilant that night. The buggy was barely faster than a person could jog. It would have been easy for the Deaders to follow them.

I still had the .50 cal so I headed to the front gate to back up the watch already there. I saw Paul and Susie head into the medical building to see if they could learn more. The buggy was sent back farther into the compound where it was kept. Lucas and the guy that was driving when they were attacked were still in medical.

I got set up, nodded to the other watch and tried to get comfortable for the long haul. He set up in a prone position with the scope looking down the road. Most of his field of vision was through that scope. Trying to see if there was any movement, he would slowly pan back and forth, back and forth.

An hour later, Paul stopped by to check and see if we had seen anything on the road. We let him know that we had not, nor had any runners been sent from the other posts.

Paul informed us that this attack seemed like a feint. That the machete and a small round pistol should not have scared off 5-6 of these things. That coupled with the fact that it happened in broad daylight seemed odd. It seemed like they had laid a trap but that level of thinking should not be possible.

"Paul, why did he looked so tired and sunk?" I asked

"Because they drained him. Took most of his energy when they attacked. But they didn't kill him. It was almost as if they let him go."

"Why would they do that? Aren't they more animal than human?"

"Typically. Maybe it was because there was abundant food sources and the gun and machete made this meal too hard? Maybe."

"You don't sound convinced." I stated

"That's because I'm not. Stay vigilant. Runners will be around with water and food as needed." Paul said as he walked off. His brow furrowed in concentration.

The watch I was working with looked at me and then returned to his scope. Back and forth, back and forth. Tonight was not going to go well.

Movement

It was crazy how quiet the nights were. No cars going by on busy streets, no planes in the sky zooming to new destinations. Sound carried so much farther than it used to. I heard doors being closed in the compound, the grass blowing slightly in the wind. The call of a bird from what could have been miles away. I could hear a rusty hinge blowing in the wind on a broken gate near the armory. You heard it all. All of the movement of the world. But we heard no screams of the Deaders, no crunching of grass or sticks being broken.

It had been 2 hours since Lucas was dragged in barely holding to life. I had not heard any news, but the people had stopped coming in and out about 30 minutes ago. It was dark and most people were probably in their rooms or the panic area in the basement, trying to stay calm.

Foodstuffs were moved to the panic area although people were trying to stay positive. There was a dark cloud hanging over the compound, would the boot drop or just hang there over us?

Suddenly, as I was ruminating on sounds, the watch that I was working with, Alejandro, stopped his slow movement and tightened his grip on the .50. Slowly he reached up and adjusted the scope to zoom in a little closer.

I perked up when Alejandro adjusted his scope. He stayed very still for minutes. Both of us were quiet, waiting to see if he saw a Deader. There were not many trees for anything to hide behind along the front of the compound, but this scope could look out almost a thousand yards. There was a bit of woods and tall grasses out that far. I slowly got up and got ready to run to tell the others that we had spotted something when he waved me back down and pulled his eye from the scope.

"I thought I saw something, but even zoomed nothing moved again. Maybe I have been here too long. You take the shift. Maybe I'm seeing ghosts. "

I took over the position and started my sweeps. I tried not to get caught stopping in the position that he had thought he saw something, but something felt off. My nerves must just have been on edge too.

About an hour later a runner came by and asked for news as they dropped off a canteen of fresh water. Alejandro informed him that he thought he had seen movement, but nothing concrete. The runner just nodded and moved to the next station.

"Why did you tell them about something you weren't sure if you saw?" I asked still keeping my eyes downrange and moving back and forth.

"Always relay information as you have it. Even if it is not concrete. Someone else may have seen something similar and it becomes a pattern. We have the best scope, so the best chance of seeing something, but others may too."

"Better more information than less?"

"Yup."

Four hours later our relief came. We had seen nothing more. We had swapped positions a couple of times as we tired, then just sat back for the last hour with binoculars. It was way past dark and the scope wasn't thermal nor night vision, so it really didn't do us a whole lot better.

We relayed what we had seen or thought we had seen throughout the night and where. Then left to debrief Susie in the armory.

When we arrived, Paul was there too. He wanted to hear everything from all of the watches. Not one shot was fired nor one Deader was seen the whole night. Maybe we overreacted.

"We will keep our guard up and not send any salvage crews out for the next couple of days. Maybe we overreacted, maybe we didn't. Only time will tell." Paul said after all the watches gave their brief.

"We reacted fast and efficiently, just like we trained." Susie said." Good job, now go get some rest. There won't be much of that for the next few days."

I headed back to my room. As I entered the door Andromeda was awake and sitting just beyond the threshold. Tail wagging, happy to see me. I patted her on the head and bent down to give her a hug. Mom asked if everything was ok. I affirmed and then crashed onto the bed. Deep into oblivion for the next four hours.

The next thing I know I hear a shot ring out in the night. Well at this point it was predawn. Either way, I jump up, still dressed from the night shift, and ran out to the armory. I needed to see if they needed help.

I get to the armory before the runners do. Susie was looking haggard and tired. She probably didn't sleep all night. The runner stated that one of the back watch stations thought they had seen movement and shot. A little trigger happy, but nothing was hit and nothing ran away.

Another person seeing ghosts at the end of the shift? No one was certain, but I went to the station and took over the shift so they could get some sleep. As the one was heading out, Brett I think, I asked him to send a runner to bring me some breakfast. The other watch, Laurie, said she would stay on until her relief showed in an hour or two.

"So what did he see, not much of a scope on this thing here. Although it is one of our only long guns."

"I don't know if he saw anything. He just stiffened and pulled the trigger. He hadn't even been on the gun very long this shift. I wonder if he really saw anything or just started falling asleep." Laurie told me.

"Well hopefully that is the case and these things weren't setting a trap to find out where we were." I say.

The day drug on. And on. Shifts came and went every couple of hours. We eventually dropped back to one person on each watch station during the day, still two on at night. Then two days after that we dropped back to normal rotations.

There were no real sightings, and no more shots fired. Everything started to get back to normal. The foodstuffs were pulled from the panic room, and life just started to go back to normal. People can't live in fear for that long, they can't live with the constant adrenaline. People like normal and structured lives. I didn't know if we would ever get away from that.

I settled into a good rotation with the watch. I didn't get all the night shifts as I feared. We ran on rotations for shifts so everyone could be off with their loved ones and have normal schedules when they could. Paul and Susie seemed to have been pleased with the way I responded on the first night.

Of course, Susie didn't tell me directly, but Jordan had heard her talking while working in the stables and told me about it.

I liked coming home to Mom and Andromeda. I liked hanging with Jordan. The time that I had spent alone, I always thought that I was happy. But being here with the people I loved and being part of something felt good.

Most of the time I could lose myself in the day. I let Jordan take Andromeda to work with her sometimes too, so she could be around the other animals and get out of the room.

There were other times that I couldn't get Paul's words out of my head. Was this was an elaborate plan by the Deaders to find us and set us up? They shouldn't have been that smart. They never seemed to have been capable of thinking along these lines. But what if that was because they were malnourished, or whatever goes for malnourished with these creatures? What if when they were fed properly they could almost think like we could? Or at least like a wolf. Wolves have a pack mentality to them and know how to close a net on their prey.

There were "ghost" sightings but nothing concrete on almost every shift for the first 4 days. Now I think people have stopped reporting them. Maybe they thought they were just imagining them.

What if they weren't? What if these things were learning our sightlines?

This deep into the what-ifs, I tried to let it go and think about something else. No use going too far down the rabbit hole. Not until there was some proof. I wouldn't fall, but I wouldn't let my guard down completely either. I guess that time on my own has not left me completely after all.

I tried to settle into a routine and enjoy the little things that I had missed in life for so long. Mainly having a Mother and friends to talk to. I just tried to take each day as it came and hoped I was ready for the day that things fell apart. I would be ready but still hoped that day never came.

Plans

The end of summer is upon us. August is here and we need to start harvesting fruits and vegetables if we want to have enough for the winter. These were the only thoughts of the people that were referred to as Bravers. The ones that live and work at the Home of the Brave compound.

The months had gone by and everyone had forgotten about the threat of the Deaders setting a trap. These things couldn't set a trap, I was paranoid. Anthropomorphism is attributing human traits to non-human entities. That is what Doctor Sal told me when I spoke to him about my suspicions. He also told me I was about Apophenia; or looking for problems when there were none.

I hate when people use big words for simple concerns.

The summer here had been great though. I reconnected with Mom became best friends with Giggles, aka Jordan, and watched Andromeda laze around and enjoy the heat of the days.

Though the thoughts of the Deaders setting a trap and changing in ways we can't begin to fathom have been weighing on it, I have found that keeping this journal focuses my mind. Seeing the words in ink helps to remove them from my brain. That is why I took the time over the last couple of months and told you my story as I remember it.

I have enjoyed my time here at Home of the Brave but as July came to an end, Andromeda started acting oddly. She would stand at the compound's entrance and look outside. She would also just stare through the doors or walls as if she knew something was looking to get in.

That was when I took my apprehension to Paul again, who sent me to Doctor Sal for evaluation. No one wanted to listen. No one wanted to hear. I had been feeling off and couldn't let it lie, but I took that as paranoia too. I had been on my own for a while and was not really comfortable in the inherent safety of this compound. Over that time, I learned to listen and watch Andromeda. She knew these things, knew when they were close. If she was agitated, then something was wrong.

Since no one was listening to me, I let them think that I had moved on and gotten into their line of thinking, but what I was really doing was planning. I had a bag set aside with all of the things that I had come with. The things that helped me survive outside this fence line. I had set aside food that wouldn't be missed and bags for Mom and Jordan. I had to be ready if no one else was. I tried to tell the people and set plans in motion to save the vast majority if something happened. But they wouldn't heed my warnings and sense. They would have to go on their own. I had to worry about my little family and everyone else be damned.

Today was to begin the harvest of the larger fields that lay in the rear of the compound. Because of this, we took guards off their stations during the day to help with moving the produce to the storage areas. Nothing was going to happen during the day. No Deaders had even been seen at night for over two weeks.

That was the plan anyway.

Today Mom was stationed near the storage area since she could not walk much. Jordan was with Andromeda and me helping move the produce from the fields. We were laughing and joking while walking back to the fields after talking to Mom when the first scream sounded.

It was short, almost too short to be heard clearly. Way too short to get a fix on where it came from. We didn't have anyone outside of the fence today. We needed everyone on the fields. So this scream had to be from inside if it was from one of us. Jordan and I picked up our pace to get back to the fields. Maybe someone was hurt and needed help.

When we got to the fields everyone else was just as confused. They swore it had come from the front of the compound, as everyone here was fine and had not screamed. I looked at Andromeda and she was staring out to the front of the compound with her ears laid back and a growl emanating from her chest.

Shit!

I grabbed Jordan and told everyone to get to safety. Something was not right and I seemed to be the only one to see it. I was ignored and everyone went back to concentrating on their work.

I ran to the front of the compound with Andromeda leading the way and Jordan following behind. I stopped and looked into the storage area where Mom was supposed to be, but she was not there so I continued to our room. As we entered the room, I threw a bag at Jordan and told her to grab the other bag behind the door. I reached for the pistol I had kept from the armory and grabbed my bag too. I wanted this stuff with me if this was really happening now.

Jordan looked confused. She moved her mouth a few times but a question never came. I paid her no heed and set my pace for the front of the compound. With no guards on the outposts or on the fence, there was no one to tell us if something was outside of the doors. I had to get up there and check for myself.

As we left the building that our rooms were in, I turned towards the front to take a look. Jordan finally dug her heels in and stopped.

"What are we doing?" she asked.

"We are getting ready to run. Something is not right here. Hasn't been for a while." I explained

"What's in the bag you gave me?'

"Rations, water, clothes. The essentials."

"So we are just running for our lives? Leaving everyone and everything else here?" she asked.

"If we must. All except Mom. Right now all I am trying to do is see what caused that scream."

"No one else is worried about this. No one else thinks that we are always under attack. We are safe here. Please get that through your head."

With that, she threw down her bags. And started walking back to the fields.

"Wait!" I yelled "Just come to the guard station with me. Let's see what is out there. What is causing Andromeda to be agitated? If there is nothing there. We will go back."

"Please." I added after.

Jordan didn't look thrilled but she decided to go with me to show me there was nothing to be afraid of. Her plan seemed to be to show me that I was wrong and then get back to work quickly.

When we reached the front of the compound, I didn't hear anything at the doors. I went to the top of the fence and figured I could see more than at a guard post. As I reached the top Jordan followed me up. I looked at Andromeda and she was now looking to the west side of the compound. No one should be there today, the storage was on the east and the gate we were at faced north. There was nothing to the west but some ramshackle buildings to hold the animals. Basically, just pole barns backed up to the fence line.

I grabbed a pair of binoculars and handed another to Jordan. I scanned the front and towards the west. I figured if anyone knew the direction they would come it was Andromeda.

I didn't see anything outside of the fence line from here. I looked slowly and made sure to check any movement in the woods.

Nothing.

Just as Jordan gave up and I was about to tell her I overreacted, I saw movement to the west. But inside the fence. As I said before no one should be there and all of the animals were stocked inside today because of the harvest.

I was looking closer at the pig area when I heard another scream. Again short, not quite normal. I then figured out why it sounded so off. It was a pig squeal. Not a scream. It was so short and high pitched you couldn't tell the difference.

Now pigs make noise. So do cows and horses on a daily basis. But this was different. Almost fearful. I locked in on the pig barn and watched for any more movement.

Jordan watched me and did the same.

Just as she pulled up her binoculars, I saw the movement again. Almost like a flash between buildings. Oddly, we haven't seen any predators in the area before now. No foxes or wolves to speak of. Plus this thing was large and not running on all fours. I had to figure out what it was.

There was nothing for another minute or two so I started scanning the fence behind those buildings. These buildings were right up at the fence line. But there were no trees or anything else behind the fence. It used to be an open field but in the past years it had grown up to over waist-high.

The Bravers never worried about cutting it because Deaders were the threat and they stood taller than the grass. There was no threat of them sneaking up on all fours.

Or was there?

We had no guard post on that side, we just relied on sight-lines from the other posts at the corners to see down the line.

Just as I thought I was letting my paranoia get to me, I saw a figure come over the top of the fence and disappear behind a building. A minute later I saw another flash between the buildings around the pigs.

Fear blossomed in my soul at that very moment. If these invaders were climbing the fence and stealthily moving into the compound they must be living. They must be raiders. One of the things that we may have forgotten about in our complacency. We have and others don't. The have-nots will always want to take from the haves.

I looked at Jordan and saw the same fear there. We needed to warn the others. So I took the pistol from my pants and shot it into the air. Three shots hoping to get the other's attention.

At the same time, Jordan and I ran towards the fields along the opposite fence line. It was farther but less likely to run into the invaders. Jordan was leading, and Andromeda was following behind. We had to make it to the group in the fields.

I then stopped so fast Andromeda ran right into me causing both of us to trip.

"What?" Jordan asked.

"Mom and the people at storage. They are right in the middle of the compound. Someone needs to warn them." I stated.

"I'll go, you warn the fields. I am faster than you and can get there easier."

I didn't want to let her go into that danger without me but we didn't have time to argue.

"Andromeda." I bent down and looked at her in the face. "You go with Jordan. Keep her safe."

I looked at Jordan and nodded. She took off at a run towards the storage area. With only a small whine and a split-second hesitation, Andromeda took off after her.

All I could do at this point was run as hard as I could and hope we had a chance to get organized, to push these invaders out. At least the armory was near the fields so we could arm those that could shoot.

As I broke into the open area of the fields I called out for Paul or Susie. Anyone to listen.

"Invaders!! Coming over the wall by the animal sheds on the west wall!" I yelled.

I was worried about what was happening with Jordan and Mom. But I had to concentrate on organizing the people here. She would do what was right and Andromeda would keep her safe.

There were looks of confusion as I hit the fields. I was still yelling about the invaders and trying to get people moving. Paul and Susie came running to meet me and see what I was yelling about. I was winded so I kept pointing to the west wall and where I saw the invaders, trying to talk through gasping breaths.

As I pointed to the area a figure broke out from behind the building. It wasn't running, it just seemed to come into the light to be seen. As we watched in horror ten more walked out into sight.

At this point, chaos won. The ones that were not fighters tried to run for the safety of the buildings. Those that normally stood watch ran for the armory. The figures seemed to be taking everything in, then fanned out across the main thoroughfare and blocked us into the fields. Everyone spun around trying to find a safe place to be.

Several of the watch that did not have the ability to grab a gun, picked up the weapons on hand and walked towards the invaders, ready for hand-to-hand combat. That was until they got close.

Up to this point, the figures behaved as the living. Jumping fences and sneaking through the compound. But as they got closer you could see our men stop and scramble backward.

"They aren't living. They are ED's. Their damn eyes are glowing!" they yelled as they scrambled for safer distances.

The figures took this as the weakness they needed and ran into the fray of bodies. As I watched this happening, I could see the animalistic movements of them now. But how had they designed this raid? And in the daylight.

I stood frozen. Susie yelled at me and pulled me towards the east fence before I came out of my stupor. When I let Andromeda and Jordan go I thought these were men, not Deaders. I would have never let them go off alone with this being the case.

Then another thought threatened to stop me in my tracks. Was this all of them? If they could figure out how to climb a fence and plan an attack, did they split up and send two forces?

This thought hit me so fast that I pulled up and grabbed Susie by the arm to stop her.

"What the hell?" she screamed

"Susie think. If these things are suddenly smart, did they just send one group to the field or did they break up into more?" I asked.

"Damn it. How did these things get smart? What is happening?"

"I don't know but let's treat this like people and get in behind them. We need to see what is going on."

I lead Susie through the buildings to get over to the pig stable. The sight was gruesome. The pigs had been fed on. They lay dead all over the pen. Same with a couple of goats that were in the area.

That is what took them so long after the first pig squealed. They fed so they had the energy to fight us. As I stopped to listen you could hear the fighting in the fields. People screamed and yelled, scared for and losing their lives but I couldn't hear anything from the storage area in the center of the compound.

We turned and headed to the storage area. The safe area was there near the housing area. If we could get people there we could protect them.

Finally, we started hearing gunshots ring out. A couple of people must have gotten to the armory and started to fight back but it was hard to kill these things when you had time to line up a shot. The adrenaline and fear made it a whole lot harder.

As Susie and I entered the main thoroughfare through the compound, we heard a scream from in front of us. The Deaders had made it here. That would not turn out well. Most of the people we left at the storage area were hurt, very young or old. The ones that couldn't walk back and forth to the fields well.

Susie ran headlong into the road and towards the scream. I knew there was not much we could do. We had to get out and hide in the surrounding areas. This was lost. Just as I had predicted. So I turned back and made my way back to the front where we had left our packs. I had to hope that Jordan found Mom and had the same idea that I was having. Andromeda would keep her safe. They just needed to find me and we could make a run for it.

Chaos

When I got back to the front of the compound it looked as if the Deaders concentrated all of their energy on the fields and surrounding areas. It was a little unnerving not having Andromeda by my side letting me know if things were safe or not.

I got the packs and found a doorway to hide in. I could see the main streets and could hear the screams of the dead and the living echoing down the corridor. Every once in a while I'd hear a gunshot go off, but they were coming less often the longer I waited.

The seconds felt like hours. How long had it been since we recognized the breach and the Deaders attacked? Minutes, an hour? I couldn't tell any longer. I just knew that we needed to find each other and get out of this prison.

For safety, there were only two ways out of this fence. The main entrance with big swinging doors to let the carriage in and out and one man-sized door in the east wall not too far from the main gate. I decided that I needed to make sure this door was opened and we could use it to escape.

As I reach the door, I can see that the coast is clear. I crouch as I run to stay as small as possible (not too hard since I am not that big to begin with). I guess being small in stature can be a blessing at times.

I reach to open the door but there is a bar latch across the door so it can't be opened from the outside. The guard post is just to the left of the door, so I duck in there after figuring out I can't get the door open with my hands full. I put everything down and then remove the door latch on the door. It will swing open easily now.

I fall back into the guard post and decide that I have to take a more active role in finding my family. They know about this post, but would they know that I am hiding here? The last Jordan saw me, I was heading to the fields. Same with Mom only at a different time. Jordan also knew about my packs, but she would think they were at the front gate area still.

I run through my options in my head. When I was a kid I was told that if you are ever lost, stay where you are and someone will find you. But am I the one that is lost or are they? Am I the one that should be finding them when they stayed put? If I leave will they come looking for me and we pass in the wind?

I take a hard look at the people that I am looking for. Neither of them are fighters. They will not be the ones leading the charge. I need to look for them, I need to be strong and lead them to safety. With this thought in mind, I take the pistol out again, remembering that I shot off three rounds so I only have four left.

I take the bags out of the guard post and put them on the outside of the door. Outside of the compound. If we have to take off quickly, those bags being outside of the fence line may be advantageous. I take a deep breath to center myself and stalk off into the street to find my family.

The last I knew Jordan and Andromeda were headed to the storage area to find Mom, so I headed in that direction. I hear a few more gunshots coming from the fields, but they seem to be fewer and fewer still. I have not heard anything from the storage area, so those workers must have run off or gone into hiding. But where would they hide? I run through the layout of this place in my mind and decide that they must have headed to the basement safety area when I started firing off the warning shots. It is not far from where they were and that is what they had been trained to do. I veer off the path that I was on towards the storage area and head to the basement.

As I reach the other side of the building that houses the basement area, I can hear something moving around inside the building. I do not know if it is living or undead. The main door to the building is open, so it could be either. Great! So I can't go inside and the only entrance to the basement is there.

But there is a window that used to be used to let light in. It is too small to crawl through, but I may be able to find out if anyone is there. I skulk around the building, keeping below the windows, and work my way to that side. The window has been boarded up but I knock on it. I do it again in the same pattern. We have designed nothing to indicate it is one of us but I hope this indicates that it is an intelligent person, not a Deader trying to get in.

It seems like minutes, but probably isn't, until I hear movement. Thank god someone is there. They pulled the plywood down from the window it was sitting in. It is a girl I recognize, she is younger and should have been at the storage area.

"How many people are in there?" I ask

"Only 4 of us. All younger ones that were working at the storage area, and 1 older runner." She replies.

This makes sense for the adults to send them to safety. But that means Jordan and Mom aren't there.

"Did you see my Mom? Where did she go?" I ask her

"She left before the shots went off. We don't know where she was going. She didn't feel good so she might have gone home." The girl said

"No!" someone else said. "She said she had a bad feeling, not that she didn't feel well. Get it right Lori." Said another voice from the basement. I couldn't see who.

"Ok, I have to go. Put the board back up and stay safe. Is the door barred from the inside?" I ask

"Yes, will we be alright? Are we safe?" another girl asks.

"Yes, you will be fine. I just need to go find the others. Do what you were trained to do and you will be just fine." I lied.

We don't have too many younger kids in the compound. Those three might be all of them. There were a couple of other teenagers to young adults like me, then mostly over 25. There also weren't very many people older than 50 in the community either. Most were working and fighting age. The ones that are built to survive an apocalypse I guess.

Mom and Jordan weren't in the basement, so they may have gone back to the rooms. But the entrance to the basement was inside the same building as the rooms were. Again only one way in or out and there may be undead walking in there. I would say someone must have left the door open because Deaders can't open doors, but they just climbed walls and stalked their prey after planning for what was probably months. I think opening a door would be child's play at this point.

I continued on, staying behind buildings and hiding spots as I found them. These creatures were smarter than we thought, yet still animalistic. They should be enjoying their kills and the energy that they drain. They should be focused on that and hopefully, not on me.

I head to the storage area, even though I don't think that they are there. As I approach I can see all the doors are still wide open and the food from the fields is still sitting on the floor in boxes. Even if the Deaders had been here, the food would be untouched. They don't eat like we do. But nothing looks disturbed or out of place. Nothing looks like a fight happened here, but nothing looks like it is being defended either.

I am defeated. I can't think of what to do at this point. I slowly sink to the ground. I don't stop until I am laying in a fetal position on the ground. Between the corner of a building and a box crate that is still empty, waiting to be taken to the fields and be filled. Which obviously won't happen now.

I am not sure how long I laid in this position waiting for an answer or waiting to die. I thought I was ready, that I had a plan. But now I have lost everything and everyone. I thought I was alone before, but now there is no one left.

Just as these thoughts pour through my head I hear something approaching. I get to my knees in a fighting stance and grab my pistol.

How many shots are left? Four?

I guess with this reaction I am not ready to throw in the towel just yet. I brace my back against the wall with the crate to my right. I set my arms, ready to take a shot and see if I can get lucky and kill one of these murderous pieces of garbage before they take me out of this world.

The sounds of walking are getting closer. It should be just around the other corner of the building. I am stationed on the short side so it will only be 12 feet from me when I can finally see it. I take a deep breath and get ready to slowly exhale as I pull the trigger.

There is movement at the corner, low to the ground. I adjust my aim and just as I get a clear picture the breath leaves me in a rush and I drop the gun to my side.

"Andromeda!" I squeal in a hoarse whisper.

Yes, I squealed ok. Stop talking about it now.

Andromeda rushes over to me and I hug her fiercely.

"I thought I lost you. Where are Mom and Jordan?" I question.

"I am right here." Jordan says as I look up from my hug. "But I couldn't find your mom. She wasn't at the storage area and I couldn't stay there long, they were everywhere."

"I know. It is ok. I spoke to a couple of kids in the safe area. They said she had a bad feeling and left before I shot the gun trying to warn everyone."

"So where would she go? I went back up front to find you and figured when you weren't there that you came looking for us. I didn't see her or anyone else alive."

"I don't know. She isn't here or in the safe area. We can't get to the rooms to see if she went there. I don't know what to do." I sobbed.

Right at that moment, Andromeda started growling and looking down the main avenue. Jordan and I duck down in the crook of the building. Andromeda huddles next to us, but still has her ears flat and hair up. Within seconds we hear multiple Deaders walk by. Not much noise but definitely not human steps. Any human alive would be running now, not walking down the middle of the street.

We couldn't tell how many there were but it was too close for comfort. We have no way to fight them off. We are exposed.

"Well, we need to get somewhere safe. We need to get out of the open. Do we hide inside the fence, or take our chances on the outside?" Jordan asked.

"I don't feel right leaving her again. But if these things have gotten this smart, maybe we need to get outside the fence for now. Hunker down and see how this plays out."

"That was my thought too. They know people are here and they aren't going anywhere until they have drained all of us. I found some bodies, but I think most of the casualties are in the fields. We need to go now if we are going."

"If you went to the front, why did you come looking for me? Didn't you see the bags were gone? I ask suddenly.

"I knew you would not cut and run without us if anything else was possible. I figured you had the bags with you or stashed them somewhere else. Where are they now?"

"Outside of the fence in case we had to jump the line somewhere else. We should head back there now and get outside to hide."

We head back to the door in the fence. It is a little easier going with Andromeda in the lead. She can sense them and tells us when they are close. We had to hide and retrace our steps twice to get to the outside. Once there, we grab the bags I threw out there and run hard to the tree line. We have to move quickly and hope the Deaders are concentrating inside the fence line. We have to hope these things weren't advanced enough to leave spotters for those of us trying to run away from death.

We were wrong.

Lookouts

How are these things smart enough to leave lookouts on the outside? These things should be so animalistic that they are just looking to feed yet as soon as we step out of the door in the fence we hear calls crying out from the tall grass. They must have seen me place the bags outside earlier and kept watch on the area.

We hit a full sprint towards the woods. Hearing the cries from these creatures just added to our adrenaline and made us run faster. The woods were not far, but it didn't seem like we would get there fast enough. We were running too hard for me to reach and grab the pistol and there was no way to get a good shot while running. We had to hope we had a head start and that it was enough for us to lose them in the woods.

Just as that thought runs through my head I get hit from the side. A perfect form tackle from my left. I go down in a heap with a yell. We tumble and roll, then finally come to a stop. Luckily I am on top of the *Deader* and not the other way around. This is the closest I have ever been to one of these creatures.

He reaches up to grab my face. One of the only open skin areas that I have since I am wearing jeans and a long sleeve shirt. I smack its hand away and try to get to my feet. I do and turn to run away again before it can get to its feet.

Then I see a brown blur and hear a loud growl as Andromeda rushes in to protect me. She bites into its hand and shakes it like she is killing a duck. Good girl! I get to my feet quickly and head off as I call to her to release and follow. She does as I ask on the first call and we are running at breakneck speed again towards the woods.

Jordan is way ahead of us now, she never stopped when I went down. Good, that is what she should do. No point in both of us losing our lives if one goes down. Everything is blurry as I am running now and I can only see basic shapes. Tears are welling up on their own. I am so scared it is hard to think. Because of this, I don't figure out what I am seeing until it is too late to yell a warning. Another *Deader* comes out of the grass to Jordan's right side. It is running hard and at an angle to reach her before she reaches the woods.

Just as I figure out what I am seeing it launches and tackles Jordan to the ground. I have no idea how many of these things are out here. Jordan and the *Deader* are directly in my line to the woods. I am trying to figure out what to do when Andromeda strikes again. This time she goes for the neck of the creature. It loses focus on Jordan as Andromeda strikes. This gives her just enough time to get to her feet and start running again.

Andromeda is still shaking the Deader as I run by. Its eyes are still glowing so it is alive, but it doesn't seem to be trying to grab her anymore. Maybe she broke its neck? Not enough to kill it, but severed the spine. Win for us I guess.

I call to her again as I streak by and she disengages and runs to my side. She has blood on her muzzle, but it doesn't seem to be hers. I take all this in as we continue to run. I am not sure how long we can keep this up. Jordan and I took hard hits when we were tackled. I can feel my muscles cramping and my adrenaline failing. The body can only perform at this level for so long.

Luckily we are actually not malnourished thanks to our time with the Bravers. If we were in the condition we were in when we got here in the spring, we wouldn't have made it this far without our bodies flagging from exertion. Jordan had also kept up a workout and training routine with me over the last couple of months. I guess my paranoia was good for something. We were probably in the best shape we had been in since before the Fall. Jordan may be in the best shape of her life.

We reach the woods, Jordan and Andromeda just a step or two ahead of me. Andromeda keeping pace, but Jordan seems to be failing. As I hit the first tree I see five Deaders running towards us. I can hear them calling out. They are spreading out and are at several different distances from us. This is better than all of them rushing in together, still not good though.

As we enter the woods the sun disappears. It gets as dark as twilight. One thing about there being fewer humans is that nature has filled itself back in. The underbrush is almost nonexistent with a strong and full canopy of leaves. Even with this Jordan stumbles and falls just a couple of steps in. Not good, since the creatures were not that far behind us, we have no time.

I reach Jordan and pull her to her feet. Her eyes have dark circles under them. Damn the Deader started to drain her before Andromeda got to it. That's why she failed so much quicker than me. So not good. I grab her arm, throw it over my shoulder and grab her waist. We stumble farther into the woods losing time with each step. We will never outrun them. We have to hide.

I see a fallen tree about 50 yards in front of us. It is partially rotten but was 4 feet around when standing it seems. We reach it and I toss Jordan over it and start to crawl over myself. Andromeda clears it in one jump. Once over we sit down with our backs to the tree. With this between us and the creatures, we should be out of their field of vision. It will only buy us time until they search past the tree deeper into the woods, then we will be visible to them again.

I can already hear the first of the Deaders entering the woods. They seem to have slowed down, probably because they lost sight of us. We are less than 100 yards into the woods. It will not take them long to get a good angle on us and pick up our electrical signals again. We have to figure out what to do.

I reach for the pistol and check the magazine again. Four shots left. Even if I hit a perfect kill shot with each one I don't have enough to kill them all. I look at Jordan, she is falling asleep. Her head is lolling to the side and she is completely out of it. That thing must have taken a lot out of her. Andromeda definitely saved her life. As I think this I look at her. She is sitting on her haunches facing behind us. Her hackles are still up which means they are getting close. I take off my backpack to grab the long knife I had picked up. As I do, I see a small pouch fall out to the ground.

It is one of the emergency blankets I picked up months ago after the canoe incident. These things saved my life back then by keeping me warm. I wonder if they can do it again. I lay Jordan down quickly as a thought comes to me. I don't have time to think through everything but these blankets are designed to keep in all body heat, which should mean that they can block out electrical signals too. Well, at least I hope the science holds up, not my strong suit. I cover Jordan up with a blanket. Then I pull another out of my bag. I grab Andromeda and lay her between me and the fallen tree. I cover us quickly and efficiently. Making sure nothing is open to the outside.

Nothing to do now but wait and hope this works.

Jordan is my biggest worry. I know the Deaders are close, if she wakes up or moves when they are close and exposes any part of her body they will find her and most likely me too. Andromeda knows they are close I can hear her whining and shaking. I need to take the time to check her for wounds from the two fights with the Deaders, but we have to survive this part first.

Another fear of mine is that these creatures just walk over the tree and literally step on us. Even if they don't see us this would definitely pique their interest in the spot we occupy. All I can do now though is lay still and try to calm Andromeda. I can hear them walking nearby. Their odd calls echoing a little in the woods. It seems like a couple of them have passed by us at the moment. I guess the true test will be when they walk back out towards the compound.

After a while, it becomes dead quiet in the woods. All of the Deaders are passed us. I have not heard them come back through towards the compound, but nothing says they have to return the same way. This may be best for us, but I can't poke my head out to see. I have to wait, which is great because patience is a strong suit of mine.

That was sarcasm if you didn't catch it.

Hours go by. I have had to pee now for a while. I haven't heard Jordan move or moan in a while and I am getting worried about her. I hope she is in a deep sleep that will help her heal. I know she needs water and food to help regain her energy. I have also noticed that Andromeda has been quiet for a little while now. That should mean we are in the good. I decide to open the blanket a bit and let her out to walk around. She is the best at detecting these things and she can outrun them if they are near.

As she wriggles out of the blanket, I cover myself back up. I can hear her sniffing around. She walks off to where I can't hear her as I wait to see if she reacts to anything near. After a couple of minutes go by she comes back and nudges my head. I guess this is the all-clear. I pull the blanket back and address my surroundings. It has gotten dark while we were hiding. This is not good since these things have better vision in the dark than we do and the thick canopy makes it even darker. I crawl over to Jordan and pull the blanket off of her.

She doesn't move. I feel for breathing and a pulse. She has one but is breathing very shallowly. I pull a canteen out of her pack and try to force some water into her mouth. She takes a little then ends up coughing up most of it. Even though there doesn't seem to be any creatures near us now that could change at any moment. We need to get farther away from the compound. I need to get Jordan on her feet. I can help her walk, but I can't carry her and our supplies, even though she is small.

After another minute or two, of coaxing water into her mouth. Jordan comes around a little bit. This is good news. Soon she can focus on my face and seems to be hearing me talk to her. This Deader really did a number on her. It took Lucas days to get back on his feet. A week or so to get back to normal. That was with medical care and IV bags. I don't have days or weeks, I don't have medical care nor IV bags. I need her on her feet now.

I feed her a little bit of a protein bar and let her rest as I configure the blankets into cloaks. I figure if we have hoods and protection on our backs it will mask our signal from the back. Since we are walking away from the compound this is where the most danger will come from. We can't outrun them now if they come for us and since I am going to have to help Jordan walk, our field of view will be limited. Any protection we can figure out is better than nothing.

I get our cloaks fashioned. Although they look nothing like the elven cloaks from Lord of the Rings, I was hoping they would protect us from unfriendly eyes all the same. Andromeda has been lying quietly while I have been working so I feel we are still safe enough. I take a second look over her with the windup flashlight in my bag. Nothing seems to be hurting her and the blood does not seem to be hers. I stand up and put my bag and Jordan's bag on my shoulders and chest. It is heavy and I do not feel like I can do this for a long time, but we need to move and Jordan cannot handle herself let alone the burden of the bag too. I then reach down and haul her unsteadily to her feet. I drape her left arm over my shoulder so I can reach around her waist with my right.

This is going to be slow going. If we walk as far as we can tonight and rest when we have to, we should be able to get a couple of miles in between us and the compound by dawn. Unfortunately, this area was mostly farmland before the fall. Mother Nature has taken a lot back in the last years, but there is still a lot of open land we will have to cross. Guess there is no time like the present. I take one long look back at the compound, there have not been sounds from there in a long while now. No one has seemed to run into the woods. The last shot I heard was before we made the run for the woods. People are either in hiding or dead. I then look forward and take the first steps in our new journey.

Leaving my mother behind. Again.

Trouble

That's been the word over the last couple of days. Jordan is still a little out of it. I do not have to help her walk any longer which is good. But we are kept at her slower pace as she heals from being drained. Each day she is looking better and able to go a little farther. Her healing is causing us to go through more water than I expected though and more food.

I had packed enough for a week of walking for three people and one dog. We only have two people, but Jordan is going through more than her share to stay on her feet. The Deader really did a number on her in a very short amount of time. Apparently when she was tackled her shirt flew up over her stomach. The creature went straight for her exposed skin. The good part of that is that when Andromeda launched at it, its hands were not in a position to grab ahold of her, leaving its neck and head exposed. When she grabbed its neck it let go of Jordan. This was what saved her life.

There should be no lasting damage to Jordan from that bit of contact, thankfully. Right now the trouble is that we are running short on food and drinkable water. We are near the north side of Slaughter Beach. I had a small bit of luck there before, but that was months ago and it was slim pickings then. Above that our way north is completely desolate. If we run out of water then, we will need to pray for rain, there will be no way to find any on our own.

So what do I do? Jordan doesn't know this area, so she doesn't know what we need. She has to focus everything on putting one foot in front of the other. Andromeda doesn't help me much with this decision either when I ask her, she just looks at me and cocks her head to the side. I wish I knew what she was thinking. Why is it that I have to make hard choices every time I turn around? Choices that may be the death of one or all of us if I am wrong.

After another day I decide we need to cut back to the west and get closer to the main thoroughfares. The average person can walk 20 miles per day. On our way up the beach, last time Andromeda and I made better than that, from what I could tell. We are not making even a quarter of that right now with Jordan still healing. I look at our packs at the next break we take and determine that we should be good for another day or two. We should be able to make it to the Frederica area in that time if she keeps improving as she has been. This area was at least populated before The Fall. It should have opportunities to find what we need. We will have to chance it, I will take less food and water to get us through if I need to.

Two days later we reach the old Rt. 1. We end up just south of the town of Frederica. It is hard to tell where you are when nothing is like it was. Landmarks have fallen, foliage has grown up.

I haven't been this far north since well before everything went down so that is not making things easy either. This misjudgment may actually work in our favor though since we came to an old sports field. They used to play soccer, lacrosse and other sports here when the world worked. Food may be scarce, but they should have kept water here. If the place hasn't been cleaned out we might be in luck.

Luck is not on our side lately though. As soon as we enter the clubhouse area of the fields I know we are screwed. The doors have been ripped off the hinges and nothing was left on a single shelf. There is not a single thing left in the area that is usable. Even the offices above the clubhouse were raided. I guess a lot of people had the same idea I did.

We are down to our last bottle of water. We will not make it long if we can't find more. Jordan is up and moving at a normal pace now and has started eating and drinking about as much as I usually do. I am taking less and less each day. I have not told Jordan how dire our straits are yet. She needs to completely heal without the added stress. I mean just being alive is stressful enough, since the Fall, but this would just add to it.

I hang my head as we leave the fields and head towards the town proper on the other side of the old highway.

"Hey, what's up? You're more down than usual." Jordan asks.

"Nothing. Just tired." I lie

"Bull crap. You could out-walk me any day of the week prior to me getting drained. No way you're more tired than me. And don't think I haven't noticed you eating and drinking less. Are we going to make it? Do we have enough food and water?"

"Yup. All good just not hungry." I lie again.

But then my stomach tells a different story by yelling out for everyone to hear.

"Not hungry huh? What is going on Ava?"

"Well. I didn't want to burden you while you were healing, but we are down to our last water bottle. And another day's worth of food. Even with me rationing." I explain.

"Is that why we detoured here and you were so frantic in the field house?"

"Yup."

We walk in silence for another 30 minutes or so before she speaks up again.

"What are we going to do?"

"We are going to go to this town and find some water or something that can get us some water. A day of thirst is not going to kill us. We will make it through." I say. Hopefully not lying again.

All is quiet the rest of the way to the town. Each of us pondering our situation and trying to come up with an answer. Hopefully one of us will soon. We pass a small little community on the way through to the town, but this was too much like the little cul-de-sac area of Milford that housed the labyrinth. Too many bad feelings with that, so we just move on. No questions asked.

Frederica was a very small town. Before, all a town needed to form was a post office and a fire department. This town had that and a couple of churches. Not even a tourist stop for the largest ball of wax or the like. This is kind of what I was hoping for. Hoping this area was forgotten and passed over by any other roving members of this broken society.

As soon as we walked into town proper I knew my hopes were nothing more than that. All of the houses were torn open. Doors hanging loosely and things strewn through the yards. Someone found this area before we did. I don't think there is anything left for us.

Even so, we walk through town and check in houses that seem more or less intact. We check the school and find it worse than most others we had seen before. Nothing is left in the cafeteria or teachers' lounge vending machines.

We start heading back east towards the main road to go somewhere else. To try another idea, when we passed the fire hall. The doors were broken open and off the hinges but the fire engines were still in place. There really was not anything for them to respond to after the Fall since most people had left the area. They couldn't help with the Deaders. Plus, in Delaware, all of our firefighters were volunteers, so they probably just stopped showing up or left when they could.

"Let's just call it a day and see if we can clear this area. We can lock ourselves in a truck overnight. There should be plenty of room in the rear part of the fire engines to lay down." I say.

Jordan doesn't respond, but she walks with me into the main bays. After a couple of minutes of clearing the area, we find a truck and climb in. It is still a little early to just go to sleep so we just sit in silence. Each of us brooding and trying to find an answer to our situation. We eat a little of the rations we have left in silence.

After a while, Andromeda whines to go out. I open the door and let her out to pee. I keep the door open so she can come back in when she is done.

As I am waiting for her to come back I hear a dripping noise coming from one of the other engines. One of the water tanks is leaking. A couple of minutes later I can hear Andromeda licking something.

I shoot up and run to her yelling at her to stop. She is licking up the water coming from the engine.

"Andromeda stop you'll make yourself sick. You don't know where they get that water." I yell

"Wait, she may be on to something." Jordan pipes in. "Don't they fill the engines from the fire hydrants in town?"

"I think so."

"Well, fire hydrants are tapped into the town's drinking water system. So it should be clean water. It may taste funny from being in the tanks, but it should be usable." Jordan surmises

"How do you know that?" I ask

"I am not sure, but I know it is true. I must have read it somewhere."

We went to the engine where Andromeda was now sitting and watching us have this talk. I swear she had a smug look on her face like she already knew this information. I took out an empty bottle and held it under the slow drip until I had about an inch of water in the bottom. It looks clear and smells clean. I look at Jordan and take a sip. It tastes metallic but clean.

"It tastes fine. Let's each take a small amount now and wait it out until tomorrow. If there are no ill effects we will fill our bottles up and hit the road. This may fix one concern, but we still need food."

"That seems like a solid plan. I'll get the blankets set up." Jordan said as she jumps up in the truck.

Hours later we are lying down ready to sleep. Neither Jordan nor I have had any adverse reactions to the water so it must be clean. That solves one problem for now. Next, we have to worry about getting some food. In the morning I am going to go out and set some traps for rabbits or other small game. Maybe we could get something. I think this place is relatively safe for now. We could stay here for a couple of days and get reset. We have been going nonstop since we left the compound. No signs of pursuit so far. Maybe we can rest and figure out our next steps.

We wrap ourselves in our emergency blankets even though we are in the truck. It has become a habit since we noticed it masked our signal from the creatures. Jordan is asleep in seconds and so is Andromeda. I wish I could fall asleep that fast. Too many worries I guess. Leaving Momma behind again is weighing heavily on me. I feel like I abandoned her again, even though I know it was the only choice.

I take this time to update the day's events in my journal. The one you are reading now. I try to do this every night now so I can make sure everything is kept current, in case something happens to me where I cannot update it any further. Eventually, the worries of the day are overtaken by exhaustion and I fall into a restless slumber.

In the morning we wake and drink a little bit more of the water. We had found a small cooking pot so we start a fire to boil the water, just to be safe. I set Jordan to boiling and filling the water bottles. As she starts that task, I set out to the area just outside and look for areas to set a couple of traps. This doesn't take long, nature has really taken back over, since the Fall. It would be kinda beautiful if not for almost dying on a daily basis.

When I return to the hall I find Jordan reading a book.

"What's that?" I ask

"It's a book on edible plants for the northeast region of the U.S." Jordan replies.

"Where did you find that?"

"I was rummaging around and found it in one of the lockers that held the firefighter's gear. I guess one was looking for a better way to survive. This could be a real help." Jordan sounded excited with her find.

"Is there anything in this area?"

"Yes, I was just looking at that. Let's go out and see what we can find."

So we did just that. We had to wait a bit for the traps anyway and I was planning on staying here for a couple more days. It was best that we try this book out and see if we can find some food. We found a surprising amount of plants without walking far. This book was a great find. I never knew what to look for and had stayed away from most plants because of that. None of them tasted good, but it filled a void and would let us live another day.

The traps didn't fare so well. I only caught one rabbit in two days. Jordan and I would have to live a little longer on the plants. Andromeda needed the meat. She would eat the plants but really needed more meat in her diet. So I smoke the rabbit on the small fire we had built and keep it as jerky for her.

Early the following morning we heard voices coming from outside the fire hall. We had not seen evidence of anyone in the days that we had camped here. No one had been seen, nor were there any traces of anyone having been by. It was odd to hear someone now. At least they weren't Deaders again.

It seemed like they were just outside the doors. All the doors had been closed when we had originally approached and we had kept them that way throughout our stay. We were huddled in the fire engine we had chosen randomly that first day. All of our stuff was inside with us. The only proof that we had been here were the footprints in the dust, the ashes from the fire we had built and the traps outside of the building.

Then all of a sudden one of them cried out. I guess he found one of my traps.

"Hey, I found a rabbit in this here snare." One called out.

"How did a snare get there? I didn't set it." Another called.

"You think someone has been here?" said the first

"Hope not. They may have stolen our water supply." Said a third voice.

Damn. They were doing the same thing as us. They would see us as thieves of their water. Maybe that is why the engine was dripping so slowly, but it hadn't become a huge puddle. We may have just missed them that day. They probably only need to get water every couple of days.

I am so frazzled that I haven't even come up with nicknames for these guys.

Andromeda is up and alert and Jordan is looking at me with a scared look in her eyes. I mime to her to pack up. We get the bags set before we hear the first door open. It seems they are hesitating coming inside, expecting trouble.

I get my hand on the pistol. How many shots do I have again? Not enough to shoot our way out. Also, I don't know if I can shoot first. I was always taught not to throw the first punch. With at least three of them I would have to go first to keep any advantage.

"Someone has been here. There are ashes in the middle of this bay." The second voice said

"Search the area. They might still be here!" says the first voice. "Doug, watch the door and tell the others outside to keep an eye out."

"What others?" Doug asks confused.

"Shhh. They don't know that you dumbass." The first voice yells in a hoarse whisper.

Good, there was just the three of them. Better odds.

"There are small prints around the ashes. Children or maybe women." Says the first voice. (I'll call him the librarian now.)

"I hope they are still here if they are women. I haven't seen a woman since the Fall." Says Doug.

As they continue to banter about women and sex, I hear a couple of the fire engine doors being opened along with the doors to the kitchen and other areas of the hall. It won't take long for them to find us. I whisper my plan to Jordan and each of us grabs a door handle to the truck.

We are going to run out of the truck from opposite sides and hope the guys are as confused as they sound. As soon as we hit the outside doors we should be able to outmaneuver these guys and get away.

I start to count to three on my fingers. As I get to two my door flies open and I fall out of the truck and land hard on my shoulder. Jordan takes this as three and jumps out of the other door. Andromeda jumps out after me, all teeth and growl. The guy is so surprised he can barely register what is happening as Andromeda jumps at him. She doesn't bite him, but does raise a ruckus and keeps him moving away. This gives me time to get on my feet and grab the gun that I dropped.

I don't take time to see much else. Jordan has a head start and I can't lose her. As soon as I am on my feet I run for the door. Andromeda takes the time for a few more warning barks and runs at my heels. I just hit the door when the biggest guy I have ever seen steps in front of it. I hit him in the chest with my face and literally bounce off of him. Back onto the floor.

Andromeda starts going off on this guy too, except he doesn't seem to care.

"Shut your dog up. She don't scare me." It was Doug.

"Well looky what we have here. You were right John. It is a woman." It was the librarian that had opened my door.

"She is mighty pretty, although she looks a little wild Billy." The third guy says.

"I like mine wild." Doug piped in.

I was working through my options. Andromeda was in protective mode. She wasn't barking but her hair was up and she was ready to pounce on whoever tried to touch me. I had not gotten back on my feet yet but had maneuvered onto my knees. I try to look cowed but get ready to move when I have a plan. If I have a plan. It was three to two and these guys are all big.

Then something Billy, the Librarian, had said hit me. "It is a woman." That means they didn't see Jordan hit the other door and run. She obviously didn't go to the same door I did and hit the jolly stupid giant. So she must have made it out some other way.

The three of them were now within feet of Andromeda and me. No real escape. I still have my gun in my hand, hidden behind my knee. They have not seen it yet.

"Go ahead and throw that gun over my way sweetheart. I saw you pick it back up when you fell from grace at that truck over there." Billy said.

Damn. He did see it.

I pull the gun from behind my leg. I guess I move too fast because the third guy pulls his gun and aims it right at my head.

I throw my hands up in an 'I give up' gesture. Barrel towards the ground, handle towards them. I place it on the ground and was just getting ready to push it to Billy when I hear a clang and Doug falls to his knees. Behind where he was standing was Jordan with a long metal pole. She had snuck up behind him while they were focused on me and smashed it over his head.

Now any normal human would be lights out. Doug just looks a little dazed and a lot pissed. Andromeda and I don't take a second to gawk. She jumps at Billy since he is the closest. I readjust my grip on the pistol and take a pot shot at the others. I don't have time to aim so I miss horribly. It does give me a second to get up and run though. Jordan takes another swing at Doug, but he is ready this time and catches it mid-swing in a great big bear paw he calls hands. Jordan looks stunned and just drops her end and runs to the door with me.

After her initial surge at Billy, Andromeda left him and takes off after us. We all hit the door at the same time and run through it hard. The guys get themselves back together pretty quickly, the door never hit the jamb after we went through. They are hot on our heels.

I guess the gunman was the first one through because I hear a bullet whizz by us through the tall grass as they come through the door. I don't take the time to look back. We just duck a bit and pour on the speed. Andromeda is in the front leading us down the game paths. We can only hope these guys don't have the speed or agility we have due to their size. I mean the average guy is faster and stronger than the average girl. But as big as these guys are they are definitely above average on the strength meter, so hopefully a little slower on the other end.

Andromeda has us running down the game trails that weave back and forth through the brush. I can hear the guys following us for a couple of minutes more. Then I stop hearing any pursuit. We run for a couple of minutes more just to be certain before we slow our pace.

I was lost in the brush and had no idea which way we ran when we left the fire hall. That doesn't matter at the moment. If these guys are part of a larger group, all they have to do is get reinforcements and push the brush until we are found. We have to keep moving and get out of the area as fast as possible. Hiding is not an option this time.

Lost

As I stated before, this area was unfamiliar to me before the Fall. Now with the growth, I have no idea where we are heading. I have to trust Andromeda to get us somewhere safe. She seems to know where she is going. I trust her not to send us into the swamp too deep to get out.

Jordan had been in front of me for most of the run from the fire hall, but she had stopped to take a breath so I just passed her to keep Andromeda in sight. I knew she wouldn't go too far, but I wanted to make sure we didn't lose her.

"Ava! Your backpack is soaking wet! Are you bleeding?" Jordan suddenly exclaimed.

I totally turned my head to look at my back to see what was wet and turned myself in a circle like a dummy. Not my proudest moment. Yet somehow not my worst either.

"Drop your backpack I think you got hit. It looks like wet blood" Jordan said.

"I don't feel anything." I stated as I shrugged out of my pack.

Once the bag was off my shoulder she could see that my shirt was not soaked through with blood. But there was a hole in the bag that was definitely not there this morning. But what was the liquid?

"It looks like I got shot in the back but the bag stopped it. The impact broke a couple of the water bottles." I informed Jordan after looking more closely.

"What stopped the bullet then? Is there an exit hole too? Maybe the bag was shot through over your shoulder."

"No other hole, just right here." I started to say and then the world dropped out from under me.

I slump to the ground and stare off into space as the realization of what must have happened hit me. I can hear Jordan calling my name. She is shaking me and looking for wounds on my arms and back. But this wound can't be found. This wound was in my soul.

I take a second to try to come to terms with my realization before I check the bag and make this fear a reality. I open the small pocket on the outside of my bag and reach in. This pocket is directly over the bullet hole in the bag. It is small but deep and runs along the outside of the liner. I reach in and my fear is confirmed.

As I retract my hand Jordan lets out a small gasp. She knows what has dropped me and rocked me to my soul.

The bullet was stopped by my old phone. As I pull it out of my bag, I still see the round sticking out of the screen. The guys must have only been using 9mm's and the ammo may have been a little old or had gotten wet. But either way this phone, this connection to my past and the way things were before the Fall, has saved my life. It stopped the bullet from hitting me in the back.

It saved my life but is still a death in its own way. It was my only link to what was. I always hoped we would get power again and I could charge it and see the pictures of my past. Of my life. Of my Dad.

Andromeda nuzzles me as I cry kneeling in the mud. Jordan is standing behind me. She knows the importance of this phone to me. Of the way it helped me feel like my old self. She knows the pictures of our last family trip and others were on here. The last remnant of my family. Now I have really lost my Dad. I have nothing to remember him by. No hope of ever seeing his face again. Even in pictures, all of it has been lost.

I try to remember as I kneel here. When was the last time I clearly pictured his face? Or Matt's for that matter? I am losing them all over again. All because the phone happened to be in the path of a stray bullet these assholes decided to shoot at me.

Don't get me wrong, I am grateful to be alive. To the fact that this phone saved me in the most auspicious of ways. But the loss is still devastating.

I don't know how long I knelt in the mud. I didn't really register much until Jordan is shaking me. Hard! Then I hear it. The guys are back on our trail. I have given them time to catch up. We lost our lead, and now we are in mud that will give away our path.

Damn it! I screwed up again.

I snap to and get to my feet. I can think about my loss later. Right now we need to get to safety. Everything seems clearer now. I needed to grieve I guess. Not just about the phone but about all those I have lost. I don't know if I have ever really let myself fully grieve. Fully feel what those losses meant.

There is the sound of water to my right. I do know that there is a creek to the north side of Frederica. We always had to pass over a bridge on our way to Dover. If the creek is to my right, we are heading west, and if we cross the water, the guys will lose our trail. We need to go now though before they can see us. I quickly inform Jordan of my plan.

"We need to cross the creek. Then head straight north. There is an old Air Force base there. A lot of fencing and a lot of old barracks to hide out in."

"Ok." Is all she said. A girl of few words that Giggles.

Without further delay, we run to the creek and wade right in. The water is not that high, but we keep sinking in the mud. It is easier to swim than to try and walk.

The creek is not that wide so we are across in no time and head off back into the brush before our pursuers are any wiser. It is warm and being this wet will not cause us any medical concerns. However, it makes our clothes heavier so running may not be an option until we dry out.

Andromeda has it the easiest. She just got out of the water and shook. Spraying water everywhere. But she was made for swimming and water like this. Never a thought for her.

As we get deeper into the brush we can hear the noises of pursuit get farther away again. They probably didn't want to cross the water as we did. Or didn't expect us to cross where we did. We should be able to put some new distance between us over the next couple of hours.

It only takes us a couple of hours to reach the Dover Air Force Base. Still only mid-afternoon by my assumption. I guess you cover a lot of ground when you're being chased by trigger-happy maniacs.

As we approach the area that the base used to be, it occurs to me that I never thought about the military still being around. I guessed that they all pulled out in the beginning. But now that we are getting close to walking onto the base, I wonder if they are still around. Or if part of it still exists here.

It is still the middle of the day and won't be dark for hours yet. The safest way to enter may be at night under the cover of darkness. If someone is here and is not expecting trouble, they will be laid back and easy. If we walk in now and there are people here they have the element of surprise on us.

With this in mind, we head to the old base museum. There are a lot of big planes and small buildings around there that we can hide in or around until it gets dark. As we approach the old entrance from across the road we can see that there is really no more fence line. At least in this immediate area.

It hasn't rotted away but seems to have been taken. Maybe by locals looking to help protect themselves, or by the military itself to make a smaller more secure and protectable area.

With the fence missing we decide that the area is most likely being patrolled if someone is staying here so we head into the museum area a little deeper. This area, as most have been, is completely overrun by weeds and grasses. As long as we crouch we should be able to move without being seen over any kind of distance.

We head to the nearest building. It looks like some kind of office building. It is solid concrete very durable. As we approach we can see some windows broken out and the doors all hanging open. This is not a surprise, but it means that we have to clear the building if we are going to stay there.

"Do you want to clear this building or move on to the next?" I ask Jordan.

"The longer we stay outside the more likely we will be seen if someone is here." She stated.

"Clear it is then." I say as we move to the nearest door.

We clear the building from the bottom floor up. We close all the doors behind us too. I know the Deaders are smarter than we had thought and they may be able to open a door, but it is better than doing nothing to protect ourselves.

Two floors later everything seems to be in order and there was nothing alive or dead on the premises. We pick an office on the second floor that has limited access to the outside and huddle down for the rest of the day. I pass out some food for us and Andromeda. Then sparingly drink some water. We lost half of our water supply when my bag got shot. The concussion must have caused them to crack. It is amazing that I never felt the hit. I guess with the fear of running for our lives some things go unnoticed.

With everything that happened I feel drained. It has been emotional and scary today. As I sit down finishing some jerky I can feel my eyes wanting to close. I can feel my body trying to relax.

"It's ok. I can keep watch with Andromeda, you take a nap. I'll wake you when it is dark." Jordan says.

I want to argue that I was fine, but we all know that was a lie. So I just nod and let sleep take me away.

Ringing

I look around and can't find my phone. For some reason, it is not set to silent as it has been since the day I got it. Only old people let their phones ring. I look under the couch cushions and under the chair. I can't seem to find it. Who is calling me anyway? No one calls anymore. Everything is messaging and text.

I find it under the blanket on the love seat. I quickly look at the caller id as I pick it up. It's Dad, I wonder what he wants. He just left for work a little while ago.

"Hello?" I say as I put the phone on speaker. If he wants to call me like an old person I'll put him on speaker like one.

"Hello?" I say again. The line is nothing but dead air. Probably just a butt dial so I hang up.

As soon as I do the phone starts ringing again. This time it is Matthew. Now I know something is up because he never calls me, or texts for that matter.

Again I answer the phone and hear nothing but dead air. What is up with the service today? They must need something. I hang up the call and immediately open the messenger app and send them both a message.

"Bad service..... What's up?"

I watch the message go delivered but not read. No big, it must have been nothing. I just put my phone in my back pocket and start to go back to my room.

As soon as I let go of my phone though it disappears. I didn't think I dropped it. I didn't hear it hit the floor. But it's no longer in my pocket. I drop to the floor to look under the couch. As I do I can hear it vibrating in the kitchen. This makes no sense.

I get up and look in the kitchen. My phone is sitting on the countertop next to a fresh batch of chocolate chip cookie dough. It's another call, but at least it is on silent now. I run to the counter to grab the phone as it vibrates off the counter and almost falls to the floor. That would have been bad. It would have broken falling off the counter like that. That's all I need to do is have to pay to replace another screen. I just had this one replaced last week. I can't remember what happened to it. I think the screen broke when

I was playing laser tag. I know I was running around and something about a gun was involved. Then the screen was broken to the point the phone wouldn't work. I am a little foggy on any other details.

As I am thinking this I look at the caller id again and it is my Mom. This time I can hear her but the signal is still spotty.

"……Left me…. behind ……..not ….. gone…. back…. away…"

"What? You're breaking up I can't hear you. I don't understand."

Then the line goes dead. I try calling her back but it won't connect. What is going on with the service here?

The next thing I know I am at my desk in school. We must have a substitute teacher today because all of the other kids are on their phones. They are all laughing and pointing at the screens about some video. I pull out my phone, but the screen is cracked. It won't even turn on. I look at Kendra sitting next to me.

"My phone won't turn on. Can you show me the video?" I ask.

She looks at me like I grew two heads and turned the other way. I never really liked her anyway.

"George, can you tell me what you are looking at? My phone got broken in my backpack."

"Who breaks their phone in their backpack? What happened? Did it take a bullet?" he chided.

"Just show me the video." I snark back.

"No, use your own phone."

Just then my Dad walks into the room. He looks pissed. Well, I think he looks pissed but I can't really see his face. I know it is him though because Mom walks in right behind him.

"You broke a brand new phone?! You only had it for a day!"

"No I have had this phone forever, I don't know what happened." I plea

"You never could take care of stuff. Get your bag. We have to go." He demanded

"What? I have to finish school."

"Get your bag. We have to go. It is dark outside." He stated.

He then grabs my arm and starts shaking it. Shaking me. I look at the room again and no one else is there. The windows are dark and the lights are out.

"We have to go. Ava. We have to go it is dark outside." This time it isn't my Dad. It's Jordan. She is trying to wake me up.

I finally rouse from the nightmare about my phone. I groggily look at Jordan and see the relief in her eyes as I come to.

"Oh thank god. I have been trying to wake you for a couple of minutes. You seemed to be having some kind of nightmare."

"You don't know the half of it. Did you see anything while I was out?" I ask.

"No, nothing. No people no lights, no Deaders. Just the wind and the grass. Kind of beautiful if you ask me."

"Good. Let's go. With the fence down as it is I don't think the commissary holds anything for us. No use going there. So let's do some quick recon of the area. See if anyone is about. Then we can find a place to stay for the night that is more secure than this place."

"Then we need a full plan on where to go from here. After losing all the water you were carrying, we can't stay here long." Jordan explains.

We get up to get moving. Andromeda rouses herself and stretches from her own nap in the corner by the door. She's ready to take the lead and be the ears and nose of our recon mission. Hopefully, it is a lot less exciting than the beginning of today had been.

We slowly make our way through the base. Nothing looks out of place. Nothing looks like it has been touched in a long while. Still, we keep to the shadows and minimize our time in the open crossing from building to building.

We make it to where the old barracks buildings were, but now they are surrounded by a fence. It is not high but it has barbed wire on the top. This may be the missing fence from near the museum. Why is it here?

We take a second to take it all in. There seems to be no movement inside the fence so it may have been abandoned a while ago. We decide to walk the fence line and look for a way in, or any breaks in the fence.

Twenty minutes later we find where this fence joins with the original fence around the base. We found no break in the line except for one man-sized gate. That must be the way in and out. While this does stop you from having a good escape plan, it also limits your exposure too.

Jordan looks at me and I look at Andromeda. She does not seem agitated, so I decide to work our way back to the gate and see what we can find inside. Jordan does not seem opposed and follows me back to the gate.

Once inside the gate, we make sure to close it as it was. There seems to be a couple of the old buildings inside the fence. We choose the first building we come to and start a sweep through. Like before we start on the first floor, we check the doors and make sure they are closed behind us. A lot of these doors are locked from the inside. We need to clear more before we start making the noise it will take to open them from here.

When we reach the second floor we find a large amount of supplies in the first couple of rooms we come to. Enough dried meat and water to last us a good long time. We take a couple of handfuls, put them in our bag and continue with our sweep. Safety first.

The rest of the building is clear, so we head back to the supplies and do a more thorough check. It is like an army was set to stay here for a while. Plenty of food, water and even a couple of magazines and books for entertainment. This is quite a find. We take this good fortune and stock up our bags with everything they will take. We need to check the rest of the buildings in the small compound before it gets too late into the night. Taking these supplies just makes us feel better if we need to run tonight. If we don't then we can come back later and hunker down for a few days to get a new plan in order.

Even with the joy of this new find, I can't help but ask the question. Why is this still here? Who left it and what caused them to run off without it? Hopefully, I will never know the answers to these questions. But that is not usually my luck in situations like this. Is it?

We head back outside with our newly full packs. There are two more buildings that we need to check out. We decide to go counter-clockwise and head to the building on the right. As we move between buildings I swear I see movement on the far side of the opening. A shadow moved in a way it shouldn't. Andromeda seems to know something isn't right too. I get Jordan's attention and nod to the opening. She seems confused so I wave my hand forward to get her moving fast to the next opening.

We get to the next doorway but there is no door. We can't go inside and close it off. With the movement we just saw I don't like this at all. With a quick word to Jordan and a soft whistle to Andromeda, we move on to the next building. This one will take us the furthest away from the opening in the fence.

We give up a little stealth to gain speed. We need to get to this building and get inside where we will most likely need to stay and hunker down for the night. As I think this in my head Andromeda drops and starts growling fiercely. She is pointing directly ahead of us. At first I can't see anything but shadows. But then I can see an eerie glow. That turns into two points, then four. We turn to make a run for the last building and see three more sets of glowing eyes looking directly at us. How did they get in and behind us? Was this whole thing a trap?

Jordan grabs my hand and I feel her shaking. The longer we stand here the more eyes I can see. All around us. There seems to be nowhere to run. It is open ground and if these things are in any kind of condition they can probably outrun us while we have the full packs. It would take time to open the gate and get out. Too much time with these creatures right on our heels.

I pull out the gun and Jordan pulls a knife. Andromeda sidles up to both of us as we try to protect each other on all sides. There is no way we are going to survive this. But we will not go down without a fight.

The Deaders are taking their time walking towards us. No hunger, no rush. It is like they know we are trapped and they are relishing that fact. They will get to feed tonight but they want to let us know it. That is not primal at all. When wolves have prey surrounded they move in quickly for the kill. This is almost a human-type taunt from these things.

The next couple of minutes are a blur. Bodies slamming us from all sides. Andromeda growling and fighting. Jordan screaming and slashing with her knife. I shoot two of the Deaders point-blank in the face. They screamed and wandered off for a minute. Then come right back into the fight.

I felt something pull at my pack and pull me off of my feet. I hit the ground hard on my back. Luckily my head is saved because it hits the pack but that was the only luck I had. Before I could turn or try to roll over I have two of the Deaders on top of me. Their nasty hands reaching for any exposed skin they can find.

One touches my face. The other my exposed stomach. I can feel my energy draining and there is nothing I can do. Andromeda flies out of nowhere and grabs one of them by the throat. It lets go and screams that shrill cry of theirs. The other staggers back at the ferocity of her attack, but only momentarily. Then it is back and draining me again.

At this point, I don't have much energy to think let alone fight. This is how I am going to go? A place that seemed protected. I look for Jordan and see that she is still on her feet fighting with her back to me. She hasn't seen that I am down and she is vulnerable. I try to yell out but I can barely open my mouth. I don't have a lot of time left.

Andromeda seems to have done something to stop the one because she is back with a vengeance on the other one that is trying to kill me. This one is ready though and let's go long enough to dodge her charge. Then it is back on me with a look of ecstasy on its face. My head drops to the side as I don't have enough energy to lift it any longer. I know it is dark out but my eyesight seems to be closing in and blurring.

Just then I see something round rolling across the ground. It seems odd and I can't seem to take my eyes off of it. When it stops rolling I can see it is a metal cylinder. The Deaders seem to see it too and don't seem to know what it is. Then there is a small detonation along the device. There was no real sound or any flames, but a very quick very bright light emitted from the cylinder. All of a sudden I feel disoriented and dizzy.

Some of the Deaders are walking away and staggering. Others are on the ground holding their heads. The Deader draining me lets go and is staggering around. As I try and get my eyes to work correctly I see new figures running into the area. They are shooting and cutting at the heads of the Deaders. The creatures are so flustered with whatever that cylinder produced that they don't seem to see the newcomers until it is too late to react.

The next thing I know I feel a prick in my arm and a warm flow in my veins.

"This will help. It's just an IV." Someone says beside me. I still can't turn my head to look. Andromeda walks into my view and lays down next to me. She saved me again. This time though she looks a little worse for wear. She keeps shaking her head and looks disoriented. I hope she wasn't drained as badly as me. It is hard to tell with my vision going dark still and the blood on her fur.

Someone walks next to Andromeda and kneels down in my view. I was expecting the military to be fully geared up in riot gear and safety equipment. You know when I pictured them in my head. This soldier is just in dark fatigues. No riot gear or helmet. I cannot focus on any details to see who my saviors are. I was wondering if there was still a military out there. I never expected to be saved by them tonight.

"Hello their Rommy. What has she gotten you into now?" He says.

"How..? How do you know her name?" I ask dumbfounded.

"I was there when you named her you numbskull." He said

And then it came crashing in on me faster than a surfer on a wave. The darkness chooses that moment to take over and then there was nothing but black.

Confusion

I wake up in a bed. A bed with rails and stiff sheets. I have wires and tubes hanging everywhere. I have no idea where I am or how I got here. As I move around I can tell that Andromeda is at my feet. Staying close and keeping me safe. As I try to sit up I hear Jordan next to me.

"Don't try to move too much, you had a lot drained out of you."

"Where are we?" I ask her.

"I am not completely sure. Some hospital in the northern part of Delaware."

"How did we get here?"

"The soldiers brought us. They had a vehicle that was somehow working. We got here in a couple of hours. You have been in bed for two days since."

Then more confusion sinks in as memories come back. The soldier calling me a numbskull and knowing Andromeda's name. The Deaders draining me, almost to death. Why were they there? Who was the soldier that seemed so familiar with me?

"The soldier that seemed to know me? Know Andromeda? Where is he? Who is he?"

"I don't know. He left and continued south. As you were being taken care of he asked me where we had been and how we got to be where we were. I told him about the Home of the Brave and how we lost your mother there. After that, he became agitated and left soon after with a small contingent of others. He made sure you and I were brought up here. I think it is Christiana Hospital."

"His actions. His mannerisms. They reminded me of my brother. Of Matthew. But that can't be."

As I try to get my head wrapped around all that had happened, it struck me. An obvious thing that should have stopped me in my tracks, but was somehow diminished from the confusion of that soldier. There was power. Lights, machines and circulating air. How was this possible? Wouldn't this attract the Deaders in droves? There was no power anywhere anymore. The power grids went down. Those that weren't destroyed by the Deaders drawing their power, were destroyed by us to keep them from getting them.

Jordan could see the confusion on my face and didn't seem to have any answers, so I didn't ask them. Yet.

Just then a person wearing a lab coat walked in.

"Oh, I see you are awake. Great. How are you feeling?" She asked.

"Who are you? Where am I?" I asked

"We will get to all of that. As for me, I am Dr. Phillips. Not really a medical doctor, but I fill in where I am needed. I actually have a Ph.D. in Biological Sciences, specializing in cell biology. I was a researcher before the Fall. Now I do whatever is needed as I still conduct my research on the Non-living Biologicals. Or NLB's. Now back to my question. How are you feeling?"

"Still a little off, a little woozy. But I think I am ok."

"Well, that is good. I will leave you to it. Get some rest, some food will be brought for you shortly."

"How do we have power? Isn't it dangerous?" I asked

"It comes from generators in the subbasement of the building next to us. We only use the power sparingly for research and small comforts. We are underground and surrounded by concrete. So are the generators. So we are perfectly safe. There is no way for the NLB's to find us." She explained.

Over the next day, I was forced to stay in bed. Andromeda and Jordan never left my side. I don't think any of us knew what to make of our saviors. We discussed the night of the attack and what happened in the hours after I was out.

Apparently, we were rescued by a branch of the military that is still functioning. Albeit a very small contingent. Since she has been here Jordan has only seen fifteen soldiers in uniform, five people in lab coats and three or four people in regular clothes.

The group that saved us was out looking for any survivors to help. Luckily they were there when they were. After I blacked out we were loaded in a truck and half of the soldiers brought us to the hospital. The other half were on foot and headed to the Home of the Brave compound to see if they could help the survivors. The soldier that reminded me of Matt headed out with the group to the south.

As soon as we arrived here they got me the help I needed and another group of soldiers headed back out to help with the Bravers. No one has seen them since. I am not sure what would take them three days to get back if they had a truck. Maybe there weren't any survivors and they just kept moving. Looking for more. There wouldn't be a reason to return until they had people to help.

I have to make peace with the fact that my mother may be lost to me again. That again I left her to save myself. To save Jordan and Andromeda too, but that doesn't help the guilt.

There doesn't seem to be more than two medical professionals in this building. At least that is all I have seen. The rest of the lab coats seem to have been researchers. Some have been trying to work on a cure for the Deaders. Others trying to truly understand what they are.

One of the nurses comes around every couple of hours when she can. Since there is no real danger for me, she just pokes her head in and asks how I am doing. I guess they are going to move the three of us to a real bedroom area later today. It will free up the hospital bed and stop them from checking on me constantly so I am all for it.

They had brought me my bag and some clothes that they thought might fit me. Mine were torn and very dirty when they brought me in. To be honest they were kind of that way before the attack. I have changed and am no longer in a medical gown, so I feel normal again. We are just finishing lunch and getting ready to move to our other room.

Suddenly, there is a bunch of commotion in the hallway. One of the soldiers runs by. Jordan and I run to the door of my room. One of the lab coats asks us to go back into the room and close the door. They have people coming in. Survivors.

We did as they asked but tried to hear what was going on in the halls. It seems like there were a lot of people brought in. Not all in very good shape from the sounds of it. As we were straining to listen and put together what was going on, my door burst open and a soldier in full gear runs into the room.

"We found Mom, she is ok." He stated as he stormed into the room.

"You found my Mom?" I asked confused.

"Technically I found our Mom." He states as he removes his helmet and goggles.

Staring back at me is my older brother Matthew. He is not only alive. He is here and telling me our mother was alive too. I was dumbstruck. I didn't know what to say. What to do.

So naturally, Matt starts laughing at me. That woke me up and I punched him in the arm.

'How?"

"To which situation are you referring? How I saved our mother, or how am I here, or the big one. How am I alive?"

"Yes to all."

"Move over on the bed and I'll tell you."

Matt tells me his story. He starts with why they were at the Air Force base in Dover when they found us. Then how he walked back to the Home of the Brave to find Mom. He tells me how they found the survivors and what transpired on the way back to cause such a commotion in the hallways. He then tells me what happened on the day we were separated and how he ended up with these soldiers and this hospital. It was not a long telling or a very intricate story. There was a lot of information that was slid over and things that did not add up completely, but the general ideas were there. We could talk about the rest later.

I tell him about how I write down my journal and keep my story and that he needs to do the same. People need to know what he has been through. What he has done. What he has become. The story left me with more questions than answers in this new world we live in.

The biggest thing in his telling was that he had found Mom and she was alive. So were about 10 other Bravers. They had all left the compound in the days following the attack and were on the road north. Matt and his team didn't see them on their pass to the compound, but Mom had left a note for me there. Matt found it and followed the directions on their path and caught up with them a day later. This is part of why it took them so long to get back. They hadn't known exactly where their backup was and there still weren't radios, so it took a while to get together with the other team. There were some problems on the way back too, but all in all, everyone was fine and they were just being checked out.

The story Matt told took about an hour. It was not very involved and was exciting. But in the end, he hadn't really told me much about this facility and what they were doing. He said that he wanted to let me hear that from the people that used the big words and actually knew what they meant.

I understood that stance I guess, but all I really wanted to do right now was visit Mom and the rest of the Bravers. I needed to know who was still alive.

Bravers

I was able to meet with the survivors about an hour later. There were ten Bravers still alive, including my mother. All but two of them were in good health. They were the reason for the hallway lockdown and the long delay in being able to see everyone. They are now in stable condition, but had been drained severely and were dehydrated. One of those two people was Susie. Of course, she would survive. I can't say I was mad though, she had fought for the rest of them as long as she could and still survived. That made her ok in my book. Even though I will never tell her that.

Others that survived were the four kids that I had seen in the safe area, three others that I had seen around the compound and Paul. Paul had been completing an inventory when the chaos broke loose. He was able to hide and stay safe throughout the whole ordeal. One was a spotter for the shooters on watch the other two were older and had been working in the warehouse when everything went sideways.

With Jordan and me, that made twelve survivors of the massacre at the compound. There had been dozens of people there at the time. That was a huge loss of life. Especially in a world where the truly living were so scarce.

I am not going to go into all of the details of the reunion with Mom and Matt together. Let's suffice to say that there were enough tears and snot to go around for a while. Matt told Mom most of his story, then Mom and I shared most of ours with Matt.

We talked long into the night to the point that Matt and I just curled up on the bed with Mom. Andromeda was on the floor next to the bed and slept. I don't know if I have slept that soundly in a long long time. The only person missing was Dad, and unlike Mom and Matt, he was never coming out of the shadows and surprising us. I saw him dead, saw his body. There was no hope that he would ever be returned to us.

I am walking around the corridors of the hospital. I have no idea where I am going. There is no one about this late at night. The halls are quiet. Not even a snore coming from any of the rooms around me.

The floor is cold on my bare feet. Colder than I remember before going to bed. I know they have to have some kind of air handler in this place, but I didn't think they would waste a lot of power to make it so cold.

I left Andromeda in the room with Mom and Matt. They need her more than I do around here. She needs to rest too. There has been a lot of excitement over the past couple of days.

As I am reminiscing about the talk I had with Mom and Matt, I found my way to the chow hall. I am not sure if they always leave food out or not, but there seems to be a ready amount here tonight. I am not really hungry. I have kind of gotten used to a low amount of calories, but the food looks good and you never know when your next meal will come.

I grab a couple of bits and pieces of different things and sit down to eat.

"That's a lot of food there. Keep eating like that and you'll get fat." Said a voice from the dark.

Not going to lie here I jumped out of my skin when I heard it.

"Damn! Don't do that." I whispered harshly.

"Always this jumpy?" He said

I still couldn't tell where he was. The voice seemed to resonate from all around the room at once. The acoustics in here are terrible.

"Only when strange people sneak up on innocent little girls in the dark."

"Innocent? You haven't been innocent a day in your life Punk."

Punk. He called me Punk.

My heart rate started running about the same as a racehorse finishing the third leg of the Triple Crown. Only one person has ever called me Punk. Not a punk, but Punk.

I drop my food on the table and get up to get a better view. It is so cold in here I can see my breath. But I can't feel the cold right now. With my heart racing and my thoughts doing the same, there is only one idea that I can hold on to.

Dad!

He is the only person to ever call me that. That was his pet name for me most of the time. I still can't find him though. A 6'3" 250-pound man should not be that hard to find.

"Daddy where are you? I can't see you."

"Right here, baby girl." He says

This time I can tell he is right behind me. I spin around so fast that I get a little dizzy.

"Daddy? Where have you been?"

"I had to go away for a little while. I am back now though. I never really left you, you know that right?"

"I know but it has been so long. So much has happened."

I think I said more than that, but it became incoherent babbles as I started to cry. I had not seen my Dad in so long, I had forgotten what it was like to hear his voice.

It was dark in the chow hall and I could barely see his face. I could tell he was smiling at me, but his features were blurred. Kind of like an old photo taken out of focus. I guess I am tired and just not seeing clearly through my tears.

"Do you want to eat your food or cry all night like a little toddler?"

"I am not hungry anymore. I just want to talk with you."

"Ok but let's talk and walk. The old legs need to be stretched a bit."

I push away from the food and just leave it on the table. By the time I get up he is halfway across the room. I jog a little to catch up and we walk in silence for a bit. As you know silence is not my norm, so within a minute or two I start talking to fill the void. I tell him about my time at the state park and my travels north. I tell him about the Minotaur village and the other escapades on the way to meet the Bravers.

I tell him about everything that had happened with Paul and Susie and my time at the Home of the Brave. He perked up a bit but still didn't say much when I mentioned Mom.

He seems to believe me when I tell him about the Deaders planning the attack. That belief was confirmed when I tell him about what happened the day I left the compound.

His affirmations or questions are mostly with nods and grunts. Leaving all of the talking to me. He used to say that I could talk enough for three people anyway, so he would leave room in the conversation for me to fill.

It seems like we talk and walk for hours. I never noticed where we were walking. Only that I had time to talk to my Dad. It seems wrong somehow. Seems like there was something I was forgetting. But I keep talking about my adventures, my dog and my friends.

Dad stops walking when we come to a big set of sealed automatic doors. The doors have a keypad and card reader to them.

"Looks like we can't go here."

"Why not?" I ask.

"This is where the scientific stuff happens. They don't like hands-on folks like us in places like these. Figure we may break something."

"Well, what are they doing in here?"

"I don't rightly know, but maybe you can find out tomorrow. After we are done with our catching up."

I nod and we turn around and head back to the rooms. Dad hasn't said much about what he has been doing all of this time. There is part of me that wants to ask, but I can never seem to voice the question.

I catch him up on all of my past adventures and start talking about the future. What we can do now that our family is back together. He looks happy when I say this, but a little sad at the same time. I am not sure why but this seems right too.

I ask him what this place is. How we got here and how he knew we were here. He just nods his head and said that he always knows where we are. He knew we would find each other again, family always does.

When we reach the rooms I open the door to walk in. Dad hesitates and stays in the hall.

"Dad come in. I'll wake everyone, I am sure they will be as excited to see you as I am."

"They may be at first. But it will make it harder later. I can't stay Punk. I have things that I need to do. That I need to accomplish now. You have done so many great things. Some scary, others downright crazy. You have made it through. Now you need to continue to do the same. Keep ahold of those people and that dog of yours too. They will get you through it."

"You have to stay with us. We are all together again. Let me wake Mom she will need to talk to you."

About this time Andromeda must have heard us talking and walks over to greet Dad too. He kneels down to pet her on the head and sides, as he always did.

"Look Punk. You know in your head what is true. This was a great night. You needed it and so did I. But you know we can't wake the family up and be happy again."

I look at him funny and have no idea what he is talking about. Andromeda must sense my confusion. She comes over and sits next to me, looking at Dad.

"Tell me about the day we got separated? You have talked about everything before and after that day."
"That was an awful day. We lost each other for a very long time. I don't like to think about it."

"Go on." He urges.

So I recap that day. I start in the morning and end with me and the other kids hearing screams from the woods. When I get to the end of the day I stop. He just looks at me and smiles. He knew I had figured out what is wrong. What is wrong with this whole night? I understand why he couldn't be there when the others wake up. What this night really has been.

As the realization dawns on my face he says one last thing before he walks away.

"Make sure you know what is behind those doors before you go too far in this place."

He then kisses the top of my head and waves to Andromeda. As he walks away down the hall he gets fuzzy. I am not sure if it was the light or the tears that causes it. But by the time my eyes clear he is gone. I also notice that the room has gotten warmer as he leaves. Like the heat finally kicked on or the Ac kicked off. But I was warm again for the first time since hearing Dad in the Chow hall.

Andromeda goes and lays back down by the bed and falls directly to sleep. Dogs can do that, but I was not so sure I could. A lot has happened tonight and I feel I need to come to terms with it before I sleep.

My brain has other ideas.

I wake to the sounds of my mother and brother talking in the room. They are whispering so I just open my eyes a little and let them continue to talk. I remember the events from the night before. I am not sure if they really happened or I just wanted them to. Then I remember the last thing my father said to me. I jump up to a sitting position so quickly that my mother let out a small shrill scream.

"Matthew, what is behind the doors? The double doors that are key coded and carded." I almost scream at him.

"How do you know about those doors? When did you walk through the building?" He asks quizzically

"I took a tour last night. While you were sleeping. What is behind those doors?"

"That is not for me to tell. I will have to introduce you to the doctor in charge of the facility. If he wants you to know he will tell you. I am just a grunt."

"Well, what are we waiting for? I need to know. Lead the way."

Doctors

They are everywhere here. I know there really isn't as many here as there used to be in a hospital this size. Just the sheer fact that this many have survived by just being here when the Fall happened is astounding. I know most of the lab coats I see are researchers. Some may not even be doctors. I just haven't seen this many people in one place in a long time. There are definitely more people here than at the Home of the Brave compound.

The first days I was here I only saw a small handful. I guess that was just in the medical wing. Now that we are out and about in the research area there is a lot more.

We walk a similar path to the one I walked in my dream. Matt asks if we want to eat and I shake my head. I just need to find out what was behind those locked doors. Also, that is the place my Dad first appeared and it is not easy to forget.

We go down a hallway that I had not seen before. This area seems to be mostly empty offices. No administrative work to be done during an apocalypse I guess. Matt stops in front of one door that looks like all the others and knocks. I hear words from inside as Matt turns to us and tells us he will go in alone and be right back out.

Matt is in the room no more than a minute or two then opens the door to beckon us in. As we enter I see a frail little man standing behind his desk. My first thought is that he would never survive outside of this controlled environment. That is probably not a fair assessment, but I have seen it and I don't think that he has.

"This is Doctor Testerman. He is the lead scientist working here." Matt announces.

"Welcome. Please have a seat. This office isn't much but it works during the apocalypse." Dr. Testerman jests. "So I hear you have some questions?"

"What is this facility and what type of research are you doing here?" I inquire.

"Since I don't know how much your brother has told you I will start with the basics."

Dr. Testerman explains that this used to be the Christiana hospital. One of the most advanced hospitals on the east coast. It was one of the largest community-based teaching hospitals in the country. It also had a very large research area, which is where most of the doctors there today were working.

When the Fall happened most of the patients and doctors went home and didn't return. No one really knows what happened to them, although they hope they got off the peninsula before it got shut down. The people we see here today had stayed to help try and find a cure for this new disease.

This of course was in the very early stages of everything so they thought it was some kind of virus. They didn't have many subjects to work with at the time so they were kind of shooting in the dark. But they all stayed. The National Guard was sent to help keep the facility safe. Eventually, they were used as gophers and sent on runs to help find specimens, survivors and food. They have all worked together here since then.

He then takes us on a roundabout tour for the next thirty minutes. He explains that some of the labs are working with living specimens, some with living tissue and others with viruses they think could be the cure for this problem. He never calls it a disease. I am not sure I would either.

Most of the facility is locked down and inaccessible because of power restrictions. The floor they are on and a couple of other labs are still running. These labs have people in them running tests or housing test subjects of either living or the Non-Living Biologicals types. These labs are all sealed and we are not allowed in, but there are windows in every lab for others to see in. We could see the Deaders strapped to beds, their brains cut open. Even in these scenarios the things were still moving and trying to get free.

Testerman makes sure to tell us that all of the locks are electrically engaged so they are secure. There are backup batteries to keep them secure for hours even after a loss of power.

"Can't the Deaders feel the electricity and drain it through the door?" I ask him.

"No. All of the doors that house the NLB's are lined with lead on the inside of the door to keep that from happening. We do throw them a couple of batteries now and then to keep them fed." He informs us and then laughs at his own joke.

He goes on to explain that the facility has been running on the backup generators for almost two years. They are working for now, but the fuel for them is getting low and getting very hard to find. Gasoline and even diesel fuel has an expiration date. The stuff they are finding is in worse and worse condition and they are having to travel farther to find it each week. Making new fuel is almost impossible due to the lack of power and the need for proper ventilation.

After we have seen enough of the other labs Dr. Testerman takes us to the lab I had questioned him about. The double door with severe security I had seen in my dream.

As we approach the doors, Dr. Testerman asks us to wait a couple of feet away and he enters the code. He has Matthew use his card as a second authorization. Whatever is in here is on severe lockdown.

As the doors open I strain to see inside. What is in here that needs to be under such a severe lock and key? As I get a glimpse I realize it was not what I expected.

There are tables like the mess hall with soldiers in different levels of uniformed attire. Some with just the pants and a white t-shirt. Some in full uniform. Others in complete civilian clothes. They seem to be just hanging out eating and talking.

As we walk farther in I can see that this area is very big.

"This is where the soldiers eat, sleep, train, debrief and where they are made." Testerman explains.

I look at Jordan and she looks just as confused...

"Then why the lock and key?" I ask.

"Safety. We bring in survivors like you. Most have no one to vouch for them. As you could see through the labs they are all locked from the inside and secure. This area had to be accessible from both sides as that is the only entrance to this area of the hospital. We can't let just anyone walk in here. They keep their weapons on hand and easily accessible in case of an emergency."

As he says this he points to what used to be a serving area or nurses station. It was hard to tell any longer because it had been made into an armory. Each weapon was just sitting in its place and ready to be grabbed on the move. There was a little of everything. Sniper rifles, machine guns, grenades, mortars, grenade launchers and more things that I had never seen before.

Looking at it now I could see why it was under heavy security. If someone with bad intentions made it in here things could go bad quickly. But then why did my Dad want me to see this area? Then the words that Dr. Testerman said hit me odd.

Where they are made? He just means made soldiers, but he also said trained. Slip of the tongue? I would have to ask Matt later. Was something a little off in the explanation here, or did I want this to be more?

As we walk through this area Matt takes the lead. He introduces us all to friends and fellow soldiers of his. I meet a couple that had been on the raid that saved us. I have never really met people in the military before, they all seemed nice enough just a little rough around the edges. But I guess that comes with the work that they have to do. One thing I did notice is that very few of them look me in the eyes while they were being introduced. My Dad was big on eye contact, especially when first meeting someone, so I tend to notice more than others. It just seems odd.

As we get to the training area, it looks like a high school gymnasium. There are wrestling mats on the ground for fight training, weights and other sorts of equipment. In the far back of the room, there is another room. It is glass-walled like the labs we had passed. There are several beds and people strapped into them. When I ask about them both Matt and Dr. Testerman look at each other and then explain that they had been hurt and were in recovery. They have separate recovery from the others brought in so they could get the care of the soldier medics along with the doctors on hand. This seems odd but I don't ask any more questions.

We come to the end of the tour and Dr. Testerman brings us back to the rooms that we are staying in. It has been a long tour and he orders someone to bring us a light lunch. Before he leaves he asks one last question.

"Do you know what these beings are? Do you really know what caused the Fall and these creatures to rise?"

Several of us answer in the negative. The news had covered very little on the cause.

"Most of the population never knew the cause of our predicament. The news liked to cover the fantastical parts and the downright gory. The media just before the Fall was about ratings and what grabbed the attention. A scientist explaining the cause was never going to get aired. What with bridges being blown up, the President being taken to a bunker underground somewhere the mask orders and curfews. There was no chance for the real story to get out."

"Do you know the story? The real story?" My mother asks.

"I do. I was there at the very beginning." Dr. Testerman says. His eyes got a faraway look as he seems to be remembering the beginning of the end of humanity as it was.

"Can you tell us? We would all like to know." I state.

"It is a long story, more than two years in the making. Let's eat lunch and then I will see if I can explain it properly."

Just as he says that the person comes back with a tray full of bread and lunch meat. We all grab a quick bite and then settle down to hear the telling of the Fall of Humanity and the rise of the Deaders.

Beginning

The doctor sits down to tell us all about the beginning of the Fall.

"You will have a lot of questions. Please just hear me out to the end. This story is long and a lot of things were happening simultaneously. I will do my best to convey this all so it can be understood."

This all started on July 18th, 2019.

On this date, there was a meteorite picked up by NASA entering the Earth's atmosphere. This in itself is not unusual as about 500 hit the Earth every year. Of the 500 most hit the water that covers more than two-thirds of our planet.

The meteor was tracked to where it landed in the barren terrain of the Kola Peninsula. Its position was tracked by monitored by the International Space Station and deemed retrievable. Although this area is very northern region of Russia, the maritime effects of the White Sea create a milder climate than expected for this latitude and made recovery easier.

Three days after the meteorite landed, the United States had research teams on site. The first thing they noticed was that it put off a blue glow. Usually, when the meteorites enter the atmosphere they can have a dim blue tail as the magnesium in their composition burns off. This one had cooled in the last three days and still had a dim glow to it. The scientific teams were confused by this yet stayed the course, set a perimeter and used hazmat suits until they could check for known pathogens and radiation.

At this point, I wanted to ask why we needed a science lesson in basic meteorites. I wanted to hit fast forward on this video because you know that science is not my favorite subject, but I decided to let the doctor tell it all in his own time. But I will add that Andromeda was yawning too.

The scientists on site expected to extract different types of metal and ore from the rock for different alloys. What they found was that the meteorite had cracked and a couple of small pieces had broken off during impact. This rock was basically a shell that housed a moss-type growth inside.

Of course, all types of safety protocols come into place at this point. A true alien life form.

Not the first contact that you make movies about typically but OK.

The area was cordoned off and no outside persons were allowed within 3 miles of the site. Samples were taken and within a week of the landing, the whole area was an international zoo for scientists. There were labs set up in plastic bubbles and large open canvas tents. The meteorite was not to be moved due to protocols, so everything had to move to it.

I feel like it looked like the scene in Thor around his hammer when it hit Earth or like E.T when he was dying. Long clear tubes with robot-like suits walking in and out.

The moss was fascinating and it would have been years before we would totally understand how this life survived the ravages of space. Every scientist in the world wanted to be part of this endeavor.

I wondered at this point if any of these people thought about the movie Evolution, you know the one where the meteorite had small alien life forms. They started small then took over a small town and tried to kill everyone?

The doctor explained that this moss spread spores at a very high rate. For moss on this planet, the pod that houses the spores can hold up to 1 million spores. Each of the pods in the alien moss held the highest amount of spores they had ever seen, over 30 million spores each. All so small that they could not be seen with the naked eye. It also reproduced too quickly to control. Even the small samples sent to the area labs reproduced with little to no source material.

Again very similar to the movie.

Within the second week, samples were sent to the area labs in Russia and some were sent here to the United States. They needed the best minds in the world working on this new discovery. The unexpected and uncontrollable growth rate of the moss also seemed to be an invasive plant dangerous to surrounding plants. The region of the original landing was so barren that this was not apparent as there was nothing for the spores to latch on to.

The spores seemed to take over weaker plants and kill them. It seemed to feed the stronger plants like trees, corn and strong grasses. Make them take nutrients faster and easier, which accelerated their growth rate over two time's normal.

One month after the meteorite fell to Earth there was a tragic car accident. One of the main researchers had been overworking themselves and fell asleep at the wheel of their car as they were heading back to town. They survived the crash but were pronounced dead at the hospital. It was a small area hospital so they had no morgue to speak of. The body was left in a cold room on a table, while the transportation could be arranged to get them back to their home country.

The body was severely mangled and the spinal cord had been severed. If they had survived they would have been a quadriplegic. This may have been what saved the hospital staff that night.

Four hours after they were pronounced dead, the researcher started making high-pitched noises and moving their eyes and mouth. The staff thought that they had made a mistake and didn't know what to do. They couldn't get a pulse to show on their equipment or see any movement in the chest of the victim.

Luckily, all the doctors and nurses wore rubber gloves to handle patients. This saved them from harm, yet delayed us from finding out what this person had become.

This subject's name was Victor Ivanov. He was patient zero.

Now we are getting to the part that I care about. What makes these things and makes them tick?

A week went by and there was no news or media leak about the reawakening of Patient Zero. Everything was to be kept quiet, under the penalty of the government, until they understood more of what was happening.

Doctor Testerman was then flown in as part of the research team to find answers. He was a leader in his field of study. He said what it was but I couldn't tell you again if you paid me for it. There were a lot of words and a lot of them ending in ology.

One week after the first reawakening of patient zero, there was a second death. This one happened in the northern reaches of Finland. Another one of the researchers from the Kola Peninsula. They had been sent home sick during the first week. This researcher got pneumonia which spread too quickly for the doctors to cure. They succumbed to this illness in days.

Two hours after they were pronounced dead, the researcher got up and walked out of their hospital room. There was no staff on this floor to see how it happened, but the patient ended up out on the street and started wandering around. They were spotted by a police officer making his rounds. When the officer approached he could see the person's eyes glowing. This seemed way off, but he followed his training and went to offer assistance. This is when he was attacked.

The researcher went for the cop and his exposed skin. Luckily he had a long sweatshirt with a high neck. His face was the only exposed area on his body.

He was trained in hand to hand so he was able to save himself and get away from the researcher. He gave himself some distance and tried to talk the thing down. When the creature attacked again the cop shot them in the center of their chest. This was a good shot but the researcher barely flinched. It was as if registering that it should hurt but not falling or even calling out in pain. The creature only stopped its advance momentarily after a third shot to the forehead. At this point, the officer lost all nerve, as he should have, and ran away until his backup arrived. The creature was taken down with some animal netting and taken into custody. Luckily there was no loss of life or any injuries to the police force.

The incident was called into Interpol as the locals had no idea what they were working with. This is how the two incidents were connected. The area was quarantined and another research team was sent to evaluate.

Unfortunately this time the incident was leaked to the media via cell phone video from a bystander that heard the shots. This is when the world first heard the term reawakened.

It was a small story then. Mostly bloggers and conspiracy theorists. All blamed on the government and new vaccines. They recalled any and all researchers and military staff that had direct exposure to the meteorite.

In the following weeks, more reawakenings started happening. One was a nephew of a lab tech, he died of a sudden brain aneurysm. He woke just over an hour after time of death. Then a girlfriend of a military soldier that overdosed on heroin. An Army officer's sister that died of complications in childbirth. Then more and more. The more that happened the weaker the link to the original staff at the meteorite site.

I had seen a couple of the news articles on these supposed deaths and reawakenings myself. In school the teachers had us do research on the newest phenomenon to back it or debunk the videos.

The media was starting to work themselves into a frenzy by this point. The happenings were coming from all over the world. Many places that the researchers and lab technicians had not gone in the past weeks. The governments had new groups put together to start conducting contact tracing on all of the infected individuals. They had to find out how they were coming in contact with the people in Russia, and if this was even what was causing the problem.

By then there had been plenty of research done on patient zero. They had found a large coagulation of spores in his brain stem during an autopsy. These seemed to be centered on the most primal instinct centers of the brain, the hindbrain and the medulla. This seemed to be a clue as to why the body was able to function while not allowing for vocal use or problem-solving. It also allowed for speculation on why the pain centers were not registering on the infected individuals.

I was so lost at this point that I did not even know what questions to ask. But I took it all in at face value hoping that all of this scientific information would eventually make some sense.

Doctor Testerman continued on by explaining that the media spun out of control calling these creatures everything they could think of out of every science fiction novel; walkers, walking dead, zombies and more.

The Center for Disease Control (CDC) had to make a statement to try and calm the public. They explained that this was just a virus and the videos that were being seen online were altered and part of a new social media challenge.

But even with this, travel restrictions were put into place. All borders were closed and flights were canceled for any and all non-essential travel. They had no idea how the spores were traveling or how they were being passed to the individuals that had never had contact with any of our people.

Studies were done with weather balloons and other atmospheric equipment. They had started picking up anomalies in the air quality over Western Europe. A new team was dedicated to just this phenomenon. They then determined that the spores had gotten into the air around the Kola Peninsula and were spreading in the wind and air currents around the globe, infecting anything and everyone that they came in contact with. The air itself was being poisoned.

The CDC then enacted a mandatory mask mandate for everyone. Inside or outside it didn't matter. If you went outside of your home you had to have a high-level mask on.

I remember that this is when cities and other large population areas started having riots. A lot of people were against the mask order and others were fighting to get more mandates put into place. As usual with our society at the time, things fell apart and everyone stubbornly stayed on their side of the issues and talked down to anyone on the other side.

Up to this point, the creatures had not killed anyone. All of the reawakenings seemed to happen in a hospital or a controlled setting. With the mask order and mandatory curfews enacted around the world, people became violent. Beatings, shootings and stabbings were happening nightly in every major city on Earth. People were fighting over mask shortages, over gasoline for their cars and generators. People were looting and hoarding everything they could think of. There came a time when even basic items like toilet paper were not able to be found.

We were only in September at this time. Three short months after the meteorite hit.

With deaths happening in the streets, and in droves, the bodies couldn't be contained. Someone would shoot another in the street for not wearing a mask. That person would then rise a little while later. Then more chaos would ensue.

There was more media coverage of the creatures, now being called Deaders, attacking people in the streets and killing them. The media and theorists were dumbfounded that the creatures didn't behave like the zombies of movies. They didn't rip and tear their victims. They didn't eviscerate the body to feed on the guts and brains. They just grabbed ahold and seemed to drain the life from the victim.

One of the biggest surprises was that these people didn't reawaken. Thorough examinations after the fact deemed these deaths as natural causes. Maybe from fear or an adrenaline overdose to the system. There was no sign of any spore infection at all.

The Deaders seemed to drain the spores, along with any electrical charge from the body. This was the theory on why the bodies didn't reanimate.

The doctor continued on and explained that they had found that the Deaders didn't exhibit any real tendencies to what we thought of as zombies. The muscle mass was good and they could run at speed with any human. They didn't respond to sounds or sights unless that sight exhibited an electrical field. They didn't moan as the movie creatures did, they seemed to have a higher-pitched sound as a form of communication to each other.

Doctor Testerman further explained that as the numbers of Deaders grew, they learned that they didn't just meander along. They hid mostly during the day and they roamed in groups that seemed to function as a wolf pack did. They worked together and surrounded prey or trapped them in some way. This meant that there was still some higher thinking to these creatures after all.

All of this was just rehashing what we already knew. I was wondering when the doc would get to the point and tell us how we can kill these things. The history lesson was starting to drag on. Most of this information was on the news throughout the whole ordeal. Or what we learned the hard way in life after the Fall.

Cities went dark throughout the following weeks. Partly because of city workers failing to go to work, but also because the Deaders were draining the electrical system. They were killing themselves by wandering into electrical substations and trying to feed. Even with their need for electricity and apparent ability to absorb it, it seemed the human body could still only take so much voltage.

I guess that was one way to kill them. Not too easy to find a functioning electrical substation around nowadays though.

As you know anything electrical seemed to draw these creatures. Towns started shutting down their power grids on purpose to keep them away. But car batteries, electric generators and anything that created a spark would find them there. So people gave up on the grid and went dark.

Eastern Europe took to the whole idea first, followed by China and most of the third world countries. By this time the research teams had relocated and set up our base of operations at the Christiana Hospital in Delaware. There was no reason to stay in the field, and at the time the U.S. was the only place with a working power grid.

Soon after, the word went out here that the peninsula was going to try and separate itself from the surrounding states. There had not been many cases on the shore, mostly because of the lack of major cities and the lack of rioting in the streets. The surrounding cities had fallen and were completely overrun with the NLBs by this point and the government officials were scrambling to do anything to keep themselves safe. Only a days' notice was given to the citizens to leave the peninsula or be trapped here when they blew the bridges.

No matter what was told to these people, they refused to listen to reason and kept with their island idea. I remember this was one of the last things that was on the television when there was still such a thing

The bridges were blown and the people felt a little safer. It still was not truly known what caused the reanimation process. But if they had power and the government was telling them that they were safe, people wanted to believe.

Two weeks later the U.S. went completely dark too. When this happened the scientists had to rely specifically on the underground generators. Only underground generators could be used since it did not seem to draw the Deaders. So they were able to continue their work. This all happened by the end of October.

Hard to tell it was only a month after the CDC mandates started and four months after the meteorite strike.

In early November the scientists figured out that by this time everyone was infected. There was no escaping it. If you died at this point any way other than by a Deaders hand, you would reawaken.

There was no way to get this information out. All of the social and regular media platforms were dead. All they could do here was keep doing research and try to find a cure.

As time went on they discovered that if the Deader didn't regularly feed they became emaciated and started to decay. One that fed regularly would keep looking like it did the day it died. Though there was no tissue regeneration, so if it was cut it would never heal.

Also, those creatures that fed on human bodies over electrical devices seemed to absorb the spores from the other body and could survive longer between feedings and seemed to retain more of its original intelligence.

But even without a source of food for over four months, patient zero was still not dead. No one knew how long these things could live without an energy source to sustain them.

This caught me off guard. Not that they needed to feed or they decayed. I had seen that for myself. Anyone remember the cul-de-sac de Minotaur? What surprised me was that patient zero was in the same building as I was. Or had been at least. Was it still alive or had they finally found a way to kill it?

For research, they needed to keep some of the creatures alive to study their habits, movements and other signs of life. Of course, this was dangerous, so they had the military create the cells to keep them contained. They took rooms and labs and turned them into study stations and quarters for them. They had to adjust the doors as most were electric and would actually feed the creatures from our power grid. There had been a couple of incidents before they figured this out. A few people were lost.

By December they had only come up with one way to kill the Deaders. The only thing that worked was a direct blow to the cerebellum. This seemed to sever the connection the spores had to the rest of the brain. The body ceased all function. You couldn't stab them in the eye or the brain like the movies portrayed. It had to be a direct shot to the specific spot on the back of the neck. Where the spine meets the skull. Even beheading them didn't work unless the beheading hit that spot specifically.

So there was a way to kill these things. You just had to be very specific. That is why the .50 cal. at the Home of the Brave worked with a headshot. It was powerful enough to take enough of the head and spine out to sever that tie.

The idea of a cure was not bearing fruit. There didn't seem to be a way to kill the spores once they were attached to the electrical system in the body. Vaccines were tried to no avail. Electromagnetic dialysis was tried, to pull the spores from the blood. This seemed promising, but only if the person then stayed in a hermetically sealed area with completely filtered air. This was not plausible for the population.

They had to find a way to cure a large amount of the population at one time. Supplies here were running low. The military had started taking ventures outside the compound to look for food, water and fuel for the generators

Meanwhile, society continued to fall. Even with no communication from the outside world, they knew that society had crumbled. More and more people were found on the missions to find fuel. The stories they told painted a very horrific scene.

That is how we found Matthew in February of 2020. He would be dead if not for our team. Frozen to death from exposure. He was a great help to our community once he was brought here though. A lot of what has been accomplished is because of him. But that is his story to tell.

Way to be cryptic Doc. I really needed to have a long talk with my brother.

As the military was taking care of the supply concerns. They continued to conduct research for a cure. They branched out on very thin limbs trying to find something they could do for the living population and about the non-living population. Nothing seemed to pan out well.

As more and more survivors were brought into the facility they found out more and more of what was happening outside of the protected walls. Civilization, as we knew it, has fallen. Gangs and villains ruled with power they never had before. All still scared of the non-living. Everything had fallen into chaos.

Doc took a second after this to look around the room. He seemed to be taking the time to look at everyone here and made one simple statement. "I do not know how all of you survived. Most of you on your own for a long period of time. There is no way to tell how much of the population still breathes and how many of the NLB's are in this world now. I am afraid to say that the latter may well outnumber the former. We need to find a way to turn the tide and give humans a chance again."

He then explained further that they had a couple of breakthroughs after the dialysis realization. Just nothing they could produce or implement on a large scale. They decided to continue on the path of killing the spores that were causing the problem.

This is where their research has led them so far. They have found a way to kill the spores living in a human host. The next part was to kill all of the spores in the plants and the air at the same time. The spores are in the air we breathe and in all of the plants and animals that inhabit the land. These spores are multiplying at an exponential rate. We need a worldwide delivery system. They have an idea, but just need to nail down the details. They are hoping it will just take a little more time.

They have a system that they are perfecting to deliver this to the world's population all at once. But with limited resources and no real communication with outside sources, it is hard to say if it will really work. It may be our one and only chance. A long shot in the dark. But a shot that needs to be taken.

The time to take that shot may be coming faster than anyone wants to believe.

As his story came to an end, Doctor Testerman looked around the room for any questions on his tale. In the end, I did not have the heart to ask anything more of him. He looked heartbroken that he had taken the last two years and was still unsure of his research and the cure to help the human race.

Since there did not seem to be any more questions we all sat there for a little while soaking in the information that he had just laid out to us. No one spoke for a while.

Time

The one thing we don't seem to have is time. Dr. Testerman went on to tell us a little more information on the current situation after we found our voices again.

The scientists have almost found what they believe to be a cure. It has not been tested on the Deaders for a long term to see how it will affect them. But if we can stop more from being created when we die, it is the beginning of the end for them.

They believe an air dispersal of the chemical they have created will travel around the world in the atmosphere, much like the spores. It will kill off the spores in the air and start to affect the production from the plant life on earth. What I didn't know was that once these spores infect a host plant, that plant also produces the spores into the air instead of their own seeds.

Once the spores are killed off in the air and the plants stop producing more, our natural immune systems should have the ability to fight the spores in our body and purge them. That is the working theory anyway.

The problem is that they don't have enough of the chemical processed to do a large-scale test of it to see how this would affect the human race and the planet long term. Entering this new chemical may alter the Earth's ecosystem irrevocably. There just isn't enough time to test the theory properly. We are skipping a lot of steps in the scientific process.

The main reason for the sudden lack of time is resources. We are out of them. The diesel fuel that they are finding is not working as well as it should. The generators are gumming up and they have to be taken offline to be cleaned. Some of the parts for the generators are running out too. They have already lost half of the generators that they started with and the others may fail at any time.

The food is also an issue. The winter made it hard to grow things. They originally had some greenhouses in the basement, but the lights were taking too much of the power to keep them lit. That had to be sacrificed for the use of the labs to make the chemical.

The other factor is Mother Nature. For this to work, they need to get the chemical loaded into a rocket to get it to the upper atmosphere. The military's best guess would be the missile silos in South Dakota area. There should still be missiles in those silos, even though they say they were decommissioned after the Cold War.

That means trekking halfway across the United States. Broken roads and loads of Deaders and bad people along the way. All the time hauling this chemical and the scientists that know how to use it along. This all takes time. It is already halfway through August. It starts getting cold in South Dakota in early November. That is just over two months to make a trip of over 1,650 miles. They cannot wait until the winter is over to try the trek as the generators and food will not hold out that long.

As I said, not a lot of time.

If all of that was not enough to throw on all of us after the long-winded story of how all of this began he then tells us that with the tests that he has run on those of us that have been outside and in the basically poisoned air for the last two years. His scientists have concluded that the spores that will reanimate our corpses once we die are also slowly killing us. The spores are taking electrical energy from us as we live. The longer we live with them the longer our bodies are having to fight the foreign substance, which is getting stronger. This is diluting our immune systems and slowly killing us in a couple of different ways.

Dr. Testerman listed a lot of the ways, but I had stopped listening by this point. Surviving the Deaders was no longer good enough. The air that we breathe is killing us. If we just keep burying our heads and try to get by, eventually we will still succumb to this poison. Only then to become one of them anyway.

I will tell you that despair set in a little at this point. I looked at my family. Mom, Matt, Andromeda and Jordan. I looked at all the other people gathered in our little group and beyond. If we just kept surviving how long would it be before we succumbed to some illness or another that would turn us? How long did the human race have as a whole?

As I stood there starting to spiral out of control with this new information. I blacked out. Well, I thought I had blacked out, it was actually the entire facility that blacked out. All of the lights went out and nothing kicked back on. It was so dark that you couldn't see the nose in front of your face. No red lights or flashlights to see by.

Another time that I miss the age of cell phones. We all carried flashlights with us everywhere we went back then.

We could hear the military and engineers running around and calling out. Trying to get people in a safe area and to get themselves to the generator rooms to see what happened. It seemed like hours, but was most likely only half of one, that the lights were off. When they came back on they were dim and stunted. There was barely enough light for us to make it back to our room and settle in for the night.

Part of the problem with living underground is that I was not really sure it was night. We had a long day and got a lot of information thrown at us in a very short time. The things reanimating bodies were alien in nature. It was protected in a stone shell well enough to make it through our atmosphere unscathed.

I looked at Jordan and Mom and asked what everyone was thinking.

"Was this sent here on purpose by some alien race?"

They both shook their heads and didn't have an answer either. Neither of them really wanted to talk about what we had heard. The old news was bad enough, but we had figured out most of that in our own way. Not specifics, but the generals. The new news is what had everyone shook. It was hard to process.

"So this place is dying, we are dying although very slowly. What do we do now?" I asked this out loud but only for my own sake.

I was surprised when I heard Matt answer from the hallway. "You go with us to South Dakota."

"Why would we do that?"

"You know that you guys survived out in this world on your own for over a year. You know how to look out for the Deaders or NLB's. You even told me yourself you were looking at going north. To Canada or somewhere else cold to get away from these creatures."

"Yeah, but with this group and these scientists it would be slow going and a death sentence if they got it wrong."

"All the more reason for you to go. Besides we just got our family back together we can't go separate ways now."

I looked at Mom, he was right. "So you come with us." I countered.

"You know I can't do that. I have to go with this team. I have to try and save the world. I think you do too. Just think about it. It is not a decision that has to be made tonight." With these words, he said goodnight and headed off to his room.

Matt as usual was wrong again.

Mom, Jordan Andromeda and I all curled up on the bed together and laid there. Andromeda and Mom fell asleep instantly. Jordan and I spoke softly with each other about different things. Mostly avoiding the decision to come and the deadly spores.

I felt as though I had just fallen asleep when Andromeda jumped up from the bed and stood growling at the door. This put me on full alert and I woke the others.

Seconds after Andromeda alerted us, there was a scream from down the hallway. This was instantly followed by boots running and gunfire. Shit, what could be happening? As this thought goes through my mind there is a pounding on the door. Matt was screaming at us to open the door. I move Andromeda out of the way and let him in.

"What's happening?" Mom asks

"A couple of the doors failed. There are NLB's moving around the facility. Luckily we have a team on it. But we need to move everyone to a central location. Now!" Matt orders.

We all grab our things with no more questions. If the doors failed it is because they didn't have any power to them and the battery backups failed. There were a lot of military here that are trained to deal with this threat. The move must be to conserve power to specific areas. The dim lights from before are now barely lighting the bulbs. This casts no light towards the floors or walls. It is not as black as it was when the generators went out, but it is not far from it. The power issue is coming to a near and final end and that is an issue.

Matt leads us to the staging area. It is dark most of the way and we are alone. Matt will move through a hallway and then tell us to stop as he checks out the next. I keep an eye on Andromeda because I trust her to tell me when there is danger.

In the third hallway Matt tells us to wait and disappears around the corner to a new hallway, Andromeda turns behind us and starts growling. We have no weapons on us and something is coming out of the dark. Andromeda moves to place herself between us and the danger as usual. I try to look around the corner for Matt. To see if he is coming back. We edge back around the corner to the new hallway. Hopefully, this is safe. As I think this I am grabbed from behind by a new source of danger we had not seen.

The Deader throws me forward into Jordan. We get tangled up and fall to the ground. Mom screams and tries to get us up. Andromeda is already moving to the new threat. But as she gets ready to pounce on this deader we see a flash and an ear-splitting gunshot goes off. It was point-blank to the cerebellum, I am guessing, from Matt as he came back for us.

The noise in the hallway is so loud that my ears start ringing right away. The bright flash of the muzzle causes me to lose my night vision too.

The danger is still not over though. There were two coming from the other direction. They are just coming into the area of light. One is missing half of its face and both arms. The other is so decayed I can't believe it is able to move. This makes them slow though and easier to manage.

As we are processing the state of these creatures Matt puts his new training to work. He moves through and around us without taking his eyes off the Deaders. It is eerie to see Matt like this. He was always in shape as a cross country runner and a varsity lacrosse player but he never had this focus. This was a new side of him that came from the desperation to help.

As Matt passes me I swear I see his eyes glow. It is almost completely dark so it must be the light playing tricks.

He walks up to the Deaders and they ignore him as they come after us. This is odd because I have never seen them pass by anyone before. As Matt gets behind them he takes them both out with a knife to the head in quick succession. Both drop immediately. He must have missed the vital spot slightly on one because he had to stab it again after it fell to the ground.

"Matt, thank god you came when you did." Mom sighs.

"It was almost not good enough. We need to go now." Matt orders.

"Why did that one not come after you? It let you go right by." I ask.

"It must have not seen me right with its state of decay. Now no questions let's go." He says.

The rest of the trip to the safe area goes without incident. Matt leads us to the double doors where the military is housed.

"Only place that still has power. Everything is depleted. We lost two more generators tonight during the blackout." Matt explains.

With that information, I knew that tonight was going to be the last night we had in this place. We were going to have to leave, one way or the other. Jordan and I just had to decide which direction we were heading.

Decisions

We are going to have to decide if we are with the scientists and the military to forge forward with the cure and the trip to South Dakota or if we are going to strike out on our own. There are a lot of factors to consider in this decision.

1. Family
2. Safety
3. Loyalty
4. Common damn sense.

I know that Matt is not leaving this crew. He is in this to the end. No matter what end that meant. But there is also Mom to think about. She wouldn't want to leave Matt again. Not after just finding him. But she is not physically able to make this trip at the pace they need to go. There would be no vehicles by the end of the trip. Even with the tech that they had developed, there was no fuel. What would we do with Mom when she was unable to go any further, or she held us back?

There is always safety in numbers. Except when these numbers showed the biggest electrical signal that would show across the areas we were traveling. The bigger the number the larger the target. Sure more of us would make it than not, but we would lose people along the way. I am not sure I would be ok with that. I have lost enough. Sure, I have found a lot of it again and gained even more but I am not sure how much I want to risk.

I have loyalty to my family. To my friends. I have a sense of loyalty to this group for helping us and giving us new information and hope. But what do I owe them? A couple of dollars for room and board. Or is it more than that? Do I owe the human race a chance to move forward? Do I need to help these people that have spent the last two years in relative safety and have no idea about the outside world? If we don't help them do they have a chance to get this cure across the country and help what is left of us?

Lastly, what makes sense? There are good people here that have worked hard and sacrificed to make a difference. To understand what this is and stop it from growing. They are taking a leap of faith that they have the answer. One I am not sure they have. Common sense tells me to go my own way. They have half an army company on their side, something up their sleeve that they are not telling us and the knowledge of the cure. What do they need me for?

With all of this information and the arguments in my head, I sit down with Mom and Jordan. We speak at length and I bring up my thoughts. Matt comes by and adds his two cents in a couple of times too. We weigh the pros and cons and try to decide if this quest, this move to the Dakotas is a pipe dream and if there really is a basis in reality for this to work. Too many variables work against it.

The cure is untested in the mass majority. It worked in a controlled lab. There has been no real-world application. The scientists will have to try and make more of this chemical on the road in less than ideal conditions and create a dispersal method. Then there is no way in this world today to track the progress after dispersal like there was just two years ago. There is no power, no NASA, no U.S.A. It will be a shot in the dark that would take years to see fruition. It is something that may never even make it to that point because of pirates and vagabonds along the way.

We go back and forth for hours. In the end, it was ended by one simple statement that could have stopped this argument seconds after it started.

"I am the mother and I am not leaving my son. We will go and you will like it. Because I said so."

Damn logic. The might of the mother is greater.

Mom does not put her foot down on much. A lot less since the Fall. So I guess we need to give her this. I look at Jordan who is not part of this family, per se. She simply nods and lays down to sleep. I guess that was the indication that she is in. I am not so sure that this is the right decision. I agree to table the discussion for now but am not convinced that this is the right course.

Maybe we would start off on this and head north with the group. Then if Mom starts holding them back or is too weak to continue I could talk her out of the trip then. Maybe we could then figure out what would be best for us.

Mom is tired and so am I, but I have some rounds to make before I lay down for the night. I look around for a bit and find Matt with a couple of the military guys. They are loading up guns and magazines for the trip. They can't take everything, so they were sorting out what would be of the best use.

I let Matt know that we are in and would be going with them for now. He looks relieved. We talk for a bit and he introduces me to his friends. He looks like he wants to tell me more, but cuts it off and tells me that we would talk more later. We would have weeks and months on the road to get reacquainted.

As I leave Matt, I go in search of the Bravers. In the last few days, I have not seen much of them and don't know where everything is going to fall when the power gives out.

I find Paul first. He is sitting in a corner reading. A lot of stress and worry had left him since he arrived here. He is no longer in charge. It suites him. He likes to read and relax. He deserves it. What happened at the Home of the Brave was not his fault, but he took it as a failure and refused to be part of the leadership here. I think that having someone else run the show is a huge weight off his shoulders and he doesn't want to bear that cross again.

We talk about the upcoming move. He doesn't know as much as I do about the course of action and the supposed cure. I keep it simple and ask if they are going to leave with us when the time comes.

"I will not, but a couple of the Bravers may. No one has given us a time frame on leaving here. If you think it is soon, it probably is. But I will not trek across the United States for a cause. I will go back, see what I can find, what I can salvage of the life before. Not the Home of the Brave, but my life before the Fall. I can't lead anymore. I lost too much to want that again. But I know Susie is looking for a fight, for a cause, she can be counted on to go." Paul explains.

I speak to Paul a bit longer and then move on. It is late and most people are rolling up in blankets and trying to sleep. Trying to see what tomorrow will bring. I am too wired for that. So I wander away from everyone else.

This area is bigger than I had first expected. It has an armory a training area, bunks and cafeteria of course too. Then there is a closed-off section that has a lot of lights running. Voices are coming from the area too. I walk up, not sneaking, to see what is happening at this time of night. Let alone all of the lights running when the generators are dying.

I see a person strapped into a chair and what looks like a surgical team around him. I guess they are continuing the experiments on the Deaders as long as they can, but then this person talked. I can't hear the words but he is definitely talking. He is human, not a Deader.

Now I am creeping. He doesn't look hurt in any way. I get only bits and pieces of the conversation.

"We will put you under… 3 minutes…bring you back..." one says

"What will it feel like?" Says the guy strapped to the bed.

"Floating…. Hurt… buzzing maybe.. "

What is going on here?

"Hey, you can't be here!" Well, I heard that.

The doctors turn and look at me. Made. So I go with it.

"What are you doing? Who is he?" I ask as I walk into the room.

"This is military business. You can't be here. You need to leave." It is one of the military guys Matt introduced me to tonight.

That is all that is said and he grabs me by the arm and pulls me out of the room.

"Go ask your brother about this room. It all started because of him. He and this project are what helped save us all. But you have to leave now." Then he turns and goes back to the well-lit room beyond the door.

Matt helped create this? Matt is no scientist. So many questions pop into my head. So many things I don't understand. One thing finally made sense though. This is why my Dad was so prevalent on me finding this room, through those double doors. I just hadn't looked deep enough yet.

Matt would have the answers. But I need to wait and talk to him later. I am tired and need to be able to think when this is explained. I go back to the area where Mom and Jordan are. Matt is here too, curled up on the floor and asleep. He would be here in the morning. We could talk then.

Morning comes quickly. Everyone in one big room doesn't make it conducive to sleep in. I am blurry-eyed and groggy when people start moving around. I notice that Matt was up and gone. No talking to him yet. That is OK, breakfast first.

Breakfast is cold cereal. With water. I had gotten used to this before but the hot breakfast was so good when we had it. Guess it is back to the old grind.

As everyone is up and eating, Dr. Testerman stands on a center table and speaks to the crowd. He is a small man so this barely puts him above the rest of the crowd. He explains the loss of the generators and the trek the military and scientists are going to take. He informs us that a few people are being asked to join them for their expertise, either in the field of science or just in survival. All others could stay here in the bunkers, no one has to leave, but most of the weapons and food are going with the scientists. They would allow whatever fuel was still here and whatever generators still worked to remain. But that was it. No more support. The military is pulling out first thing in the morning the following day. Those that chose to leave today would be given what food could be spared and weapons if they wanted them. Anything that would help them on their journey.

The military is in the other rooms packing up and getting ready to evacuate. There are a lot of things to do and not much time to do it. He goes on and speaks about the captive NLBs.

"They have all been euthanized. There would be nothing to fear from them any longer. So it will be safe for those that want to stay."

I look around the room as he is talking. I see Paul talking to a couple of Bravers, Susie in particular. From the looks of it, he is telling her to go and that he is not. I wouldn't be able to tell this if I had not known them so well, or hadn't talked to Paul the previous evening. Susie is coming with us. Oh well, a piece of entertainment I guess.

After Dr. Testerman stops talking he goes away. Back to the area that I saw last night. The crowd breaks up and goes to their own separate groups. Some you can tell are leaving. Not with us, but just to go on their own. They are not waiting until tomorrow. They are speaking to others about where to go and how to get the supplies promised by Dr. Testerman.

Others are packing up and talking to other military soldiers. I guess these are the people going with them. Very few people were asked to accompany them by the looks of it. We will get a briefing on the moving parts later I am sure. Then there are the people that are settling in. Nowhere to go. This place is safe and would be for a while until the food and generators run out. But they may have at least a couple of days to make a decision. Maybe turn this into their own bunker.

Then there are the groups of people that seem angry about the whole ordeal. The ones that don't like being asked to go or being told to stay when they would no longer be taken care of.

Jordan sits beside me and taps me on the shoulder and points. I look to where she is pointing and see Matt motion me over to another room. This is when I will talk to him. I need more information today, especially if everything is going to happen in the morning.

I get up and feel my ever-present shadow, Andromeda, follow me to meet Matt. He motions us in and we sit down at an old desk. At first, he just stares at his hands, looking for the words.

"Look, I know you have questions. There are things about me now that are different. I am sure you have noticed it some. It goes deeper than you think. But all I will say right now is that there is time to talk about this and time for me to explain all of it to you the way it needs to be explained. This is not the time or the place."

"So you just pull me in here to tell me you won't tell me anything?" I ask exasperated.

"Yes and no. I know you are perceptive and that I couldn't keep you from asking questions for too long. Just know that the differences in me and my team are for the betterment of our group. They help keep us and others alive. I am sure you have noticed that yourself. I pulled you in here though because there may be unrest in our group here at the hospital. Some of the ones being left behind are not happy. They like the safety of what we have built here. They don't want to understand how it is coming to an end either way. They also don't like that we will not tell them what our plan is and how we are going to cure the world. They think we are just leaving them to their fates. I am afraid that things will go the way they did at the Fall. When people are scared and don't like the way they are treated they lash out. I don't like that Dr. Testerman told those that are leaving today that they can get weapons from us. I think some may use this as a guise then try to force their way. I am not sure, but others think this is a possibility. We also think that some in our group, some of the other military will help them. They don't believe in this trek and the cure. They want to stay safe. Feel safe." He states.

Matt tells me about what his team has seen and what they have heard. He is aware that the Bravers are not part of the dissention as they have not been here long enough to feel safe. We felt safe before and that fell apart. He wants me to talk to them and make sure they are ready if something is to happen. I know most of them are packing up and getting ready to head out, very few were asked to go with us. I told Matt that I would talk to them and let them know what is needed from them.

The doctors and scientists can't fight for themselves. They never learned. They have been here or places like this for the entirety of the pandemic. Matt is not sure which of the military's other members can be trusted and his team can't be everywhere at once. He wants the Bravers to be the last line of defense for them.

It was way too early for all of this. We had to watch for people that we just met. We don't know who to watch for or what they really want. The good thing is that it will only take the rest of today for the area to be packed up. We won't be able to carry much with us. We are taking some of the vehicles for the first part of the trip, they are being loaded now. But they won't last long with no fuel. We can hope that there will be areas where we can salvage some working fuel along the way. But we pack light to move quickly just in case this isn't the case. We will have to find other things that we need on the way too.

I leave Matt, still not happy with no answers about him and the military team he is with or what the hell was happening in the room last night. But he is right on one thing we will have plenty of time over the next couple of weeks to hash this out. At least as long as the vehicles hold out and Mom can keep up. I will know the truth soon.

I tamp down my frustration and find Jordan. I will need her help to talk to some of the others more quickly. I tell her the cliff notes and she just nods and heads off. As she walks away I hope that this will all be for nothing and we will leave tomorrow without a hitch. The trip itself will be dangerous enough. We need a last day of rest. A day I know we won't get.

I sit there a couple of more minutes petting Andromeda and zoning out. Then I decide to go ahead and get the day started. We never really unpacked, so grabbing our stuff from the old room will not be a problem. I decide to go find Paul first and bring him up to speed.

Last

Last day of safety again. I think this one is just as hard as the day I packed up and left the state park. I haven't been here long, yet I feel a little safer and a bit at home. The long trip to get here is getting to me I think, I like staying in one place. The state park was nice but lonely. The Home of the Brave was good but even with Mom there it never felt like home. We were too exposed. Now I have what's left of my family back, along with another member I found along the way. This place is safe and secure. Not exposed and we can control all of the exits. I used to love the outdoors. Running through the woods, hunting with my Dad, camping on those cool autumn nights while sitting around the campfire. Now the outside only brings fear. Fear of Deaders, fear of other humans that only want chaos. Inside where the exits are controlled lets me feel safe and forget the world has fallen apart, at least for a little while

Now we are leaving again and putting us all in danger of the unknown. Walking into it willingly, towards places I have never been, seems wrong. There is nothing to be done though. The big guy says we are moving out. It is go with them or find my own way again without my brother and my mother. I need to stay with my family, so I will go along, for now.

Sitting and thinking about the what-ifs is not doing me any good. I can never plan for every eventuality and I have no idea what we will find along the way. The military and the scientists are good at planning so I'll let them do it now. I just need to keep my eyes open and keep Andromeda close so she can tell me when she senses something off. Today it is all about getting through with no violence breaking out inside the bunker. I can hear the low whispers that stop when others come near. The sideways glances that stop when you look directly at them. These people know who I am and who my brother is. They know where my brother stands so they are not going to approach me or talk around me if they are planning something.

Some people have already headed out. I am not sure if they are just ready to get on the road or if they have heard about the dissension and are not willing to be participants in it. Not all of the people that are still here are a danger. They just don't have anywhere to go. They have no plan so they stay put. These are the ones that I worry about if things go wrong. They will be in the way and the line of fire. I am really hoping people have learned from our past, learned from the Fall and know that the violence will not solve anything. It only causes more problems. The main one being the Deaders. There are none in this basement now. But if violence breaks out there will be deaths. That leads to Deaders and possibly more deaths. I did learn from the Fall. I learned that people that are scared do dumb things out of that fear.

Andromeda and I are already packed and ready to go, Jordan too. So instead of staying idle I walk around the small area with power and keep my eyes on things. After a while, I figure this is the same thing the military is doing so I decide to venture out. Back to the old barracks areas to see if maybe there are people out there planning things. Although I really hope not.

As I walk out of the double doors Jordan walks with me. I look at her to make sure she wants to be part of this. She just nods and no words are needed. She is staying with me, so we move on. She has been especially quiet and somber over the last day. The explanation of how this apocalypse started and the cause has her shook. She seems to be taking a little longer to process things than me. I wonder what that says about me.

The first thing I notice is how quiet it is outside of the doors. Before there was movement and labs and just ambient noise now there is nothing. You can hear our footsteps echo down the hallways. We come upon the dead bodies of the Deaders Matthew killed to save us. That seems like days ago now, but it was not even one full day. I have never seen a body that had been turned into a Deader actually dead afterward. Nothing much is different than when they were walking, except their eyes. Their eyes of blue are now just white. They look like a blind person's eyes or a seers in the old movies. No color at all, just milky white all the way around. It is kind of eerie and creepy. I don't like the feeling I have looking at them so we move on quickly.

Back in the old barracks rooms, we hear movement. We stop and listen for a while until we realize it is some of the people that are heading out on their own. They are going through all the things left behind to see if they can find anything of use. It is harmless if unethical. These people had to leave their things in the pitch black, and now they are going through and stealing it. That is what it takes in this new world to survive though, so we move on. After about an hour of walking and looking around, we decide that there is nothing here to do. This is our last day of rest for weeks, so we head back to the military area and find a place to rest. Sleep tonight will be nil so we might as well rest now.

When we get back, small things were passed out for lunches. It was kind of a menagerie, but I guess we won't have refrigerators or anything on the road, so we might as well eat it all now. Keep the dried and canned items for the road. Jordan and I eat and I feed a lot of mine to Andromeda. I am not that hungry. Nervousness does that to me.

The rest of the day continues on in the same manner. As it progresses I should feel better, but I don't. Andromeda seems to feel it too. I am not sure if she is picking something up in the air or if she is just nervous because I am. Either way, we can't seem to sit still.

Jordan has given up on us and just stayed laying down in our bed for tonight. She does not seem to think there is any danger. I hope she is right.

Dinner comes and goes, same as lunch. More people leave and say short goodbyes. Others beg to be able to come on the journey with us. Plead that they can be helpful. All are turned down again and again.

The military have become scarce as the day progressed. Either being sent out early as scouting parties, or set on shifts to load supplies. The scientists are packing the equipment they will need for the trip. They are also packing up the equipment they are not taking so that time and dust will not harm it. They feel this may be needed later when the cure works and we need it to get society back on course. There were a lot of people in this basement when I arrived. More than I thought. But now the area is bare and everyone is in this one area, now with the scientists and military out of the picture you can tell we are down to a skeleton crew.

A couple of people are still side-eyeing me and the military members that are still here. But now it does not seem like they would have a reason or force enough to make any kind of real trouble so I start to calm myself down and stop my imagination from going off the rails.

As the evening sets in, we all find our bed areas and settle in ourselves. Matt is still here and will stay with the main convoy. He is usually a forward scout but decided to stay with the main force so he could be with Mom and me the entire time. Matt always seems distant. He seemed like he really didn't care, but he did and still does. The time away and the military have changed him more than most people know but he is still here and wants to be part of our family. Be here to protect us when we need it.

Jordan is already asleep. She has a way of turning everything off and resting when she needs to. I am a bit envious of how she can sleep at any time. Mom is still up and about. Trying to help pack in any way she can. Always trying to be helpful and pay her way in this world. She will be up for a while longer because she can rest in the truck tomorrow. I, on the other hand, will have to walk most of the way. Keeping my eyes out for danger. I need to rest and be fresh for tomorrow. It is early but I lay down next to Jordan and Andromeda lays at my feet. I concentrate on Jordan's breathing to let myself settle. It helps and I am asleep quickly too.

Suddenly, loud noises and screaming jar me awake. I can't get my bearings and just see people with guns running around. Some on one side of me some on the other. I can hear them yelling at one another, but I can't get a clear idea of what is happening. Jordan and Andromeda are awake too. Mom is still not next to me. She must still be helping the load up. We were not asleep for long.

I start to gather a little of what they want. We have a few vehicles going with us that are loaded with supplies. The raiders want one of the vehicles, loaded with food for them to leave. The military is not letting them have it. Precious resources in the fuel and food. There is a lot of yelling back and forth. One of the civilian raiders says the trucks are rigged with explosives and they will blow up all of them if they don't get one. Stupidity. Another bout of fear ruling one's actions. If they blow up the trucks with the supplies they are cutting off their nose to spite their face. They will lose the trucks and supplies too. But as history can tell you, they will do it in the heat of battle and not think about the repercussions until later.

Tensions are running hotter and one of the raiders is waving a gun around. This guy does not look stable. Jordan and I find a table and turn it on its side for at least a little protection. In the movies, the tables can provide protection from anything and everything. I know this is not the case but, hopefully, we don't need to see how wrong the movies are.

That hope runs out almost as fast as I think it. The raider with the gun loses it and starts shooting. He is not a very good shot and the soldiers have time to get cover. I don't think he hit anyone. But then they fire back. The noise is deafening and we just close our eyes and cover our ears to try and block out the mayhem.

The walls here are all thick concrete which causes bullets to ricochet around. Our table is hit either directly or hit with these ricochets multiple times in the first minute. I feel my arms and face get cut with a few splinters from the material of the table. I can't see Andromeda or Jordan, I can only hope they are ok.

Just as I think this I feel Jordan grab my arm. I look at her and she looks at me. Her face is clear of blood and scratches. I think I got the worst of the splinters. I guess she was just trying to reassure me that we will be ok. The look on her face is serene and calming. More gunfire erupts so I put my head down again and curl a little tighter to Jordan.

After a couple of seconds, the shots stop abruptly. I put my head over the table and it seems the military soldiers won. The raiders are either on the ground or lost their nerve and left. I can hear footsteps running down the hallway away from our position. A few soldiers run to the trucks to make sure the explosives part of their tirade was a lie and the others move forward to take possession of the fallen weapons.

Andromeda noses my elbow and whines. I look to make sure she is alright. She is but she is looking at Jordan. Jordan's eyes are still closed. As I shake her shoulder to get her attention, she slumps over to the floor. I scream for a medic and lay her on the floor. Something hit her in the middle of her chest. It must have come through the table. There is blood all over her shirt and running onto the floor.

The medic is close and comes over to check her out. A couple of the soldiers are walking through the bodies of the raiders making sure they will not rise again if they are dead, taking the ones that are alive into custody. Others are bandaging up their friends and others in the room.

I look back at the medic and see the look on her face. She looks as though she wants to tell me something but doesn't have the words. I know what is happening, Jordan is dead. She is small and there was so much blood already on her and the floor. I can't speak so I just nod and lean down to hold Jordan one last time. The medic moves on to help any others that she can.

Matt finally shakes me out of it and is able to get my attention.

"She is gone. If we don't take care of her now she will turn." He says.

"Can you take her away and do it? I can't see you do that." I say through tears.

He just nods and carries off my friend. My sister. I grab Andromeda and hug her tight. I am aware that Mom has grabbed me in a hug too and is holding both of us. I don't know where she came from or how long she has been there. I also don't know how long we stay there. Time is nothing to me right now. I have no way to think, no way to process what has happened here. When I finally break the embrace, Matt is standing over us. I look at him quizzically and he just nods. Jordan is gone and she will not rise again as her parents did. That at least is a relief.

He tells us what happened with the raiders, although I really could care less at this point. These people in their fear and greed have taken a bright light from this world. Taken one of the few lights of my world away from me. Jordan did nothing to these people and still paid the ultimate price for just being here with me.

Matt tells us that one soldier and five civilians that were not part of the raiders were killed. There were fifteen raiders in all and eight of them were killed or wounded. The others ran off. Since they were not sure what weapons they had or if there were others, they have decided to put some distance between us and them. We were leaving now.

I can't grasp this. I was just asleep. Happy that my family was together.

Before I can leave I have to say goodbye. I tell Matt as much so he nods and points to the room with the beds that housed the injured soldiers. Andromeda and I slowly get up and walk to the room. They have covered her with a sheet. The sheet covers her body and face, but I can see the blood soaking through at her chest. She is going to be left here to rot on this table. We don't have the ability to take her body, or the others that died here tonight and bury them properly. That is a sadness that is part of this new world.

I stand there saying my goodbyes to her until I can't cry anymore. The time to grieve will come, anger is taking hold tonight. We need to go. Need to get away from the people that caused this tragedy, caused this pain. So I turn and walk out of the room and leave her behind. Andromeda takes another second of her own and then follows me out.

Matt and Mom are waiting for us on the other side of the door. They look at me and I just nod once. They understand and we all walk towards the exits.

Mom finds the truck she was assigned to. I think I have had enough of this place after tonight. I think I have had enough of people in general. We learn history in school and have lived history ourselves over the past years. Yet people still refuse to learn from it. They do the same things and react in the same ways that the human race always has. This place felt safe for a while I thought I would miss it, but now I would only miss Jordan.

As we walk out of the lower levels for the last time I look up to the sky. It has been a while since I have really looked at the sky. It had been days since I had even been outside. The night is bright and a little cool for this time of year. It is still August so maybe it is just me feeling a chill. The road will be a lonelier place without Giggles. I will miss her every mile, but the trip must go on. Maybe if we can cure this disease, kill these spores from some other planet, maybe we can get some civilization back into this world.

I turn around one more time and look at the entrance to the hospital. There is nothing for me here. I make the decision to be part of the fix, part of the cure. Jordan wouldn't say it to me but I know she wanted to see this through just as my brother does. Mom, Andromeda, Matt and I need to look after one another better than we have in the past. Better than I just looked after Jordan.

The trucks pull off and I can see Mom wave to me through a window. They will drive a few miles down the road and make camp. It will be ready when we get there.

I bend a little at the waist and pat Andromeda on the head. The future is forward and if this goes right it will be a future worth fighting for. A future without the Deaders. I turn to look at the stars one more time and set my backpack a little higher on my shoulders. Just then a shooting star cuts across the sky towards the northwest. Is it telling us to head that way to save what is left of humanity?

Guess I shouldn't keep destiny waiting.

Author's Note

Eyes of Blue is a work of fiction as should be perfectly clear from the subject matter. Many of the events occur in real places. Delaware is a place that I have lived most of my life. I have traveled across the country and back and have not found a place quite as unique as our little peninsula. I wanted to share some of that with others instead of creating a land all my own. I have taken the liberty to change them to what bests suits the course of my story though. I hope that readers will not be too upset with my creative tweaks to reality in places that are dear to them.

In particular I would like to address the Home of the Brave. I used this place as a safe place for Ava and her family. A place for her to recover after being on her own and living in places that should not have to be a home. In reality the home of the Brave foundation in Milford, DE does this for our veterans. They serve those who served us by providing temporary housing, food, guidance and support to US military veterans. They develop programs to serve veterans in their journey towards permanent housing. To help reduce homelessness among our military veterans.

This is a worthy cause and one that hits close to home as I myself am a veteran that comes from a long line of military volunteers. Please look into their program and donate to their cause if you can.